Up a Yum Bum Tree

Martin Pilcher

ISBN 978-0-9556819-0-5

AADVARK-ZAP PUBLISHING (UK)

For my critics

Into nothing, nothing can go, from nothing, nothing can come . . . but there are exceptions.
                    Titus Perilous III Roman Emperor

1

Effie Bannister was contemplating another orgasm in the bath. It would be her second one that week. Needless to say, Dale would be on the job again. What a lover and what a find. Thirty years her junior with the body of Adonis and hung like a Thracian ram. He was just a happy-go-lucky carpenter without an ounce of aggression in his entire being. Divorced of course. Lovely lad. He owned a clapped out old motorbike with a sidecar. He called it Oil Slick. Effie thought that was terribly sweet.

Dale leapt up the stairs two at a time and burst into the bathroom in his usual care-free manner sending the door reeling on its hinges.
"Nipples on parade!" he yelled, making Effie guffaw with her usual full phlegm forty-a-day smoker's cough, "go on then, spit in the bath."
More riotous convulsions at soapy suds time.
"Oh dear God," said Effie, "pass the gin."
Talk about Saturday night hysterics. And why not?

Effie's scientist husband Freddie was in Tunisia for the weekend at some boring old missile conference. All expenses paid for by his employer, the Defence Evaluation and Research Agency, part of the UK Ministry of Defence. DERA for short, or Auntie Vera as Dale called it. It didn't matter that he was educationally challenged because he was such a fantastic lover. So inventive. "This little piggee – wheeee!"
Dale's strong, knarled, carpenter's hands snaked through the water and up the mount of Venus like a U-boat in fjord. Effie started frothing below the waterline, beating the side of the tub with her thighs. Thump, thump, thump. Ooh yes! Grab ye pleasures whilst ye may.

It had been going on like this for months now. Freddie had his suspicions but he'd got more important things on his mind. What really turned him on was his ballistic missile research. It wasn't his fault he was a genius. The trouble was, the Ministry of Defence had kicked his latest project right in the goolies. Politically unacceptable they said. The bastards. So, the normally mild mannered Freddie had become a seething cauldron of anger and bitterness.

A dangerous state to be in.

2

"God, that's amazing," said Loretta to Freddie.

They were in bed together in an hotel in Tunis. Freddie was drugged to the eye-balls and had just spilled the beans about Project Cassandra, his politically unacceptable ballistic missile plan.

"I know, I know," he said wearily, "but nobody believes me."

"But I do," said Loretta, "you can trust me."

It was then that Boris nearly wetted himself. He had got a video camera running behind a two-way mirror. Boris Blodvrinsky. Russian Mafia. A big bear of a man with a finger-on-the-nuke-button personality. He was incredibly rich and wanted to control the international arms trade. He loved opera and ballet too and was equally fascinated by men in tights or quick drying cement. But for now he shut the camera off and tip toed out. He had got everything he needed and watching sex was boring, besides he had seen Loretta perform so many times before.

Meanwhile, Freddie had an erection. At his age it didn't happen often so he was quite impressed. So was Loretta. And given that she could fall asleep counting the number of dicks she had seen, both flaccid and erect, it was a pleasant flip side to what was fast becoming an occupational draw-back. She swung herself on top of him. Black pussy in action. She had lips as big as dolphins and eyes you could dive into.

"Okay mission control, we're in a definite go situation for an all systems shag."

When not on the game, Loretta Regina was a beautiful mixed up jazz singer.

Come the morning and Freddie was still in her bed. Comatose. The little white powder that Boris affectionately referred to as his Dacha Dandelion could be alarmingly potent at times. Some clients could take it, others could not. Loretta checked Freddie's pulse before taking a shower. She had to leave for a lunch time gig at the Hilton in Hammamet (Boris managed her singing bookings too) so there was no time to coax Freddie into consciousness. She scribbled him a note and placed it underneath his spectacles. Boris would get heavy if he knew about it. The point was however, that Freddie flew home today and last night he had told her what Effie did for a living. She ran a professional theatre. Top cat on the Board of Trustees. Quite an entrepreneur by all accounts. When Freddie mentioned Effie's plans for a late night cabaret, that was it. Bugger Project Cassandra. She wanted out of the game and into the spotlight. Loretta craved artistic success.

Desperately.

3

Dale could hardly believe his luck. He had really fallen on his feet this time. Regular job. Good crowd. And no need for wanking. He thought Effie was great. Life and soul of the party, always got something on the go. She ran a flower shop as well as the theatre. There was no end to her energy and enthusiasm. The shop was called Cascade Ornamental Gardens. Effie had been quick to spot a market opportunity in the midst of all the Feng Shui mania. Dinky little interior numbers that brought nature into the living room. Yin and yang in a box of veneered yew. Dale made the bases. It was the first job she gave him and the lad done brilliant. The shop just happened to be sited inside the theatre.

The Haystack theatre in Fropsham was a weird building. No so much an architectural folly as a mutant conception. It had a little thatched roof straight out of Hansel and Gretal which was plopped on top of a glass observation post that looked like the lamp bit of a lighthouse. That bit was then stuck on top of a wooden slatted building that resembled a windmill minus the sails. This in turn was crudely grafted on to an enormous square warehouse big enough to hold the Seventh Cavalry.

Effie rented Dale a one bedroomed flat above the shop. If you went out of the back door you would find yourself inside the theatre workshops and scene dock. It was really quite spooky. Not surprisingly, the scene dock was where Dale first met Gaspard the stage designer. Effie said Gaspard was a frightful snob but very talented and lonely. Most of the actors said he was a screaming queen. Gaspard fancied Dale like mad.

It didn't take Effie long to recognise Dale's carpentry skills and before long he was making the scenery. He had such an amiable disposition that occasional stage hand duties came his way too. One evening he was operating the curtains. He loved to sneak a peak at the audience. He had spotted a really foxy young blonde sitting in the front row with a Versace safety pin stuck in each breast. It certainly wasn't the street fashion along Burnt Oak Broadway which is where he had spent most of his life sizing up the talent. He remembered the time when he had been waiting in the casualty department of Edgware General Hospital for a tetanus injection and seen a hysterical young woman, the victim of a staple gun attack, half naked on a stretcher. Streams of blood flowed across her breasts like the Ganges Delta. The duty nurse told him that the woman's husband was a carpet layer who was convinced that the bruises on his wife's knees were attributable to clandestine activities on top of a stretch of industrial weave that she was supposed to be cleaning during the night shift. Well that explained everything. It was sadistic madness but what Dale was looking at now was something entirely different. As he adjusted his position, Gaspard crept up behind him, the smell of Sweet Martini heavy on his breath.

"Just one pin is an abhorrence, but two is obscenely excessive," whispered Gaspard, in his plummy voice, as if straining to pass a cut glass faeces through a perfumed sphincter.

"Well, there's no accounting for taste is there?"

"Unfortunately not, but even tribal society has transcended that level of mammary mutilation."
Dale sort of half got that.

"She's just a show-off with big tits, no harm in that, is there?"

"The point is Dale, she is sitting in the auditorium of a professional theatre, not performing in some tacky strip joint in Soho."
Anyway, they ended up having a cup of tea in Dale's flat because Gaspard said he'd got something important to tell him.

"I've run out of biscuits," said Dale, "d'you wanna packet of crisps."

"No thank you."

"Catalan Goose and Pimento Sauce flavour?"

"No thank you, please sit down and listen to me."
Dale did as he was told. It was his nature. Compliant. Easy going.

"Dale," said Gaspard, placing his hands together like a Catholic priest about to give unction, "I think you should be aware that I am fully cognisant of your affair with Effie."

"Say that again?"

"I know that you and Effie have sex together."
Dale was gob-smacked. Gaspard said it was none of his business but it could lead to bad publicity especially with Freddie being a top government scientist. So they finished their tea like two Aberdeen spinsters and Dale promised to be discreet like. Gaspard was dying to bugger him but he had to make an important phone call instead.

He tore himself away and slipped out the back door. He crossed through the scene dock, out the other side, round the building, across the shingled car park to a public telephone kiosk. There was no way he could risk using his mobile for a call of this nature. He dialled a number from memory.
A male voice answered.

"Yes?"

"You recognise my voice, of course."

11

"Yes."

"I have achieved a temporary holding position."

"Good. Let me know when it becomes permanent."

"I am fully aware of the requirements of my assignment, thank you."

"Good night, number six."

"Will you kindly refrain from such drollery."

But the line had gone dead. Ignorant peasant, muttered Gaspard to himself.

It was only to be expected now that MI5 recruited its agents through the Guardian.

4

The sunrise over Tunisia was tumultuous.

Cocks crowed, dogs barked and donkeys brayed. As the sun grew ever stronger a gerzillion insects sung in cacophonous exultation of the day. It was very stimulating but Freddie didn't appreciate a word of it. He had got a massive hangover. He didn't know he had been drugged but he was beginning to recall the night before. That big booming Russian Boris. A General Lebed look-a-like right down to the gold tipped cigarette holder. He remembered consuming several bottles of champagne at the night club preceded by cocktails at the bar. Then there was that banal cabaret act with the sweaty boss-eyed belly dancer and eventually Loretta. God, what a voice she had. What a figure. What a fuck! He knew he was thinking liking an eighteen year old. He put on his glasses and winced at the pressure on his temples. It was too much. He was about to take them off when he saw Loretta's note. *Freddie, you're fabulous, believe in yourself, ring me soonest, love Loretta.* It was followed by a central London telephone number. He took off his glasses and found the bathroom. Stumbling, fumbling, shaking. There were lots of nice things about, including smells of Loretta. And hello, what was this? A morning erection at his age? He turned on the shower and stood beneath the steaming cascade squirting perfumed goo all over the place. It was lovely, lovely. He thought to himself, yes, I believe in myself. Project Cassandra is a goer and so is Loretta. I shall have both.

A new man emerged into the courtyard below. It was eleven o'clock and the sun was blinding. Freddie bumped into Achmed a local cab driver. There was a strong whiff of donkey piss and goat's cheese.

"You have hangover?" said Achmed.

"Yes."

"I fix it."

Achmed led Freddie to a table with a sunshade and had a quick throaty jabber with a waiter wearing a white and gold tunic. It was a posh hotel. Very soon, two small cups of strong black coffee arrived with a little glass of gungy brown liquid on the side.

"Corpse revival," grinned Achmed, his breath wafting like a drain, "one swallow, is good."

Freddie was still feeling rather fragile so he did as he was told. It nearly made him puke. Achmed gave another big wide grin like Yasser Arafat with bad teeth.

"You want to see genuine Bedouin village?"

"No thank you."

Half an hour later, Freddie staggered out of Achmed's beaten up old Toyota.

"Original bread ovens," said Achmed proudly, pointing to a filthy hole in the ground."

"Fascinating," murmured Freddie, squinting at the desolation that surrounded them. A toothless old hag emerged from behind a pile of bricks.

"Meet my mother," said Achmed.

Now ballistically speaking Freddie might be off his trolley, but when it came to manners, he was still an English gentleman. Achmed's mum was obviously charmed and offered him another invitation to coffee that he couldn't refuse. The three of them entered her hovel. It was like a born again builder's skip but her coffee was surprisingly good and compensated for

14

the lack of decor. Freddie sneaked a look at his watch. His flight was due to leave in two hours. He fumbled in his pocket and found a little pink paper parasol, a remnant of last night's cocktail. Amazingly it was still in one piece. He opened it and gave it to Mrs Arafat. She beamed and jabbered away.

"She would like to give you present in return," said Achmed, obviously touched by the proceedings.

"I would be honoured," said Freddie.

Her horny hands scrabbled around inside an old pot eventually producing a filthy rag which she opened reverently.

"The seeds of the Yuchallaballah tree," said Achmed portentously, "they will bring you luck."

Freddie thought they looked like a load of goat's dung. Time was marching on however, so he thought it best to accept them gratefully; he would give them to Effie to stick in a pot or something.

"Thank you so very much."

"It is our custom."

"I am definitely honoured."

By the time Flight BA276 took off for London Heathrow, Freddie was feeling a lot better. Even the nasal twitterings of Ian Trubshaw his wimpish assistant were somehow bearable.

"If only you'd told me beforehand you weren't attending the final plenary session," he whinged and whined, "the Libyans asked some terribly embarrassing questions."

Freddie ignored him, eased his loins and ordered a vodka and tonic.

There was no doubt about it, the devil inside him had discovered an alternative bang.

5

"I have never been so insulted in all my life," said Effie, pushing the seeds of the Yuchallaballah tree across to Dale, "and I told him so."

"What did he say?"

"He suggested I might ask you to plant them for me and see what came up."

Dale took a sharp intake of breath. Did Freddie suspect something? Maybe Gaspard was right? Perhaps he really was a hair's breadth away from causing a national security scandal. He didn't want anything sensational to happen because he knew the kind of mayhem that could erupt. When he had bought the Oil Slick off George Jolly, who wasn't allowed to ride it anymore following his third angina attack, George's daughter Noreen had just been caught giving a Monica Lewinsky to some married geezer who worked at the RAF Museum in Hendon. His wife went for Noreen big time and there had been blood all the way from Colindale tube station to the Graham Park Estate. The Mill Hill, Hendon and Finchley times had even run an article on women and violence in today's society under the tacky headline: *Joystick ride propels girl into blood bath.* Dale knew when not to over-react.

"I'll find a pot out back then."

"Apparently they need a lot of sunlight."

"That figures, being Tunisian like. Cor, these seeds don't 'alf pong."

"Precisely, I think they're goat's dung."

"Well, I've only seen sheep shit in Wales, so no comment."

Effie started laughing then lit up a fag. It was a good sign.

"D'you wanna cup of tea before I start potting?" said Dale helpfully.

"I'd prefer coffee."

"Okay," he picked up the seed pods and rolled them around in the palm of his hand, "how about an After Eight choccie?"

Effie convulsed with a big honking guffaw, "Ooh yummy." Things were back to normal now. In the back of the shop Dale fixed an instant.

"How about a pick-me-up?" said Effie, producing a bottle of Remy from amongst the til rolls, "it's nearly lunch time."

"Yeah why not?" said Dale, who was quite the hedonist these days.

Effie produced two paper cups, uncorked the bottle and with a reassuring glug glug, they were ready.

"Mud in your eye," she said.

"Up yer yum bum," he replied.

Cough, splutter, hoot, snort. It was what you might call a defining moment - the Yuchallaballah had been anglicised.

"Right, best be getting on with it," said Dale, "I know the very place for maximum sunlight."

"Don't tell me, in the lighthouse."

"Got it in one," said Dale, heading towards the back door. The telephone rang. Effie answered it. He left her to it knowing that she would be nattering for hours.

Dale mounted the circular wooden steps that rose inside the building just like in a windmill. They spiralled around a large gaping hole where some sort of milling gear used to be. As he reached the floor above the scene dock, he saw Roslyn de Winter tucked away in a corner reading a book.

17

"Hi Roz, what yer doing?"

"Learning my lines, how about you?

"Gonna pot a Yum Bum tree upstairs."

She grinned. He didn't know she found him fascinating. She didn't know that he liked her too.

"I've never been up there," said Roz, " what's it like?"

"Come and find out."

So off they go, the pair of them.

The steps were narrow and steep, room for single file only. Roslyn's pert arse wiggled close to his face. Her jeans were so tight they could almost have been painted on. Dale had seen her in a mini-skirt too. Fantastic legs. After a long climb they eventually reached the top.

"Gosh!" exclaimed Roslyn, "I never knew it was so high up."

"Beats the Eiffel Tower," said Dale, having never been there, but remembering Effie's remark which made him feel worldly. While Roslyn gazed at the rolling countryside around her, Dale set about filling a terracotta pot with compost on top of a rickety old wooden table.

"Don't you need a little trowel or something?" said Roz.

"Nah, I'll use me fingers."

He spread Mrs Arafat's rag on the table, it was Freddie's idea of an ethnic gift wrap. He started to make a hole with his finger.

"Here, use my biro," said Roz, offering her red bic.

"Oh ta."

Well it made sense really. By now they were standing quite close and her perfume mingled with the rank odour of the pods.

"Phwoar, have you farted?" she said.

"No it's them Yum Bum seeds, better cover 'em up quick."

"That's not their real name surely?"

"No, some Arab word that sounds like you're about to honk up a load of greenies, but I can't say it. Anyway, they're supposed to bring you good luck."

At which point the sun came out. The vibes were promising.

"Shall we talk to it like Prince Charles?" said Roz.

"You go first then."

She recited a poem by John Donne. Dale didn't know who it was by but he was seriously impressed. He couldn't help thinking how beautiful she was, in spite of her tortoiseshell glasses.

"Your turn now."

He shuffled around a bit, trying to hide his embarrassment. He was a chippy not an actor. In the end he just blurted out.

"For what we are about to receive, may the Lord make us truly grateful."

"Amen," said Roz.

Then they both got a fit of the giggles. It was good fun and they sensed their growing attraction for each other.

"D'you fancy a pint then?" said Roz.

"Yeah, why not?"

Down the steps they went which seemed steeper in descent. Roz put her hands on Dale's shoulders as he led the way. She liked the feel of his muscles. He enjoyed the warmth of her hands.

The Villain's Noose was opposite the theatre. From a second floor window, Gaspard saw them cross the road. From behind the shop counter, so did Effie.

She was not amused.

6

Boris wasn't amused either. He had been playing his secret video tape of Loretta sticking her note under Freddie's glasses; it was amazing what could be revealed by a micro-camera hidden in an hotel smoke detector. What he couldn't understand was why she had done it. He provided for her every need, what more was her life lacking? He was angry and hurt. That was women for you. He didn't understand them. He had first viewed the tape while Loretta was singing at the Hilton in Hammamet and Freddie was on his way back home. He had got on the phone to Dimitri straight away and told him to bug her London apartment in the Bayswater Road; he knew he should have done that ages ago. Freddie was a major catch, a top scientist and definitely one who was in a pissed off, if not totally disillusioned mood. Project Cassandra was going to make Boris mega-rich and mega-powerful, even the White House would defer to him. Clearly, he was going to have to knock Loretta about a bit. Make her see sense. It was a shame really because he was rather fond of her. It was no good asking Dimitri to do it. He was one helluver mean bastard but soft on women. Every time he got drunk he would start crying about how much he missed Svetlana his wife and

Anita his daughter. He was on the phone to Boris now, working himself up for a big emotional dump. They went back a long way so Boris did his best to cheer him up.

"How many times do I have to say it, Dimitri, bring them over here, London is where it's all happening, you said so yourself. I can fix both of them up with something."

"And I've told you before, Boris, Svetlana won't give up the dog fighting syndicate and Anita's making really good money stripping at The Rasputin."

"There's a lot of Pit Bulls in Leeds, send Svetlana a postcard, you can get coloured ones at the Saturday market. And tell Anita about our protection contract at the Mermaid's Cutlass in Soho, she'd be a real hit there, hairy girls are making a big come back."

"Maybe, I'll think about it."

Boris knew he would have to slap Loretta about himself. So be it. He got the vodka out, took a hard slug and then lit a huge Havana cigar. Time for some music. With a deep sigh he took a rat-tailed mop from the cleaning cupboard and propped it lovingly against the hi-fi deck. He selected a CD, pushed the play button and swept the mop into his arms as the music flooded the room.

"It's Glinka, mummy, your favourite."

'Ah yes, A Life for the Tsar, and can I still manage the mazurka?'

"With me you can manage anything."

'The flowers were lovely Boris, you're such a good son.'

"I do my best but at times it's difficult."

'Well I don't like dancing with a cigar in my face, have you forgotten your manners?'

Boris plucked the cigar from his lips and carried on dancing.

"Me and Loretta, we've danced this one too."

'I know, I watched the pair of you.'

"She's got a natural sense of rhythm."

'Yah, and look what she did to you in the Polonaise.'

"Mummy, this is Boris you're talking to."

'Yah, well you'd better slap her into line before she gets the better of you.'

"Mummy please."

'The cigar or sabre, Boris, you only got one choice.'

That was too much. Boris threw the mop on the floor and switched off the hi-fi. It was always the same. His mother had to have the last word. Even when dead. Well, nobody was going to cut *his* balls off, especially a woman. He was in a blind rage when the door bell rang. That bloody commissioner, thought Boris to himself, he paid him two hundred and fifty quid a week to give him the nod before anyone arrived and still he goofed up. It was typical of the service in the Albert Hall Mansions. That was where Boris leased a huge apartment with a superb view of the Albert Memorial, the best in the block the agent had assured him. Boris was a sucker for gold leaf. Stepping over the mop, he checked his Luger in its holster and peered through the spy hole. There was Loretta with an armful of red roses. Blood red, his favourite colour.

"Boris darling, happy Easter," she breezed through the door and kissed him on both cheeks, Russian style, "these are for you."

"Loretta baby."

He forgave her disloyalty immediately. There were tears in his eyes. His mum always sent him roses at Easter. Crucifixion was no longer an option. Loretta got straight to the heart of the matter. There was no point in blackmailing Freddie because his marriage was a disaster. More significantly, Effie was a big noise in the theatre. A provincial one it may be but what an opening, for both of them!

"I know it's not the Bolshoi, Boris, but this time you could really fast track on the inside."

She was right, of course. When Boris had tried to muscle in on the Moscow musical scene he had only succeeded in controlling the theatre supply lines. The people influence had somehow eluded him. Surely his love and knowledge of the subject were as valid as anybody else's? Privately he had felt insulted. Admittedly, there had been the occasion when it had become necessary for an artistic director to have his head crushed by a falling stage weight, but that was only because he had slept with Dimitri's daughter who happened to be under age at the time. Boris had a moral code of sorts. He was now thinking how best to approach the situation between Freddie and Effie. He knew Loretta was ambitious and show business was the same the world over. Now if Effie had contacts with the Royal Opera House.

"Perhaps I should pay this Effie Bannister a call sometime?"

"Why don't you wait until I've seen Freddie again.?"

"When's that happening?"

"This Friday, at the Great Cumberland Hotel."

Boris chuckled. "You're quite a little mover, aren't you?"

"I'm gonna be a big mover too, Boris."

She was right again. He took her in his arms and saw the glow of ambition in her eyes. With a voice as sensual as a barrel of honey, she could excite on stage the same way as she did in bed.

She had her own rockets and now he wanted his.

7

Roz and Dale were sitting in the saloon bar of the Villain's Noose.

"So how long have you been an actress, then?"

"Actor."

"What?"

"I'm an actor."

"You ain't a bloke."

"Well you don't say Doctress, do you?"

"What?"

Roz giggled. Dale was so gauche. But lovely and natural with it.

"It's alright, I'm only winding you up. Actor is the politically correct term these days and it was Edith Evan who said the bit about the Doctress."

"Who's Edith Evans?"

"Dame Edith Evans, one of the greats."

"Oh yeah, she played the queen in Shakespeare in Love, didn't she?"

"No, oh Dale, you're hopeless."

"Yeah I know."

Roz knew he wasn't. His carpentry was fabulous, everyone in the company agreed. And everyone knew that Gaspard was chasing him too. But Dale was handling it, which was no mean task when it came to an uptight, spiteful bitch like Gaspard. Dale was so easy going that quite unconsciously he could diffuse every one of Gaspard's attempts at a public put down. Roz knew a red blooded male when she saw one, as long as she had her glasses on. Sure, she wanted to shag him but she knew there was more to him than sex. Anyway, they had both had two pints of Old Wallop which helped.

"Dale, you're not hopeless, okay?"

"Cheryl thinks so."

"Who's Cheryl?"

"Me ex."

"Oh well, say no more."

"We couldn't have kids 'cos I'm infertile like."

"You sure about that?"

"Oh yeah. I did all them tests, you know like wanking into a little bottle. Couldn't even get that right. Kept coming all over her watch strap."

The thought of Dale coming anywhere turned Roz on so she pressed ahead with the obvious question.

"So are you divorced?"

"Yeah. In the end she just give up on me. She said I was a useless chippy full of mastic and as far as she was concerned I could go stick me prick between a couple of skirting boards."

"Sounds like you're better off without her."

"Yeah. She had the Cortina and I kept the Makita cordless drill."

Roz thought that was hilarious but she didn't laugh out of respect. The last thing she wanted to do was hurt his feelings and there was something about his vulnerability that made him even more appealing. What she really wanted to do was to feel him all over in bed. She was aching for it. The bell for last orders went. It was loud enough to wake the living dead. Cedric the publican was a bit of an exhibitionist. He wore a blue blazer, a lemon polka-dot bow tie and sported a nicotine stained handlebar moustache.

"Come on my lovely luvvies," he said to the rest of the cast who were in the snug bar. It gave Roz a moment to consider her strategy.

"D'you wanna another pint then?" asked Dale.

"No thanks, I don't want to become legless."

Dale immediately got an image of her legs. He was about to ask her back for a coffee when he remembered he had only got a packet of PG Tips.

"How's the Yum Bum tree?" said Roz.

"Dunno, haven't been up there since we planted it."

"Perhaps it needs some tender loving care, you shouldn't ignore it."

Dale got the message and they were out of the pub and across the road in a jiffy.

The others were still clamouring for their last orders as Dale picked up a torch from the Oil Slick's sidecar which was parked inside the Haystack building on the ground floor; the Seventh Cavalry assembly area, as Effie called it. Gaspard spotted them entering via the back door and immediately put himself on snoop patrol. He followed them in the darkness as they made their way upstairs and through the workshop and across the scene dock to the wooden staircase that snaked like a merry-go-round to the lighthouse. Damnation, he cursed to himself (he was far too well-bred to use the F-word). But now he was confronted with an even greater problem. Ever since childhood, when his Governess had pushed him rather too recklessly on his swing, poor Gaspard had acquired a pathological fear of heights. He remained transfixed to the ground, gibbering like a jealous baboon and watching helplessly as Dale followed Roslyn into the heavens.

It was a clear night and the stars were twinkling brightly as they finally made it to the top.

"It seemed to take longer in the dark," said Roz.

"Well, now we're here, let's have a look before this torch conks out."

They moved closer as the flickering beam pointed the way to the potted plant. They peered over the rim anticipating nothing in particular beyond enjoying the intimacy of the moment. What they saw made them gasp. In the mere space of twenty-four hours the Yum Bum seeds had sprouted into a vigorous looking stem which had pushed its way through the surface and now had two leaf buds on the point of opening.

"I'm no green fingers," whispered Dale, but this is bloody amazing."

"Listen," said Roz, her voice almost trembling, "you can practically hear it growing."

At that moment the torch went out. In the moonlight their senses switched from the Yum Bum tree to each other, somehow the phenomenon they had just observed seemed to add magic to the atmosphere. It was as if the Yum Bum was willing them to move closer together. And so they did until their bodies touched. Dale could feel the soft warmth of Roslyn's breasts through his T-shirt. Roz could feel Dale's erection against her stomach. There was no holding back now. Their lips smacked together like two hungry octopi at a suckfest, their tongues thrusting back and forth in an orgy of saliva. Gaspard meanwhile had beat a frenzied retreat to grab his ultra-sensitive long range listening gear - a pair of hi-tech headphones and a long furry proboscis. He was just about to set things up when he heard them coming down the stairs again, and, by the sound of it, in one hell of a hurry. In the nick of time he ducked behind some scenery and watched them enter Dale's flat through the back door. It slammed shut. He crept towards it and positioned his microphone. Inside, Dale and Roz were stripping off. No need for overtures and niceties now. Dale had hardly got his Timberland boots off when Roz was on top of him. She was totally rampant, urgent and panting. Gaspard heard everything.

"God, I want your cock, I want your cock."

"You got it, you got it."

Outside, poor Gaspard was practically incandescent with frustration. If only, if only. He remained glued to the spot. It was a form of torture but he could do nothing about it. Roz and Dale were going at it with such unbridled frenzy that Gaspard found it embarrassing. Was this really what men and women did together? All those sounds. All those positions.

And Roz was crying out for more. Ye Gods, was Dale really going to put his head between that degenerate harlot's legs?

Talk about conspicuous clitoris, no wonder men had lost their sense of direction.

8

Boris loved England.

He didn't love it as much as Russia because at least in Russia they didn't close their opera houses for lack of money or a viable business plan. Admittedly, these days the average Russian would rather sell their grandmother for a bottle of vodka than buy a ticket to the Kirov but even so, at least the notion of culture hadn't been irrevocably pissed down the Volga.

Boris loved the English too. So undemonstrative and so polite. You could crush a person's fingers in a car door during broad daylight and nobody called the police if you said the magic words 'just a bit of domestic'. Whatever the papers might say, the English had kept their sense of family values. And the restaurants were good, the clubs were good, and so were the museum and art galleries, apart from occasional excursions into baseless vulgarity. Notwithstanding the legion of traffic wardens who couldn't be bribed, you could more or less do what you liked, and that's what Boris liked doing best of all.

He hadn't been to Moscow in over a year because there was no need to, he could control everything from his apartment overlooking Kensington Palace Gardens. After several bottles of Stolichnaya he even imagined that the renovation of the Albert Memorial had been sanctioned by HM the Queen specifically to satisfy his lust for gold and fondness for operatic grandeur.

Boris enjoyed the gentle English spring too. A pleasant alternative to the wild and ferocious Russian version with its cracking ice and turbulent waterfalls. Nevertheless, little traditions lingered on. Any day now he would place his mother's silver samovar on the balcony and invite Loretta round for lemon tea and caviar. He was glad they had got things sorted.

However, he still intended to carry out surveillance of the Haystack Theatre and make the acquaintance of Effie Bannister before Loretta's next liaison with Freddie. Having played the tape of Freddie in Tunisia he was aware that Effie had a young lover, and by the sound of it, the same age as Loretta. He knew what theatre people were like too. Oh yes. Instinctive animals. It all added up to a high risk scenario. He needed to know what really made Effie swing, apart from sex that was. A woman of her age with those kind of urges clearly had more than one string to her balalaika. Besides, Loretta had yet to persuade Freddie to play ball his way. But she would do that. She knew who buttered her bread.

Boris stopped musing and put in a call to Dimitri.
"Bring the Bentley round, we're going for a ride in the country."

At the Haystack Theatre, Gaspard and Dale were in the workshop discussing plans for the next production.

"Are you suffering from ear ache or something?" enquired Gaspard.

"Nah, just a bit of loose wax that's getting on me wick."

"Perhaps you should use a cotton bud, your fingers could be carrying all sorts of germs."

"Are you saying I don't wash me 'ands after a dump or something?"

30

Gaspard recoiled at the vulgarity.

"May I suggest that we discuss a more tasteful topic."

"Yeah okay. Who's this geezer wiv a beard then?"

Dale was referring to a book of naked men that Gaspard had been showing him. He was trying to feign interest because Gaspard was always banging on about music, art and literature. It wasn't that he didn't want to know, it was just that most of what Gaspard said went straight over the top of his head. Take the pictures for instance. Some of the blokes had got their arms chopped off and in one case even their head which Dale thought was a bit out of order until Gaspard explained that they were photographs of ancient statues, relics from the Greek and Roman civilisations. Whatever. They all looked like a bunch of posers anyway.

"That's Socrates, a philosopher," said Gaspard pointing to one of them.

"He don't look too happy."

"He was sentenced to death for his beliefs and died of hemlock poisoning."

"Just goes to show then, too much thinking don't do you no good."

"Most people don't think at all, which is why the world today is full of philistines."

Dale decided not to ask Gaspard what a philistine was because obviously he would get worked up about it. He'd been touchy all morning.

"Well, I just keep me nose clean and get on wiv it, know what I mean?"

Gaspard knew exactly what he meant. If only Dale had been given a proper upbringing he might not have chosen to have those ghastly tattoos on his arms. If only he had received a decent education he could appreciate the finer things in life. If only he would bend over and stop being so vaginalatrous.

"Have you given any more thought to our recent conversation?" asked Gaspard innocuously.

"You mean about Effie?"

"Precisely."

"I shan't break me promise, I'll be discreet like."

"I'm relieved to hear that, please tread delicately, I would hate to see her get hurt."

"Trust me, as if on egg shells."

Gaspard felt it was inappropriate to bring Roslyn into the equation just at the moment. Besides, he was still trying to erase that image of unfettered fornication which he found so utterly repugnant. He decided to proceed carefully.

"What I'm trying to say Dale is that, prior to your appointment, I had to endure the most ghastly riffraff, local unskilled labour who wore hideously ill-fitting jeans and malodorous trainers and were obsessed with football. I was obliged to watch them run amok with their electric screwdrivers and bad manners, scuffing the hessian and firing the staple gun in every direction. Needless to say I dismissed every one of them but it was a tiresome duty that caused me considerable vexation. Your presence has changed all that. You are a craftsman Dale. I recognise and value that. I would hate to see you go just because of an ill-judged relationship with our mutual employer."

Once again, Dale was gob-smacked. It was the first time in his life that anyone had cared a toss about his welfare. Admittedly, the old king and queen had done their best but they had lacked imagination. They were both dead now. The old king died of cancer after smoking sixty a day and old queen collided with a moped when she jumped off a bus. Well, that was life, wasn't it? Still, they had enjoyed it while it lasted and that's what it was all about. In a funny way they had their standards though. Honest and straight, the pair of them. Both hard grafters too which was a quality Dale had inherited in abundance. It impressed Gaspard and Effie in equal measure. His work duties bounced freely back and forth between the two of them, there was not set pattern, it just sort of happened.

He left Gaspard gazing moodily at his naked men to make a few local calls in the Cascade delivery van, after which he planned to nip up to the lighthouse at lunch time with Roz to inspect the Yum Bum tree in daylight. After yesterday's love making he had got an aching jaw but he wasn't going to tell anyone about it. But everything went smoothly. There were no awkward customers and he enjoyed talking to them and telling them all about his job. Effie said he was a natural marketing asset which was an improvement on Cheryl's view that he was a natural arsehole.

After his morning delivery round he drove the van into the Seventh Cavalry assembly area just as Boris and Dimitri arrived in their big green Bentley.

"You take the back and I'll take the front," said Boris.

They were a good team. They could read each other's mind. Boris was wearing a Savile Row suit with an expensive silk handkerchief tucked in the breast pocket. With his broad shoulders and military bearing he was really quite handsome. He charmed a lot of women. As Dimitri made his way round the back of the theatre Boris walked into Effie's shop at the front, a Gauloise burning merrily from his gold cigarette holder. Effie perked up instantly. She had been down in the dumps all morning following a blazing row with Freddie last night. He had told her he was going to a special conference in London and couldn't reveal its whereabouts for security reasons. She knew he was lying and told Dale about it.

"I shouldn't be at all surprised if he's become infatuated with some blonde bimbo in Admin who's convinced him she's doing an MBA in research ethics or something equally stupid."

"I didn't think Freddie was interested in other women."

"That's the trouble with men, they never tell you the truth."

Fortunately for Dale, Gaspard entered the conversation just at the right moment, but Effie was still smarting, until she saw Boris, that was.

"Good morning," he said expansively, "what a lovely shop."

"How kind of you to say so," replied Effie, warming instinctively towards a fellow smoker who exuded confidence and wealth, "we do our best."

She had an unlit cigarette between her lips and started to scrabble around in her handbag.

"I couldn't possibly trouble you for a light could I? I've been walking around for hours trying to get one on but to no avail."

"It is my pleasure," said Boris, producing his gold Dunhill, "and please will you join me in one of these?" he proffered his Gauloises.

"Ooh, high tar and no tip, you do live dangerously, but thanks very much."

"Well, let me put it this way," said Boris, admiring her figure and the cut of her dress, "I like to live."

"Oh yes, don't we all, in spite of the government health warnings," said Effie, nearing a self-induced hoot, "thank you." Boris held the lighter in his huge hand while Effie drew long and hard as was her custom. When the nicotine hit her stomach she started coughing violently. Boris offered to get her a glass of water as if he were a perfect gentleman but Effie waved his offer aside, preferring instead to bask in the attention.

Meanwhile, at the back of the theatre, Dimitri had found his way across the scene dock to the foot of the staircase. He was alarmed to see Gaspard loitering at the bottom surrounded by hi-tech listening gear. Clearly he was spying but why didn't he climb the steps? He smelt a rat and sank into the shadows, his micro-camera at the ready. Up above in the lighthouse, Dale and Roz were speechless. They were staring at the Yum Bum which had grown nearly a metre high and had started to develop branches. Thick dark leaves sprouted all over.

"Fantastic."

"Incredible."

"Amazing."

"Also probably abnormal."

"Let's check it out again after the show tonight."

Roz and Dale descended the steps after a deep throat snog. Dimitri watched Gaspard whisk his surveillance gear away and got a quick mug shot with his micro-camera. He snapped another one of Roz and Dale as they scampered along their separate ways.

Dale entered the shop from the rear just as Effie was concluding business. She looked ecstatic.

"Dale, can I introduce you to Mr Blodvrinsky, he's just bought fifty water gardens and I said you'd be delighted to carry out the installation."

"My pleasure," said Dale, who was always positive about everything.

"Mr Blodvrinsky's an impresario, isn't that marvellous?"

"Yeah great," said Dale, who wasn't sure whether that meant Boris was something to do with the circus.

"Naturally he's interested in our theatre," said Effie, who was bubbling away like a hot water spring, "and I said we'd be delighted to give him a guided tour ."

"Sure, no probs," said Dale, wondering whether the Yum Bum was off limits; he had not even told her about its incredible growth yet.

Just then, Boris spotted Dimitri scowling in the corner of his eye and decided it was time to conclude the charm offensive. It had not been hard work though because Effie was a natural when it came to socialising and clearly the entrepreneurial culture was alive and kicking. He had already made up his mind. She was a woman he could do business with. Freddie must be mad not to be happy with a woman like Effie. But Boris soon changed his mood when Dimitri gave him the low-down about Gaspard.

"Let's stick around a bit and watch him," he growled, " we've got plenty of time."

It took the best part of ten minutes to disengage with Effie, she was that hyper, after which they hung around in the car park until they both got pissed off and plumped for a bottle of Stolichnaya and six rounds of prawn salad sandwiches in the lounge bar of the Villain's Noose instead. Cedric made a big fuss of them. He was about to bore them rigid with his bogus Falklands Conflict stories when Dimitri spotted Gaspard walking across the Haystack's shingled car park towards the public telephone kiosk. So, much to Cedric's chagrin, they settled up smartly and disappeared round the back of the pub where nobody could see what they were up to. Dimitri put some headphones on.

"You wanna go hi-tech, I give you hi-tech," he muttered angrily. He was so competitive.

"Stay cool Dimitri, don't lose it," said Boris as they picked up a signal.

Inside the telephone kiosk, Gaspard looked around cautiously before punching in a number.

"What a prick," hissed Dimitri.

"Just concentrate on the sequence," snapped Boris. They watched and listened intently as Gaspard made his connection. A male voice answered.

"Yes?"

"You recognise my voice, of course."

"Yes."

"Cassandra has a rendezvous in London tonight."

"Who with?"

"I don't know."

"Where?"

"I don't know."

"Why?"

"Look, this may sound tedious but I don't know that either."

"Time for a smack botty then."

"Must you be so childish?"

"Just follow him, dear chap, and try not to lose him."

"Please don't patronise me, I know what I'm doing."

"I'm relieved to hear it, the section needs a success. Goodbye number six."

Once again Gaspard was left with the mocking sound of a dead telephone. But there was another sound which he did not hear.

It was Boris choking with rage.

9

Freddie was in his office getting all paranoid about his assistant Ian Trubshaw. He was convinced that the only reason Trubshaw accompanied him on the trip to Tunisia was to keep an eye on him, no doubt on the orders of Reginald Ponsonby-Spratt, the Controller of Projects. A devious bastard if ever there was. But Freddie had got the measure of him. Ponsonby-Spratt, or The Sprout, as he was more popularly known (because of the shape of his head and poxy complexion), had asked to see him about Project Cassandra yet again. In a previous meeting he had requested that Freddie sign a note confirming that no further copies of the computer programme existed now that it had been removed from the hard disk and all papers shredded. Freddie gave his signature, barely able to conceal a smile. What kind of fool did The Sprout think he was? An idea like Project Cassandra came once in a blue moon. Freddie had seen the move coming a mile off and had taken copies of everything a month before the Tunisian conference. He knew the only reason he was sent to Tunisia was to get him out of the way while they ransacked his office. Everyone knew that The Sprout was sleeping with Gloria

Fitzbagley the recently appointed Director of MI5. And being the slimy creep that he was, he would often nip from between her sheets for a quick drinky poo's and free lunch with Sir Rodney Snodder the Head of MI6. No wonder Ian Trubshaw was flitting about like a demented butterfly. He thought Freddie would spot a tell-tale sign any moment and go ballistic. Most of the time Freddie was very quiet and reflective, always lost in his thoughts. But when a raw nerve was touched, well, say no more.

"What time is your appointment with the Sprout?" asked Trubshaw, for the umpteenth time.

"Four o'clock, and I'm fully aware that he likes to get away promptly for the weekend, thank you."

Freddie despised Ian Trubshaw. A weasel. A wimp. A snivelling little apology for a human being. Not a patch on his father Ted. Now there was a scientist for you. Died of a heart attack induced on the squash court. Silly man. At his age. Freddie was very close to him. They shared each other's research. He was the only one by his hospital bed when Ted finally popped his clogs.

"Don't let the bastards grind you down, Freddie."

"I won't Ted, I give you my word."

"Here's my safe key Freddie, take it and - "

Zonk. Kaput in mid-sentence. Freddie practically leapt for joy when he opened Ted's safe and read the contents of his paper: 'The Ergonomic Psychology Factor when applied as a Human Behavioural Analysis to a Political Hypothesis'. Dear old Ted had cottoned on to a line of thinking that was almost identical to his own but had been unable to translate it beyond a complex mathematical equation. But Freddie, no mean slouch when it came to figures, had cracked it. Now all he had to do was build an integrated programme, system test it and draw up an implementation plan. That was when The Sprout put the boot in.

"I'm sure it will all be for the best in the long run Freddie," said The Sprout with a leer insincere, "and now we must talk about next moves."

"Oh really?"

"Indeed yes. Onwards and upwards as they say."

By the time Freddie had returned to his office Ian Trubshaw had departed. Just as well because Freddie was mortified with humiliation. The reality of onwards and upwards was backwards and sideways. The Sprout had appointed him as Senior Project Evaluation Officer. Freddie had practically gagged on the words. After all these years they could put him to no better use than that. A sifter and filterer of younger scientist's ideas. The bastards. His time would come. He grabbed his briefcase and headed for the station. Tonight Loretta. Tomorrow the world. He believed in himself.

"Don't lose him," said Boris.

"I lose bugger nothing," said Dimitri, as he tailed Gaspard who was following Freddie at a safe distance into the station.

The three of them were still in sync as Freddie arrived at Waterloo and hailed a taxi.

"Follow that cab," said Gaspard, elbowing his way past a waiting stranger.

"Follow that cab," said Dimitri, kicking some poor bastard in the groin.

Freddie's cab jumped the lights but Gaspard's didn't. By the time Gaspard caught up with him, Freddie was already inside the Great Cumberland Hotel. Gaspard was all of a fluster. He arrived just in time to see Loretta kiss Freddie on both cheeks. He was so stunned by her beauty that he nearly forgot to stay out of their eye-line. No goofing up now, the section needed a success. He was about to position himself when a foreign looking woman with a ridiculous hat and three weeks Mediterranean make-up approached him. He tried to avoid her but with little success. She had a stupid looking miniature poodle with a frizzy pink perm like freshly spun candy floss. It pranced up and down on its pom-pommed paws in some kind of neurotic attempt at doggy dressage.

"Excuse me," said the woman, in a thick Viennese accent, "please hold onto Maximillian vile I speak to reception, I don't sink zey like doks."

"Madam, neither do I," replied Gaspard.

"Ach, he's a pussy cat as long as you don't give him crisps."
Gaspard was too flabbergasted to protest further.

As Maximillian began to yap hysterically, a Japanese couple focused their cameras for a jolly holiday snap. Talk about centre of attraction. A hotel flunky appeared from nowhere.

"I'm terribly sorry sir, we don't allow dogs in the hotel."

"The stupid animal is nothing to do with me, as far as I'm concerned you can give him to the chef, now please take him away."

But Maximillian had other ideas about becoming Chien et Poisson Pie and ping ponged across the foyer in a bid for freedom. Gaspard shrunk back from the commotion with the awful realisation that he had also lost Freddie and Loretta. There was no sign of them anywhere. He threw his hands in the air and strode out of the hotel in a fit of petulant exasperation. In a dark corner, Dimitri fell about laughing.

Outside it was raining cats and dogs. A liveried doorman was shielding guests from the deluge with an umbrella the size of a Maharaja's tent.

"Would you like a taxi, sir?"

"Well of course I would, only a fool would set off in a monsoon like this."

A taxi was duly hailed. Dimitri, having composed himself, moved in again to watch. The doorman was still being kindly even though Gaspard was muttering under his breath that the serving classes ought to have elastoplast across their lips.

"Where to sir?"

"The Trappist's Tool, Old Compton Street."

Dimitri relayed the address to Boris via his mobile as soon as the taxi pulled away.

"Stay at the hotel," said Boris, "cover Freddie and Loretta and ring me if they make a move, I'm on my way to Old Compton Street."

Boris was familiar with The Trappist's Tool. He managed their protection. The Bethnal Green boys cut up rotten when he had first muscled in on their contract but eventually they came to an understanding. It was amazing how a strategically placed pint of sulphuric acid could iron out those difficult clauses. Well, let's face it, there was no street cred in being a burnt out eunuch in Bethnal Green.

By the time Boris arrived, poor Gaspard was drowning his sorrows in gin. After his third double he was seriously into melancholia. By the fourth, the focus of his introspection had shifted away from his incompetence as a secret service agent to his failure as a stage designer. Why wasn't he up there with the best of them? The fact of the matter was that he was too good for them. Yes, that was it.

As a cloud of delusion descended, he poured the remains of his tonic over a saturated slab of lemon which sat in the bottom of his glass like a jelly fish with a hangover. Was it really asking too much to be served with a delicately cut slice that could float on the surface where it would titillate the taste buds as it mingled with the bubbles? Wasn't there anyone who knew how to do things properly these days? Didn't anyone have a sense of style?

Only last week he had endured the Royal Opera's production of Rimsky-Korsakov's The Golden Cockerel, the sheer aridity of which had reduced him to tears of rage and indignation. Oh, if only he could have been the driving force, how he would have dazzled everyone with the magnificent opulence of Tsarist Russia. King Dodon would ride into battle in crimson and garlic whilst the Queen of Shemarka would sing her famous sunrise aria bathed in orange and gold, the whole stage ablaze in glorious colour. And instead of that, what did he have to put up with? Monochrome throughout! Dull swathes of grey on vast imageless flats that rose like storm drains into the sky. All the magic of a sewage farm on a rainy day. No wonder the advertised conductor had stayed in bed. Even the Golden Cockerel itself had been reduced to a tacky cardboard cut-out on an elongated broomstick. And was King Dodon pecked to death by this apology for sado-masochistic magic? No, of course not. At the very moment when the audience should have been brought to the edge of their seats by the bloody spectacle of splattered brains and disgorged entrails, a little plastic gun had gone off pop. The paucity of imagination defied comprehension. The philistines had infiltrated everywhere. Artists such as he might just as well retire to another planet.

Back at the Great Cumberland Hotel, Freddie was marvelling at the beauty of Loretta's body. It was only the second time in his life that he had seen a black woman naked, apart from all those African documentaries on television. He was fascinated by the pinkness of her tongue, the smooth chocolate allure of her breasts. And he was more than happy with the erectile performance of his penis.

"Hmm, some rocket," whispered Loretta, gently sliding her hand up and down its shaft.

Freddie let himself fly with the sensation. It felt incredible. Fantastic. He was about to come prematurely when Loretta suddenly let go and swung herself on top of him. Such amazing grace, such dong riveting action. And this was only the beginning.

Gaspard on the other hand was having some difficulty in holding his glass. Ever since some idiot in Whitehall had presented a paper entitled 'The Cross Fertilisation between Security Agencies' things had gone from bad to worse. He knew that Sir Rodney Snodder, the Head of MI6, was jealous of his superior intellect, and when this buffoon's paper had gained the backing of three cabinet ministers it wasn't long before he was the first to be offered a unique career development opportunity in MI5. But all the fertiliser in the world couldn't hide the deeply embedded suspicion between the two departments. After his transfer, he was vilified by both. When he complained that he was in an impossible position, his remarks were forwarded to the author of the paper who concluded that somebody with their head in the freezer and feet in the fire could, on average, be said to be reasonably comfortable. Needless to say, the author of the paper was an economist seconded to Personnel. Gaspard knew he was being deliberately squeezed out. But help was at hand.

"Here, let me get you another," said Boris, who had been watching Gaspard's slow descent into self-pitying inebriation from across the bar.

Gaspard mumbled incoherently. Boris thought he heard the name Rimsky-Korsakov. Could this really be a kindred spirit? Strangely, he no longer wanted to annihilate him. He knew Dimitri would be disappointed but the fact was, rock solid though he may be in the friendship stakes, somebody whose musical appreciation peaked at Oasis did rather leave a yawning gap, culturally speaking. Boris repeated his offer.

"That's very kind of you," said Gaspard, rallying to his senses, "I'm on gin."

"Let me improve on that," replied Boris, gripping his cigarette holder between gold capped teeth.

He strode to the bar leaving Gaspard to admire his broad shoulders and ram rod posture. The fact that in between his move from MI6 to MI5 he had been conveniently dropped from each department's Eastern Bloc Agent Familiarisation Programme was neither here nor there. He could spot a Russian a mile off. Well, so what? Nobody paid any attention to his reports, in fact it was widely known that Sir Rodney Snodder had ridiculed the passages he had helpfully included about the richness of Russia's religious icons. He was past caring and anyway, a glass of glasnost was hardly a dismissable offence.

Meanwhile, back at the Great Cumberland Hotel, Loretta was riding gently back and forth on top of Freddie. Her legs were opened wider now which gave her a lovely burning sensation as more of her pelvis engaged with Freddie's rising crutch. There was no denying it, he had the thrust, she had the ignition.

"Oooh Freddie," she gasped, seasoned pro that she was, she could hardly believe that she was coming, "I'm all for an early blast off!"

"Me too!"

By mutual consent, they had arrived at another definite go situation for an all systems shag.

"And as if that wasn't bad enough," said Gaspard, as Boris topped up his glass with more pink champagne, "the soprano singing the golden cockerel was dressed like Norah Batty."

43

"A travesty of taste," replied Boris sincerely.

"Precisely," said Gaspard, who was finding the ambience most gratifying, "and the rising sun, instead of matching the brilliance of Rimsky-Korsakov's orchestration, was reduced to a painted canvas no bigger than a card table."

"That is practically a crime," said Boris, identifying totally with Gaspard's seething indignation.

"One simply cannot piggy-back satire with pretension," continued Gaspard, "unless of course one is a philistine."

"We are surrounded by vandals."

"Ignorant peasants."

"We should shoot every one of them."

"Personally, I would prefer to run them through with a sabre."

"You know," said Boris smiling as sweetly as Stalin as he produced yet another version of his opulent business card, "you and I have a lot in common."

Gaspard could hardly believe his eyes as he focused on the heavy gold lettering.

Boris Blodvrinsky - *International Opera Production.*

Loretta let rip with a deep throated gasp as Freddie erupted inside her. Up until now, mutual orgasm for both of them had been a distant memory, but tonight it had been revisited and with stunning effect. She flopped on top of him. She could feel the pace of his heart pounding against her breast. Her nipples still as hard as his penis inside her. It had been good. Surprisingly good. It was a pity in a way that she would now have to steer the conversation towards Effie.

Poor Gaspard. The combined effect of alcohol and the chance meeting with an international opera producer was just too much for one night. Before Gaspard passed out altogether, Boris rang Dimitri and told him to come on over. They chatted in the gents while Gaspard pissed down his leg.

"Drive him home," said Boris, "play him my CD's, he loves opera, he's one of us."

"You mean he's one of you."

"Dimitri, we've had this kind of conversation before, just get him home safely."

"You want me to tuck him up in bed?"

"I want you to bug his place."

"Okay, he's gonna hit the sack, believe me."

"Yah, well take it easy, he's gonna be real useful. Ring me tomorrow, I'm going home."

"What about the other two?"

"No problem, they're in Suite 42."

Dimitri chuckled. He had bugged that one too.

In Suite 42, Freddie wanted to talk about rocket science rather than about Effie but Loretta was too insistent. After such great sex he couldn't understand why but then the penny dropped. Loretta was ambitious, she'd had enough of the small time in foreign hotels and wanted a gig at the Haystack Theatre, it was only thirty miles from London. Freddie was becoming aware that he had said more in Tunisia than he realised. The trouble was he couldn't remember what. He recalled Loretta's singing though. Utterly fantastic. Every man had been completely pole-axed by her mesmeric sultriness. But trying to sort out the next best steps was causing him a bit of a problem.

"It was bad enough trying to conceal where I would be tonight," he said, "my wife is very astute, so how on earth can I introduce you?"

"You don't have to," said Loretta, softly padding her long fingers across his chest like a tarantula on an away day, "Boris will take care of all that."

"Ah yes," said Freddie thoughtfully, "....Boris."

He could remember Boris right enough. That big Russian who looked liked General Lebed and had bought endless cocktails at the bar followed by several bottles of champagne during the hotel cabaret. And then another penny dropped. A bigger one this time. Freddie cursed himself for being so naive but then just as quickly rationalised himself out of it. His formal career was over. The Sprout and his political cronies had made sure of that. His marriage was over. Effie and her insatiable urges were to blame for that. Now it was his turn to indulge in some

45

animal instincts, not to mention an unquantifiable measure of cunning.

The bottle of champagne that had been delivered by room service earlier was deliciously chilled. Freddie proposed a toast.

"To your singing career."

"To Project Cassandra," replied Loretta.

As she drained her glass she knew that, from now on, she alone was not enough.

10

"Did you enjoy your scrambled eggs Freddie?" said Boris, the following morning.

The four of them were breakfasting in Boris's apartment with its beautiful view of the Albert Memorial.

"Yes thank you."

"I was taught how to cook real scrambled eggs by a French chef," said Boris proudly, "just beat them lightly with a fork and serve on a hot plate with a touch of black pepper."

Dimitri had already wolfed his eggs down and was mopping up the HP sauce with his bread.

"Boris is a man of many talents," said Loretta quickly, noticing Boris's irritation with Dimitri's plebeian manners, "as I said last night, there's not much he can't do when he puts his mind to it."

Dimitri burped.

"Go wash the Bentley will you," snapped Boris, "I'll ring you when it's time to take Freddie to the station."

Dimitri left without comment. Anyway, scrambled eggs always made him fart.

"So tell me about Project Cassandra," said Boris, beaming confidently beside his mother's silver samovar. He had already played the video several times but wondered whether Freddie had said anything of vital importance while his head was under the sheets. Freddie paused before replying, as was his manner, and took note of the opulent surroundings. He could smell the real leather of the Bentley again. He recalled the taste of Loretta's tongue, all her juices and delights. He caught an imaginary glimpse of The Spratt's patronising sneer. He heard Effie's phlegm laden cough, Ian Trubshaw's nasal whine and all his colleagues' stifled mirth. He believed in himself, he had to, no one else did. He had the balls and he had the brains. And with the flag of St George virtually synonymous with racist bigotry, why should he have a conscience about selling England down the river?

"Well, it's both straightforward and complicated," he began.

An hour later he had finished. He had revealed everything except the very last twist, the sheer bit of genius that was the ace to keep up his sleeve. Nobody present was any the wiser. A bit of skewered emphasis here and there and Project Cassandra had become a piece of leading edge research as opposed to the diabolical concoction that it really was.

"I think a cognac is in order," said Boris, seriously impressed.

Three glasses appeared. Three generous measures. One big toast.

"So what happens now?" said Freddie, "they'll be watching me closely."

"And we'll be watching them," said Boris, warming his brandy glass in the palm of his hands, "don't worry about a thing, just give me a list of your requirements and I'll be in touch."

"I'm afraid my wife is already suspicious."

"I'll see to it that she has an appropriate distraction."

"She's already got one."

"So tell me about it."

Freddie launched into another saga but not so long this time. There was only so much you could say about massage oil on

48

the chaise-longue and youthful pubies on the bathroom mat, not to mention Effie's new found enthusiasm for playing Chopin on the piano again.

"I think it's lovely that Effie has music in her blood," said Loretta.

"Yah," agreed Boris, "a soul without music is a soul in vain." Freddie being tone deaf made no further comment.

Dimitri was listening to Oasis on Capital Radio when Boris rang him.

"Make sure you're not tailed."

"You know I got eyes in the back of my head."
This was true. He had also got the aural reception of a bat and the olfactory sense of a tiger. Dimitri was Reconnaissance Man not Renaissance Man. Nevertheless, he was still eyeing a long-legged blonde swanking about with her Afghan hound when Dale drove round the Royal Albert Hall in the Cascade delivery van. As soon as he spotted Freddie with Loretta he quickly carried on round the building. Loretta did not look like a fellow scientist, that was for sure, and if Effie's suspicions were correct he'd be better off keeping a low profile. He double parked the van round a corner and nipped back on foot in time to see them climb into Boris's Bentley and drive off. A few minutes later he pulled up outside the entrance.

"Delivery for Mr Blodvrinsky," he chirped, "I'm expected."
The problem was that Boris, somewhat untypically, had forgotten all about it. After her biggest ever single sale, Effie had moved quickly to despatch Dale and now, here he was, in Boris's hallway wondering whether the remaining forty-nine ornamental water gardens were all going to be installed up several flights of stairs. By the time he reached the top he was relieved that today's visit was just a one-off installation.

Boris, in spite of his memory lapse was unfazed by events. With Project Cassandra occupying his thoughts he was already dreaming of the deals he would be making the world over, the Balkans, the Middle East, Israel, Pakistan and China. He, with a schnapps and Rum Baba in a Viennese coffee shop, Dimitri with a Big Mac on Clapham Common.

"I'm only installing one today," said Dale helpfully, "just so's you can get the feel of it like."

"Yah, sure, go right ahead."

Dale was not ready for such a green light go-ahead as that. How did *he* know where to put it? Boris wasn't ready for it either, he was still fantasising about being Goldfinger. Fortunately, Dale remembered Gaspard's advice about set design - 'conceive the whole first and the details will follow naturally'.

"Most people put them in their living room but that don't mean to say that's always the right choice. Perhaps I could have a look around first?"

"Yah, you do that, I'll be in the lounge."

Boris left Dale standing there. Even for someone as casual as Dale, it struck him as a dose of excessive trust, after all, they had only met once before for a couple of minutes. Effie had clearly been impressed with Boris and definitely charmed. And if Dale had read her body language correctly, charmed right through to her knickers. Perhaps this was turning into a lucky turn of events, what with Roz and all that stuff. After Boris had departed from the Haystack, Effie had kept asking Dale silly questions like did he think Boris was a millionaire or a billionaire? Perhaps he would make a donation to the theatre and if so, how much? Maybe he would fund a much needed face-lift or, better still, a total refurbishment? And what about that Savile Row suit and beautiful silk shirt by Loosehound & Hasser?

As Dale wandered from room to room it struck him that Boris had one helluver swanky pad. The furnishings were fabulous. Everything was rich and lavish. IKEA and MFI it was not. The furniture was made by a bloody good cabinet maker, as a chippy he could tell that. There were curtains and drapes and posh looking carpets all over the place. Just like a picture out of one of Gaspard's books, in fact Gaspard would love it. Come to think of it, Effie would love it too. And Boris didn't know where to put his water garden? It was as if the FA couldn't spell football.

Dale was wondering where to go next when the waltz from Eugene Onegin flooded through the apartment. He didn't know what it was but he vaguely remembered hearing it on Classic FM. Gaspard had urged him to tune in when he had said that he couldn't understand the introductions on Radio 3 which Gaspard listened to continuously. Whatever the case, the music sounded beautiful and seemed to suit the surroundings. Dale traced the source to the lounge and tapped politely on the half opened door. Manners maketh a man, the old queen used to say. The music was going full belt and since there was no reply he peered in. There was Boris in velvet smoking jacket, dancing to the music with a rat-tailed mop in his arms.

"Is that a good investment mummy or is that a good investment?"

Dale was about to say pardon when he realised that he was not Boris's mummy. So what was going on then? Dale stood in the doorway non-plussed watching Boris dancing whilst having a singular two-way conversation.

'It's only a good investment if he delivers and you don't know if he can do that.'

"But he's one of their most senior scientists mummy, years of experience behind him, this is his latest project."

'So how come they don't want to know about it?'

"It's too political, you wouldn't understand."

'Huh, and I suppose you do?'

The music swelled and Boris started to shake the mop in mounting anger.

"What am I? Stupid? Is that what you're saying?"

'Yah, that's right, take it out on your poor defenceless old mother.'

"Everything's under control, I can manage it."

'Sure, sure, like where's your gun for when the SAS comes crashing through the window?'

Tchaikovsky was piling on the climax now as the brass and percussion began to kick the shit out of it. Boris was purple in the face, yelling and screaming - the rat tails flailing.

"SAS, MI6, MI5 nobody moves without I know about it!"

'Ha ha ha, what do you know about anything?'

"Stop it mummy, stop it, don't do this to me!"

'So where did you stick your microphone son, up their arsehole?'

"Dimitri fixed everything."

'Ah Dimitri, Dimitri, now there's a real man talking.'

As the music crashed to its final climax, Boris flung the mop violently across the room. Dale eased himself back into the hallway. Best not to get involved with a bit of domestic, let things settle down a bit, maybe put the kettle on? That seemed like a good idea so Dale made a bee line for the kitchen to suss things out. There on the shelf was a packet of Twining's Broken Orange Pekoe Tips, one of Gaspard's favourites. He could see Boris and Gaspard hitting it off. Then it occurred to him that that might make Effie jealous. Perhaps not. A bloke what dances wiv a mop is more likely to be a nutter than a stern-tube artist, thought Dale to himself.

While the kettle boiled, Dale returned to the lounge and tapped politely on the door again.

"Excuse me, Mr Blodvrinsky."

"Yah, yah, come in, come in, and call me Boris."

"Oh righto, ta, um, I was just wondering what it was like in here, for the water garden like."

"Probably the best, this is where I do my thinking, whaddya think?"

"Very nice."

"Good, we have it in here then. Now sit down and tell me all about yourself. You wanna iced tea and vodka?"

Dale thought it would probably cause offence if he said that he'd already put the kettle on.

"Ta, just a small one then, 'cos I'm driving."

"Ah, the English, so responsible, that's why I like them."

Dale gave his best friendly smile in return and Boris seemed to take it as a cue to commence chatting about this and that and any old other. It was all very cosy and some while later Dale accepted a second drink. Boris served him a fresh glass in a delicate silver holder that Gaspard would've gone potty over.

Boris noticed that Dale was sinking back into the cushioned sofa. So, this was Effie Bannister's toy boy was it? He could be useful. Any moment now the Dacha Dandelion would kick in, after which he would be positively singing; Boris was a dab hand at slipping the powders. Dale suspected nothing. In fact he was tripping out on his life history already. Boris just prodded gently here and there to bring him right up to date. Dale even told him how he had shagged some actress whilst planting a tree. So, Boris concluded, here was a divorced and penniless chippy with a roving dick and an arse that Gaspard fancied. He seemed to have led an aimless life and somehow ended up with no real enemies. A slag of an ex-wife by the sound of it but with no hassles as long as he paid the tax and insurance on some old Cortina. Freddie wouldn't be a problem as long as he got his secret missile research station and could slip a length to Loretta every so often. Handling Effie could be a bit tricky but there again, everyone had their price. Quite what Effie's was, Boris had yet to establish.

"Sounds like the Haystack theatre has got a lot going for it," said Boris, when Dale eventually drew breath.

"Oh yeah, definitely. Mind you, it needs more than a lick of paint and I'd love to have a go at replacing them rickety old steps."

"The ones up to the lighthouse?"

"Yeah."

"Demolish and rebuild, that's my answer."

"Well that's mega bucks and planning permission innit?"

Boris chuckled. No wonder the lad was a drifter. No vision. By the time Project Cassandra came on stream there might not be any necessity for planning permission.

There may not even be a Houses of Parliament.

11

Spring was in the air but that wasn't the reason why certain relationships began to shift and slide around a bit. Amazingly, when Freddie got back home, there was no blazing row with Effie. That was because Dale had rung her beforehand to say that he and Boris were getting along like a house on fire. Boris loved the water garden and Dale reckoned that if they played their cards right, Boris would probably cough up some serious dosh for the Haystack. Effie forgave him for being pissed and assured him that she understood entirely the need to accept hospitality from such a wealthy sponsor. She was also terribly excited about a further visit from Boris and was most impressed that he had made arrangements to return Dale and the Cascade delivery van separately on account of Dale being legless.

Freddie, for his part, was equally excited about the prospect of having his own secret missile research centre, not to mention certain pencilled-in dalliances of a ballistically sexual nature with Loretta. So the bottom line between Freddie and Effie at that juncture was pure fragrance, unheard of in the Bannister household. Such was their conviviality that they transferred it to the Villain's Noose.

They were still there when Dale staggered in, having been driven all the way home by Dimitri, on Boris's orders of course. Dimitri wasn't too happy about that. He was suspicious of Dale. There was something about him, he couldn't put his finger on it, but it was there. Anyway, he had bugged the Cascade delivery van while Dale was installing the water garden. And there was something else that bothered Dimitri too, so he mentioned it to Boris before driving Dale to Fropsham.

"How come he could think straight enough to fix up that fish tank after two Dacha Dandelions?"

"It's not a fish tank Dimitri, it's a water garden."

"Well something stinks and if it isn't fish then it must be him."

"There's no need to get paranoid Dimitri, he's got a strong constitution that's all.

"*I'm* the strong one, remember?"

"Yah, sure, have you fixed the van?"

"Yeah."

"Good, so what's the problem?"

"Nothing's a problem."

Boris gave Dimitri a big bear hug and smile. He knew he was missing Svetlana and Anita. Underneath the hard shell was a sensitive man, he just needed reassurance now and again.

"We go back a long way Dimitri, you're rock solid."

"Sure no problem."

"D'you fancy a jar?" said Dale, as the Bentley drew up outside the Villain's Noose.

"Not while I'm on duty," replied Dimitri tersely.

"Okay, see ya around then."

Dale was oblivious to the snub and sauntered straight into the pub.

"Dear boy, how lovely to see you," greeted Effie effusively, " are you beyond drinking?"

"Never, I thought you'd 'ave one lined up already."

Effie hooted with the sheer merriment of it all.

"Well you look as if you're about to collapse, sit down, I'm sure Freddie will do the honours."

"Okay then, ooh, that's better, cor, that Boris don't 'alf pack a mean vodka, at one point I thought I was going to throw up in the water garden, puke and pebbles all together like."

Effie convulsed, Dale grinned, but Freddie was suddenly alert. Boris? Did Dale say Boris? It wasn't a name to brush aside a consequence. Freddie was quick to remove the glint in his eye.

"What's your poison Dale?" he said, as innocently as the first crocus in spring.

"Pint of Old Wallop, thanks."

"My sweet?"

"I'll stay with the gin, thank you."

Freddie went to the bar. Cedric was beaming. As a publican he thought Freddie and Effie were a star turn, very important people to have in the pub, art and science together, movers and shakers in Fropsham, good for business. He wasn't sure about Dale though. Somebody who didn't shave every day and spoke like they were in East Enders was a bit iffy. Cedric was a snob who had learnt to patronise the rough end of the trade in order to sustain his beer turnover. Freehouse or not, he believed in a policy of deliverables which manifested itself in a clientele that was as pissed as a newt regardless of their pecking order in life's great urinal.

"What'll it be Freddie?"

"Gin and tonic for Effie, lager shandy for me, and a pint of Old Wallop for Dale, please."

Cedric wafted into action, the combination of Old Spice and Old Virginia propelled together by the Spitfire wings of his polka-dot bow tie.

"Haven't seen you around for a while Freddie, how goes it?"

"I've been very busy but it's nice to get out a bit."

"Top government business eh?"

Poor dear Cedric would shit in his Tory Y-fronts if only he knew what Freddie was really up to. Freddie offered an enigmatic smile.

"Oh yes indeed, the future of mankind held in the balance."

Cedric snuffled sycophantically into the amber fronds of his handlebar moustache.

"Well, in that case old boy, have this one on the house."

"That's very kind of you, thank you."

Cedric hadn't got where he was today without an unerring eye for the future, that future being the market pull of celebrity status. He had a nose for such things.

Back at the table all the vibes were functioning. Effie was effervescent with Dale's success.

"So, can I expect a call from Boris on Monday?"

"Yup, I reckon so, in fact I think he's got the hots for you, no disrespect to present company."

Freddie chose to remain conspicuously uninformed.

"Sounds like there's a great opportunity in the offing, my sweet."

Effie was bubbling over with gin laden incaution.

"I think it fair to say that Dale has cemented an entrepreneurial connection of the highest standard."

For the first time in his life, Dale experienced a kind of smugness.

"Yup, forty-nine water gardens to install and a major investment in the Haystack as a definite possibility."

"A definite possibility," said Freddie carefully, "is something of a contradiction in terms, would you care to be more specific?"

"Oh for God's sake Freddie, who needs to be specific? It's obvious that Dale has sown the seeds for an investment contract and all I've got to do is nurture it and sign it."

Dale was glowing at his hitherto unrealised accomplishment, he wasn't sure however, how much up to speed Freddie was on the seed sowing bit.

"Is this an investment or is this an investment?" he intoned, recalling a strange conversation he had witnessed that seemed to hang in the air to the sound of music.

"I appear to be missing out on something," said Freddie innocuously.

Effie snorted at Dale's re-inebriation before launching into a meandering tale that effectively confirmed to Freddie that Boris was not be trusted. What Freddie could not understand was how Boris knew how to find Effie in the first place. He knew he had said a lot about her to Loretta but that was only last night, wasn't it? His mind began to wander. Then Effie chimed in.

"So, what do you make of that?"

"Er, pardon?" said Freddie.

"I dunno, a pint of lager shandy and he's anybody's," quipped Dale.

Effie tried again.

"Freddie, it's about those seeds you brought back from Tunisia, apparently they're taking off, we're going to have a look at them, do you want to come?"

"Er, no thank you my sweet, I've got some paperwork to catch up on."

There was a splitting of ways.

"Can you make it, dear boy?" said Effie, as they climbed the steps to the lighthouse.

Dale swayed a bit and then concentrated on Effie's form as he followed her upwards. He noted her lovely calves, not a hint of varicose veins, beautiful ankles, so finely chiselled. Dale wondered what Effie must have looked like when she was Roslyn's age. How on earth did Freddie make it with her? He was ever such a nice bloke really but most of the time he seemed to be somewhere else like. Both Dale and Effie were out of breath when they reached the top, but they had enough to gasp at the sight of the Yum Bum which was definitely now a tree and not a plant.

"Good gracious me!" exclaimed Effie, "I don't believe it."

Somehow Dale just managed to stop himself saying 'yeah that's just what we said when we saw it last' and said instead,

"I told you, it's gone bananas."

"You're playing games with me," said Effie, "this isn't the same one, it can't be."

"It is, it is, I swear it."

"But how can it be? These dark leaves are typical of a succulent, plants like that aren't native to a desert, I reckon it's a common old crassula obliqua and Freddie's been taken for a ride again."

"Well, crass or not it's certainly thriving and if it keeps up like this I shall have to re-pot it and move it down a level, I mean look at them branches, they're thick as two fingers."

Effie and Dale spent a few minutes in silent wonder and then Effie said:

"Well, talking of fingers, are you up to it?"

Dale, who was swaying around with the effects of alcohol and drugs of dubious origin, couldn't quite cotton on to the question. A quizzical grunt was the best he could manage. Effie tried again.

"The 'gone to lunch' sign is still on the shop door window."

Dale finally got it. Effie was feeling horny. It could be a problem. The excesses of the day were catching up on him, yet he knew that a refusal would offend. It could open a door to a lot more as well, so he took the passive route out.

"You lead I'll follow."

"Is that a yes or a no?"

"Let's just go with the flow."

Effie was happy with this and some while later she was lying naked in his bed. Dale was trying to maintain his balance while discarding his pants. He moved towards the bed. As yet, no erection.

"Have your feet got an inferiority complex or something?" she said.

"Oh sorry."

He bent over to remove his socks and promptly collapsed face down on the floor. Out like a light. Bloody hell, cursed Effie, as the reality of the situation dawned. She lay there in a state of frustrated limbo. Seconds became minutes and then her hand drifted slowly downwards across her stomach. She thought of Boris and began to play with herself until Dale started snoring. That was it. She stopped, eased herself off the bed and took a close look at him. Dead to the world. With a sigh she dressed and went downstairs to the shop and opened up. As long as no bugger came in she reckoned she might just about get through the rest of the afternoon.

Freddie was on the phone to Loretta.

"Freddie I swear I didn't even know that Boris had met her," said Loretta, and she was being dead honest.

"But Dale was at Boris's apartment this morning installing a water garden, he may even have seen us."

"Did he say anything?" she asked, sensing that Freddie was becoming a tad agitato.

"No, he was rather incoherent."

"Was he drunk?"

"I believe so."

Instinctively, Loretta knew what Boris had been up to but it was what he was up to now that bothered her more.

"Look Freddie, trust me, there's nothing to worry about. Sometimes Boris moves very quickly, he's always one jump ahead of everyone else, that's why he's so rich and successful. I'll talk to him, I'm sure he's not going to do anything that will jeopardise your plans."

She was careful not say our plans. It was important to put Freddie back in his own comfort zone first and then deal with Boris later, not that she knew what to do next. Usually they chatted things over first but this time he had clearly taken the initiative on his own account. Did he really want to see her career take off? Perhaps he was afraid of losing her? Surely not? Controlling the international arms trade was the real goal. Deep down she knew that Boris was just a screwed up megalomaniac.

"Well, I just wanted to register my concern," replied Freddie, reasonably.

"Of course, I understand that Freddie, we must feel free to confide in each other, that's very important."

"Quite so, quite so. I'd also like to point out that Effie is a shrewd and ambitious woman and she can be quite vicious if things don't go her way."

"Don't worry about a thing Freddie, Boris is used to dealing with difficult personalities, I'm sure he'll handle things wisely, anyway, nothing's happened to stop us enjoying ourselves has it?"

He could not but agree.   With a few more whispered thoughts from Loretta their parting had the essence of sweet tomorrow.

That bastard Boris, she cursed to herself as she rang off, he was up to his tricks again. Maybe he fancied Effie? What kind of woman was she? She needed to know. When it came to women, Boris was nothing if not ambivalent.   Ever since Loretta had first met Boris in Rio, when he was licking his wounds after a failed drugs deal, they had had a close but platonic relationship. He would often smother her with gifts and kisses, sometimes even passionately, but she knew his real mistress was power and control. So what was going on?

She lit up a spliff and inhaled uneasily.

12

Gaspard was feeling uneasy too. Unlike Loretta however, he had more than Boris to consider. Who was that stunning black woman who embraced Freddie in the Great Cumberland Hotel and what was Freddie up to? He had lost them both and how could he make a report to the section without incurring yet more ridicule and humiliation? And his head ached to the point where a guillotine was beginning to seem like a better option than another horse-sized capsule of Nurofen Advanced. And he was aching for Dale to the point of pain. He doubted whether he would be able to watch him plane another piece of wood stripped to the waist without serious emotional damage. And now there was this complication with Roslyn de Winter. Bloody sex starved actress. Tits and fanny on offer twenty four hours a day, no wonder poor Dale was bewildered. Why couldn't she be a lesbian and go vibrate with somebody else? And where did this leave Effie? God forbid, the whole scenario was going pear shaped.

Pour Gaspard poured himself another glass of milk and tried to get a handle on the meaning of existence. How did he get home last night? He could not remember. And how come he awoke naked in bed this morning? His Chinese silk pyjamas were his constant companion and never before, in his entire life, had he retired for the night with his tasselled dressing gown cord draped in a lazy bow around his dormant penis. Something was not quite right, of that he was sure. Even his milk tasted sour.

He staggered to the bathroom and tried to freshen up. Instead he puked into the sink. Après la spew he observed his image in the mirror. For a fleeting second he was fascinated by the delicate lattice work of blue veins that straddled his nose and ran towards his eyes in a translucent membrane. How very rococo, he muttered to himself and fumbled for his bottle of L'homme Lumiere mouth wash. A gradual process of recovery took place. As time passed he found himself sitting in his cobra shaped rattan chair surrounded by pots of variegated geraniums and Icelandic poppies. The intensity of the colour was almost unbearable. In his shaking hand was an opulent business card. His heart almost missed a beat when he focused on the lettering: *Boris Blodvrinsky - International Opera Production.*

Another heart beat was almost missed when his mobile rang, he didn't even know that it was on. He struggled to sound in control but it was not easy.

"Yes?"

"Good afternoon number six."

"You know the time of day?"

"Sarcasm will get you nowhere, have you nothing to report?" It was at times like this that Gaspard was grateful for his superior intellect and cultivated imagination. Nymphs and shepherds became instantly sorted as Gaspard concocted an instant scenario.

"I have to be sure of my facts."

"Which are?"

"The CIA are involved."

"Nonsense."

"I have photographs."

"You'd better meet us on the common."

"It is not safe to do that yet."

63

"The section needs a success, we cannot tolerate procrastination."

"I shall ring you when I am ready."

"We may ring you first, goodbye number six."

The line went dead. Gaspard was grateful for the silence. But how would it solve his problems? How would it cover his lies?

Dale had a problem too. He felt awful and couldn't remember a thing. He didn't know what time it was and didn't know what day it was. He knew it was daytime because the sunlight was hurting his eyes. Neither could he understand why he had woken up on the floor naked except for one sock. He took it off and headed for the shower. The water was cold but it didn't matter. He squirted some Tesco gunge over his head, frothed it up and spread the lather over his body. He towelled down afterwards and having decided that it was a no-shave day was about to put the kettle on when the door bell rang. He deduced therefore that the shop wasn't open. He opened the window and saw Roz standing in the street below dressed in a mini-skirt, a micro-top and those huge tortoise shell glasses. She looked lovely. She gave him a big smile.

"Hi."

"What time is it?"

"Midday."

"What day is it?"

"Sunday."

"Oh, what happened to Saturday?"

"If you let me in perhaps we could talk about it."

Since he couldn't work anything out it seemed like a good idea.

"Be right with you."

Effie and Freddie were having breakfast in their conservatory. Yesterday's unprecedented bonhomie had long since vaporised.

"Must you stir your tea for so long?" remarked Effie.

"We've got more than one teaspoon, surely?"

"That is not the point I'm trying to make, and what's more, if you remember, I don't take sugar, unless of course thirty-five years of marriage has completely ruined your senses."

64

Freddie carefully considered the statement and concluded that Effie still hadn't grasped the principle of the differing specific gravity of the two separate solutions and hence the need for stirring.

"I am aware, however, that you do take milk."

"I am perfectly capable of enjoying my tea without going to the bother of stirring it, thank you."

Freddie decided not to pursue this point. He recalled the last time he mentioned taking a horse to water it had led to accusations that he had suggested she needed a face lift. Instead he finished stirring his tea and drunk it. At least the morning sunshine was agreeable even if his marriage was not.

"I think I'll inspect the tomatoes," he said.

Effie ruffled the newspapers, they fell to the floor but she couldn't be bothered to pick them up; that was the trouble with the Sunday Times, it had so many sections. As Freddie rose to go she fired one last shot.

"Am I to assume that you are still not prepared to tell me what you were doing on Friday night?"

"I've already told you, I was attending a classified conference."

Effie realised she was getting nowhere and his insouciance infuriated her. Then she remembered a social engagement which set her mind spinning. Muriel Carrington's cocktail party. Ian Trubshaw was bound to be there with his silly wife Melissa, showing off their new-born baby. She would corner the little prat and find out what Freddie was up to, no problem.

Boris was on the telephone. He had been on it all morning and most of the night for that matter. He had been organising Freddie's requirements for a secret missile research centre and there had been one hell of a lot of arm twisting and string pulling, not to mention the calling in of multi-various favours. However, the time had now come to get a bit more serious. He had located a warehouse not too far from where Freddie worked in Farnborough. It seemed like an ideal situation except that the owner of the warehouse was reluctant to free up the top floor office space; some stupid excuse about spoiling the aeroplane spotting. The point was that the warehouse shifted a substantial amount of illicit liquor, courtesy of Boris, of course, and so this unwillingness to co-operate had rather niggled him.

"So what happens next?" said Dimitri.

Boris twiddled his cigarette holder in one hand, it was a sure sign that he was hatching a plan. His fingers were surprisingly dextrous for a man with such huge hands. Dimitri waited patiently. He had watched this process many times before. The bit he liked best was when Boris did this drum majorette thing and then flicked his cigarette holder up in the air to land in his mouth. When that happened it meant he had thought of a plan, after that it was all action. The telephone rang. Boris answered it but kept on twiddling. It was a long conversation. Dimitri reckoned it could only be Loretta. They often spent ages chatting together. He waited patiently. Whoever it was they were certainly doing the lion's share of the talking. Suddenly Boris flicked his cigarette holder up in the air. Up it went in wild convolutions. Down it came, clunk-click straight between his teeth.

"I gotta business lunch," said Boris, into the telephone, "why don't you put on a nice dress and join us?" there was a pause "okay, we'll see you in ten minutes."

Dimitri grinned, "where to boss?"

"Put on a suit and tie, we're going to Tzarbinski's."

Dimitri chuckled and loped off to his stash of posh clothes. Tzarbinski's meant business, *his* kind of business. He flicked through a rack of suits that Boris kept available for him in one of the spare bedrooms, he was treated like a king.

Meanwhile, Boris put in another call to Frank Files the reluctant warehouse manager. Frank understood the suddenness of the occasion and naturally was delighted to join them all for a five course lunch to hear what Boris's request was really all about. Of course his wife would understand the short notice, they'd had them before hadn't they? In any event, Mrs Files didn't go in for fancy foods and would prefer to stay at home watching football. Dimitri returned as the conversation finished.

"How'd I look?"

Dimitri had chosen the worst colours in the wardrobe. Ruddy brown mohair with mustard tie. With his squat frame, barrel chest and deep-set eyes, he looked every inch like an orang utan. But the man had feelings so Boris was ever the diplomat.

"It's fine, just fine, it matches the weather."

"Yah, that's just what I thought."

"But can you move easily?"

Dimitri tried a few karate kicks and a leather pouffe went flying.

"That's great," said Boris, "as long as you can climb the steps of a warehouse crane on a full stomach."

"No problems."

They were still laughing when they picked up Loretta in the Bentley.

Roz and Dale were having breakfast at Dunkerbell's in Fropsham High Street. Dale hadn't any food at home so it seemed like a good idea, besides, he was ravenous and Dunkerbell's did a great English breakfast as well as the poncy continental stuff.

"Do you always mop up your egg with your bread?" said Roz, fascinated.

"Every time, wipe the plate, that's my motto."

"The French do that with their sauce and gravy."

"Well, there's no sense in washing the best bit down the sink, is there?"

"No, but why do you think the English consider it bad manners?"

"Dunno, as long as you don't lick the plate it don't matter do it?"

Roz dabbed her croissant in the last bit of his yellow goo.

"Gotcha!"

They always ended up mucking about like that.

"So, getting back to what I was saying earlier," said Roz, "it sounds like this Boris guy has got some serious dosh."

"You're not kidding, you should've seen his apartment, it was like a palace."

67

"So what does he do for a living?"

"I'm not sure, Effie said he was an impersonator or something."

"You mean he's a variety artist, some sort of performer?"

"I dunno exactly but I saw him dancing wiv a floor mop."

"A floor mop!"

"Yeah, and talking to it too."

"Jesus, sounds like a bit of a nutter."

Dale was pleased that he was not alone in thinking that. He guzzled his tea and wiped his mouth on a Dunkerbell tissue.

"Well anyway, I've got to show him around the Haystack tomorrow and he'll probably turn up in a chauffeur driven Bentley like last time."

"I bet that will impress Gaspard."

"It's already impressed Effie, in fact I think she rather fancies him."

"Maybe he fancies her."

"That won't please Gaspard."

"Why not?"

"Well, as I see it," said Dale, mustering all his powers of deduction, "Gaspard is a bit lonely and insecure and if this Boris bloke sort of takes over, he's gonna become jealous like,"

Dale paused to scratch himself as another permutation of human behaviour dawned on him, "on the other hand if Boris is queer, then Gaspard's gonna be all over him and not wanting Effie to interfere."

"What makes you think Boris is gay?"

"I dunno really, but I can sort of see the two of them hitting it off like."

Roz smiled with her usual big grin, "well at least that stops him chasing you and we can get on with it without him treating me like a bad smell under his snobby nose."

"Yeah, but Effie won't be too chuffed."

Dale suddenly realised he'd dropped a bit of a clanger and started to drain the tea pot for a third cup that wasn't there.

"Why not?' said Roz.

"Well, her being a control freak and giving all the orders like," he added quickly.

Roz gave him a sort of funny fixed look.

68

"I guess you know her better than I do."

Dale tried to shrug nonchalantly but his shoulders nearly struck his ears.

"Maybe."

"Anyway," said Roz, "there's something else I think you should know."

Dale braced himself.

"What's that?"

"You've got egg on your nose."

13

Effie was powdering her nose in readiness for Muriel's cocktail party. Although she was about six hours in front of herself, trying out various shades seemed the only thing left to do after her breakfast spat with Freddie, particularly as reading the newspaper all day was not her idea of fun. She was sick of ploughing her way through yet another exposé of greed and corruption, another grisly tale of refugees fleeing from disaster and more cancer-inducing food on the supermarket shelves. God, it was all so depressing. Gaspard had rung to say that he was feeling unwell and would she please give his apologies to Muriel. She didn't press him any further as she knew how sensitive he was about enquiries of a personal nature. However, she concluded that he couldn't have been totally pole-axed because, before ringing off, he launched into a bilious invective over the news that some unemployed oik dossing under an inner city railway arch had been hailed as an artistic genius for defecating on a plate glass window and illuminating it from underneath with ultra-violet light. Effie had expressed the view that at least it hadn't involved dead animals, soiled bed linen, or plagaristic videos, although admittedly on balance it sounded marginally worse. All the same, Gaspard was inconsolable. She had noticed how moody he had been of late. The thought struck her that perhaps she should mention it to Dale. He was good at cheering people up. Come to think of it, putting aside her own personal frustration, she wondered how the dear boy was following yesterday's collapse. This was her foremost employee that she was ignoring. How callous was she becoming? A visit was a must.

"And please try not to cover yourself from head to toe in potting compost just as we're about to leave for Muriel's," she said to Freddie as she headed towards the front door.

"I presume you'll be spending your usual three hours in the bathroom?" he retorted.

"Probably yes, and if I feel like it I shall drain the entire house of hot water."

Effie slammed the front door feeling good about getting the last word in.

The sun was high in a clear blue sky as she approached the Haystack theatre. Dale's bedroom window was open, which was promising, nevertheless she decided to use the back entrance. Entering the shop on a Sunday was not a good idea, there would always be some prat who would appear from nowhere with a stupid grin and tap on the window expecting service. Effie strolled happily round to the vast wooden doors of the Seventh Cavalry assembly area. She was happy because it was sunny. Happy because she was going to see Dale again. Happy that the amazingly rich and charming Boris Blodvrinsky was going to visit her tomorrow. She was also happy that she was free of Freddie for several hours and that tonight at Muriel's she would find out from that weak little wimp Ian Trubshaw exactly what Freddie was up to.

Effie opened the little catch door that was set within the big doors and crossed the vast ground floor to the stairs in the far corner. As she neared the scene dock the smell of wood glue and paint hung in the air. She loved the aroma. Mix it with hot spotlight gels, theatrical grease-paint and dust laden curtains and she had her fix for the day. Up the stairs she

71

went and across the big creaky floorboards. She was about to knock on Dale's back door when the unexpected sound of fun-laden laughter tinkle pinkled down from above. Effie moved sleuth-like towards the sound of innocent merriment. She heard Dale's hearty guffaw but who's was the female voice? Was there hanky panky afoot? Was there treachery? Was there what? She moved closer, creeping up the narrow steps. From above came more thuds and cluds and laughter, male and female together. Too much together. Then she saw them. Dale and Roz covered in compost. And the Yum Bum tree bigger than ever before, ridiculously bigger than before. They had transferred it to a larger tub and now it was sitting one floor further down because of its height. Huge scaly python-like branches hung in random curls like Medusa on a bad hair day and Roz and Dale were playing peek-a-boo within its deep green fleshy leaves. Dale was stripped to the waist and sweating. Roz was radiant and with so little left to reveal that she might just as well be stripped too. And she was laughing with a full throated, projected-from-the-diaphragm, actressy type gusto.

Effie was frozen with jealousy. She struggled with her emotions. Was she really surprised at what was happening? No she was not. It was inevitable really. How could she, a married woman, hold onto a man a generation younger than herself when he was surrounded by attractive, creative, sexually active people who were already propelled into a state of heightened emotion by the very nature of their profession? All the same, watching Dale, who was now tickling Roz in the navel, was a major bummer. It was all very well being philosophical but how could she match a rampant young actress with lovely legs, a flat stomach and a pair of cutesy-tootsy tits? She wondered how long the liaison had been going on for. The prospect hurt her. Nevertheless, on the cusp of a hellish fury she backed off and quietly retreated downstairs. She hadn't got where she was today by behaving like an impulsive drama queen. Let them enjoy their fun, she held all the cards anyway.

Effie decided to make a second and more audible entry. Crash bang wallop. A deliberate commotion downstairs.

"Yoo hoo, anyone about?" she cried.

There was a scrambling of feet.

"Yo there," shouted Dale from above.

Well the lad's got presence, thought Effie, as she clumped up the stairs in preparation for a hearty isn't-it-a-gorgeous-day-not-to-be-working salutation. She arrived at the Yum Bum tree just as Dale and Roz had brushed themselves down and reconfigured their body language.

"I say HELLO, and goodness gracious me, is this really the Yum Bum tree, how extraordinary, how fantastic and ooh Roslyn too, I say, how amazing, hello, how are you?"

"Hello Mrs Bannister, have you ever seen anything like this before?"

"No my dear, I most certainly have not, I can hardly believe it."

"It took the two of us to lift it," said Dale, still a little bit fidgety, "I took the weight like and Roz held the branches."

"I'm so glad you managed it, I hope you haven't pulled a muscle."

"Well Dale did most of the work while I sort of watched him," said Roz breathlessly.

"Yes I know the feeling," said Effie cheerily, "but the lad done brilliant as they say."

"It's growing so fast I didn't think I could leave it any longer," said Dale.

Roz was still a bit fluttery and not quite sure which way the wind was blowing. She knew there was no clause in her contract defining who she should or should not have a relationship with, but these days, with everyone jumping into bed at the drop of a hat, you were lucky to keep something under wraps for more than a day. Quite apart from that, she was mindful that Effie was the queen bee, and the name of the game was survival. It occurred to her that it was just as well they hadn't started to muck about with water because she wasn't wearing a bra and what with Dale's lovely glistening muscles her nipples would be standing out like raspberries on parade. But phew all the same.

"This is really remarkable," said Effie, becoming genuinely amazed at the Yum Bum's phenomenal growth, "I've never seen anything like it. Look at these heavy, lush leaves, they've got such a tender, downy feel to them, and what about these peculiar branches, it's almost as if they were made of rubber, and the whole plant has this peculiar energy about it."

"Yes, I feel that quite strongly too," said Roz.

"Yeah," added Dale, "and when I was re-potting it, the roots kept touching me hand like they wanted to shake it."

"Well, even if it's some kind of mutant freak, if we can cultivate it, we could be on to some kind of commercial success, so not a word to anyone, okay?" They were a gang of three now. Effie was very manipulative.

"right then, drinks are on me."

In the Villain's Noose everything continued to be chummy. Effie decided to play along with it all, even though, deep down, she knew that her relationship with Dale had shifted irrevocably in the wrong direction. Well, there was always Boris. In the meantime, as with Freddie, it was a case of flushing things out. Revenge did not lend itself to spontaneity.

"Listen," said Effie, as they started another round of drinks, "why don't you two come to Muriel Carrington's cocktail party tonight? A few people have dropped out at the last moment, including dear Gaspard, and Muriel loves to see the house full to the brim and it looks like it's going to be a beautifully mild evening and the garden is quite something to behold, absolutely acres of it, and she always invites interesting people and never cut corners on the catering, and I bet you've got a gorgeous little cocktail dress that you're just dying to show off."

Roz and Dale exchanged glances while Effie hammed it up with bonhomie.

"I haven't been to a party in ages," said Roz, her eyes twinkling behind her spectacles.

"Me neither," said Dale, wiping beer foam from his mouth with the back of his hand.

"Great," said Effie, lighting up another cigarette, "and remember, not a word about the Yum Bum, it's our little secret."

14

Tzarbinski's was very busy and the service had become a bit frayed at the edges.

"Dimitri, there's no need to pass Frank the mustard," said Boris. They had reached the cheese and biscuits stage and the main course condiments were still on the table. Frank wasn't bothered about etiquette however. He had spent the entire evening ogling Loretta. As always she was dressed to kill. Boris knew that was her way and it was all part of his strategy. The meal had been a very light hearted affair. Boris and Dimitri had deliberately kept the wisecracks flowing. Frank had lapped up the hospitality. He wasn't really bothered about Boris's reasons for wanting the warehouse because as far as he was concerned, he'd already told him that he couldn't run his business without a minimum of administrative floor space and naturally, whilst he was obviously grateful for the business Boris was putting his way, floor space was floor space and he was no magician. End of story. Frank was nothing if not blunt. Boris said that he appreciated his position and maybe Frank wouldn't mind driving over to the warehouse with Dimitri for a little update on dimensions, just to give him a fresh perspective on his requirements, after all, he could only do so much on paper.

"Sure, I understand Boris, a bit of hands-on assessment never did anyone any harm," said Frank pompously.

"That's what I like about you Frank, you're so accommodating."

"My door is always open Boris."

"Okay, so listen, Loretta and me, we've gotta catch up on some business, she's a busy girl, she's going places, even as her manager I have to grab my moments, you understand?"

"Of course I do," said Frank, understanding only that his wife was a couch potato and he would give his right arm for a moment with Loretta, alone and interrupted.

"Okay, so Dimitri can run you over to the warehouse in the Bentley, take a few measurements and then we'll all join up afterwards, how's about that?"

Loretta gave Frank an I-ain't-wearing-any-knickers kind of smile and Frank's eyeballs nearly jumped into his Tzarbinski special coffee (freshly ground Colombian beans mixed with neat vodka and Arabian Mocha douched with a tablespoon of rich creamy milk still warm from the cow's udders).

"It will be a pleasure Boris."

"Frank, the pleasure's all mine."

Boris snapped at Dimitri in Russian. Frank thought Dimitri was getting a bollocking for sucking the remains of his Tzarbinski coffee through a straw but Boris was actually giving Dimitri the green light to show Frank exactly what he thought of his open door.

"Okay, I bring the Bentley round," said Dimitri, like an orang utan who'd just been offered a bunji jump with a mile of knotted jute.

There were smiles all round as they made their exit.

"Okay Boris," said Loretta, taking a pre-rolled spliff out of her handbag, "what the fuck's going on?"

Boris gave her a big you-can-trust-me smile, "we gotta pull Frank into line, he's getting a bit out of order."

"I'm not talking about Frank, I'm talking about Effie Bannister."

"What about her?" Boris pulled on his Gauloise, he didn't like it when Loretta got all shirty.

"Why didn't you tell me you'd been to see her?"

"So who's running the show, you or me?"

"Freddie rang me, he's very agitated. You should've told us that Effie's toy boy was paying you a call, he may have seen us, it was too close for comfort."

Boris blew a slow arc of cigarette smoke across the table. He wasn't going to admit that he had totally forgotten about Dale's visit until the moment he arrived. Losing his marbles? It was unthinkable.

"Look, everybody's gonna see everybody else before too long, it's inevitable, and don't worry about Dale, he's gonna be real useful."

"Oh yeah, how come?"

Boris realised he had boxed himself into a corner. He could hear his mother laughing at him. *I told you, she's got you on the run, you've lost control, now what are you gonna do?* Loretta was giving him the steady gaze treatment. It was a difficult moment. Who needed who the most? Maybe they both needed each other? Okay, call him a softie but they'd been together a long time now. What with Dimitri, it was practically like being married to two people. Boris decided a bit of honest explanation would take the heat out of the situation.

"He's got influence but he doesn't know it."

Loretta thought hard, she hadn't met Dale yet, nor Effie.

"I know he keeps Effie happy," she said, fencing around a bit, "so what's the big deal?"

"It's no big deal, but the trouble is he doesn't keep Gaspard happy."

"Who the hell's Gaspard?"

"He's the stage designer."

"So?"

"He also works for MI5."

"Jesus shit Boris, this is one helluver fine mess!"

Boris didn't quite see it like that. As a secret service agent, Gaspard was an incompetent prat. He had practically fallen into his arms. Other people were falling into place too. Those he didn't know about, he soon would. So what was the problem? Sometimes he thought that Loretta's aversion to opera in favour of jazz was a problem, a problem for him but at least he had come to terms with it. Maybe the problem with her now was the time of the month? Well, if he said as much it certainly would be. So he didn't.

"Loretta, it's not like you to fret," he reached across the table and took her hand, "there's no need for it - hey, what's this? you're shaking."

"With anger Boris, think about it."

"Listen babe, let's not have any scenes, huh? Dimitri won't be back for a little while, let's chill out at the bar, huh?"

So they chilled out at the bar until Dimitri returned. He looked pleased with himself. On seeing them he could hardly contain his laughter. He had a weird sort of laugh, like the last gurgle of bath water.

"Everything's ready boss," he gurgled.

"Good, let's go then."

Off they went in the Bentley. Loretta wanted to listen to Jazz FM. Boris acquiesced. By the time the raw sax of Scuzzy McCane had reached the final bars of All Roses Got Prickles, they were at Frank's warehouse. Loretta lit up another spliff. She was still into chilling out.

Boris and Dimitri strolled round the outside of the warehouse and entered through a small side door that opened directly onto the main storage area. And there was Frank, hanging upside down from the hook of a loading crane. The crane gantry was very high, almost sixty metres, and there was a huge, slow, swing to the cable which was fully extended. At the bottom of the pendulum there was a blood-stained streak on the ground which Frank's head cleared by only a few inches. He screamed on the approach.

"Took a few go's to get it right," gurgled Dimitri.

"Nobody's perfect."

They watched fascinated as Frank flew by.

"I got grease on my jacket while hanging him up," remarked Dimitri casually.

"Don't worry, it'll come off in the dry cleaners."

"He threw up over my shoes too."

"What did I tell you about wearing Hush Puppies?"

"He said he'd buy me a new pair."

"Well he would, wouldn't he?"

Frank came screaming by again.

"I think my socks have had it as well."

"Okay, we'd better talk to him about it, take him down."

Dimitri clambered into a fork lift truck and raised the arms about ten foot in the air. Then he drove into the line of swing at the point of the perpendicular. Timing was everything. There was a tremendous clang as the cable struck the arms of the forklift. Frank was whipped upwards and over in a perfect arc. It was very gymnastic, almost balletic. It reminded Boris of Nureyev in his hey day. The cable and hook snapped back. Frank's trouser's ripped off like a grizzly bear skinning a salmon in one go. Magnificent. As everything came to a clanging rest, Frank just hung there, whimpering like an injured dog.

"You know what I can't stand, Dimitri?" said Boris, drawing on a freshly lit Gauloise.

"What's that boss?"

"A man who doesn't wear clean underwear on a Sunday."

15

Some say opportunity and need are the same thing. Three months after Ted Trubshaw's fatal heart attack, Muriel married Christopher Carrington, a merchant banker with execrable taste. They lived in his twelve bedroom mock-Georgian mansion called Shangriluv. It was set in fifty acres of private parkland complete with two floodlit tennis courts, three heated swimming pools, a Ten-pin bowling alley and a golf course with its own driving range. The carriageway to the house was lined with huge, red, illuminated plastic toadstools which were activated by a light sensor at the main gates. There was a floodlit fountain at the front of the house, a vulgar kind of splasharama whose design origins owed much to Disneyland in Florida.

In spite of such excesses, Muriel and Effie remained good friends. They had been party girls ever since schooldays and Christopher threw a lot of parties. This alone was a good enough excuse for Effie to forgive Christopher for refusing to invest in the Haystack theatre.

"He won't even touch Andrew Lloyd-Webber," said Muriel, in his defence, "on the other hand, if you want to import pickled sheep's eyes from Saudi Arabia, he's your man."

Effie had accepted that Muriel had married a philistine because when all was said and done, a party was a party. It didn't stop Gaspard accepting the odd invitation either, although he bitched incessantly about the conspicuous grossness.

"An alabaster elephant on the main terrace is bad enough, but to replace the mahout with the Virgin Mary is a heinous sin not even Salvador Dali would contemplate."

Effie was too pissed on champagne at the time to take much notice and suggested that Gaspard might like to paint Mary's toe nails if he thought it would make it artistic. He was testy with her for ages. Freddie remained mute on the subject and indeed about the marriage. He had never like Muriel and thought she was a bad influence on Effie. Ted, on the hand had been a life long friend and a great scientist. If it wasn't for his untimely death, Project Cassandra might even have been given the go-ahead. Ted had always been better at the politics than he had. Those were the days when The Sprout would never come out of his office because Ted had swamped him with paper after paper. Nowadays he was snooping all over the place. He might even be at tonight's party, perish the thought! After Ted's death, Muriel had kept in with the MoD crowd partly because of Ian and partly because she was a snob who loved rubbing shoulders with people in high places.

Effie and Freddie arrived at Shangriluv in a beaten up mini cab because Freddie's car wouldn't start and the fourth emergency service appeared to be on some kind of extended siesta.

"I suggest we go round the back to avoid embarrassment," said Effie. Freddie made no comment, he didn't want to be there in the first place. He had no capacity for small talk and loathed the prospect of meeting people who had probably had a hand in his demotion, something he had yet to tell Effie about.

Effie knew the layout of the house well and they soon found their way into the main reception where Christopher

Carrington, already drunk, was hee-hawing away with a mouthful of canapés, his pot belly constrained by a lurid waistcoat that had gone out of fashion with Kojak.

"Effie my love, how are you and why haven't you got a drink?" - a waiter came running - "and Freddie, do try one of these giant red chillies, they've been marinated in llama's piss or rocket fuel or something, ha ha ha, bloody delicious though and guaranteed to cure your dandruff, ha ha ha, what?"

Freddie cautiously took a chilli, "thank you, but I don't suffer from dandruff."

"well, you're a bloody lucky old sod, aren't you? ha ha ha, how about crabs then? and I'm not talking about marine life either, ha ha ha."

Freddie turned away in disgust, trying to find a means of escape, Effie however, joined in like the seasoned party girl that she was.

"Christopher, you're too crude for words, now do be a good chap and give me a light, it's been at least ten minutes since my last one."

There were clouds of smoke and more hee-hawing as Christopher joined Effie with a huge Monte Christo cigar. Freddie slipped away in search of a glass of mineral water while Effie got stuck into the cocktails. There were loads of people and loads of everything and things were hotting up. There was no sign of Ian Trubshaw or anybody from the MoD, much to Effie's annoyance and Freddie's relief. Freddie was despondent though. He was dying to get started on Project Cassandra and wished that Boris would contact him soon with news of the arrangements, all this partying nonsense was a waste of space. Generally he loathed socialising although he could not erase from his memory the sheer pleasure of Loretta's cabaret performance and how much his senses had been stimulated since meeting her. She was like no other woman he had met before.

He looked about him and saw Effie on the far side of the room hooting and coughing with Christopher Carrington who was an obnoxious buffoon by anyone's standards. The entire place was choc-a-bloc with Hooray Henry's and Funny Fenella's, everyone of them stinking rich and shallow as a fish pond. What on earth did Effie see in them? Pound notes in place of personalities. Well, let her make a fool of herself with Dale. Who cared if their affair became public? Not he. His future was with Boris and Loretta and sod the lot of them.

"Cocktail sir?"

"Er...yes, I think I will, thank you," said Freddie, "and I'd like that one with the large maraschino cherry."

The flunky did his number.

Freddie was wondering whether he was obliged to stay sober when there was a bit of a kerfuffle at the front door. Minor celebs making an entrance and there was Muriel making a fuss of them. But just a minute, Freddie could hardly believe his eyes, it was Dale and Roslyn. Did Effie know about this? He gulped his maraschino cherry in glee. Serve the silly bitch right. All eyes were on the pair of them. They must have raided the Haystack wardrobe. Roslyn looked like a model straight off the cat walk. The back of her dress was slashed to the crease of her buttocks and her breasts were covered with a see-through stare. Dale had a swanky, silvery foil tuxedo with glittering lapels like the heat deflectors on the space shuttle. His spiky, gelled, blonde hair stood up like electrified maple syrup.

"Effie give us the nod like, so we got our act together and come," he said, oblivious to the attention, "Roz done me 'air special, so I took a chance and give the ol' crash 'elmet a miss."

"And lovely it looks too," said Muriel, the consummate hostess, turning quickly to Roslyn, "and that is quite the most stunning dress this season."

"And not much of it either," said Christopher, moving in for a lecherous ogle.

"Well, one never knows when one might get thrown into a fountain," said Roz, realising she was in the company of a pig.

"Take no notice," said Muriel, "have a drink and let me introduce you to a few people."

Christopher Carrington stuffed his face with more canapés and continued to dribble over Roslyn's bare back. Effie was chatting not too far away but with half an eye on the action. She wondered whether Dale compared her and Roslyn in bed.

84

There was no actual proof that they had slept together but her intuition was seldom wrong.

More people were piling in now and it was all getting rather silly. In fact everyone was stoned out of their skulls. Roslyn and Dale became separated for a while and when they met up again, they had tales to tell.

"Some cocktail party," said Roz, "it's more like a film premiere full of air heads."

"Dunno about air heads," said Dale, "some bird just asked me if I fancied sticking me dick through her doughnut ring."

"What did you say?"

"I said I was saving meself for a melon."

"Maybe you should've joined the ten-pin bowling instead."

"Why's that?"

"Christopher Carrington and his pot-bellied banker friends are all playing stark bollock naked."

"You're joking?"

"No, I just had a look and there's more balls than bowls swinging about."

"This place is a nut house."

"More like an acid house, I could do with some fresh air."

"Me too, let's go outside for a bit."

As they fed their way through the revelling throng and out across the terrace to the landscaped lawns, Ian Trubshaw tottered into Effie who was ladling a goblet of punch from a bath sized bowl.

"Why Trubshaw junior, I do declare."

"Hello Mrs Bannister."

"What no Melissa?"

"No, I'm afraid she's got a slight headache."

"Oh dear, such a shame, and how about little Sebastian?"

"He's sleeping well so I thought it would be alright to pay my respects for an hour or so."

"Why, has somebody died?"

Trubshaw junior gave an embarrassed titter, he hadn't much sense of humour, "Well, no, but you know what I mean, must support my step-father's gigs."

"Most commendable, now do have some punch and come and talk to me, there's something I've been meaning to ask you about Freddie."

Ian Trubshaw, Trubshaw junior, looked uncertain. He had only just arrived and yet already his brain felt as if it was in the air. He wasn't too happy about Effie asking him questions either, he knew that Freddie had been acting rather strangely of late and what with The Sprout asking him to keep an eye on things, he wasn't sure where his allegiances lay. It was such a strain. He decided to get stuck into the punch, it might wash the weird taste of those canapés away.

"I'm worried about Freddie,' said Effie, steering him into a corner and standing inside his personal space rather too personally, "he's been acting rather strangely of late and I wondered if you might know why?"

"I don't think he's quite come to terms with the cancellation of Project Cassandra," replied Ian, at the same time thinking what an extraordinary punch it was and what enormous eyes Effie had.

"He's had disappointments before," continued Effie, not knowing what the hell Ian was talking about.

"Yes, but this project was so visionary, I believe my father was working on it too, but Freddie will never discuss it."

"Is that why last Friday's special conference in London was so hush hush?"

"What conference? I mean yes, I mean no, I mean probably, er - I don't know." *God, this punch is seriously weird, Effie has blue hair!*

"Freddie seemed very preoccupied after Tunisia, why was that?"

"Why is everyone taking their clothes off?" Ian Trubshaw's head was spinning.

"I beg your pardon?"

"Why is my mother dancing with an ape?"

"Probably because she's fond of animals, now tell me about Freddie in Tunisia."

"He missed the final plenary session."

"Why?"

"He had a hangover."

86

"Rubbish, Freddie never drinks to excess, in fact he never does anything to excess."

"Then why is he climbing that white elephant?"

Effie looked through the french windows towards the terrace in the direction of Ian's incredulous stare. She saw something different.

"That's not an elephant, it's a giraffe."

"I think I'd better go home, Melissa might be fretting."

"I doubt it, she seems to be enjoying herself."

"Where?"

"On top of that giraffe."

"But that's Freddie on an elephant kissing the Virgin Mary."

Tangerine skies and cinnamon pies. Effie and Ian were punch drunk and hallucinating madly. Just like everyone else that evening.

Ha ha ha, what?

16

Boris was of the opinion that people who couldn't get their act together on a Monday morning were losers. Loretta, on the other hand, reckoned that anyone who rose before midday, any day, was a sad workaholic. She was strictly a night-bird and catching the morning sun was something to be avoided like a vampire. In contrast, both Boris and Dimitri possessed round-the-clock stamina and would enjoy the breaking of dawn regardless of how many bottles of Stolichnaya they had consumed. Loretta had been so perturbed by Boris's recent actions that he had decided it was necessary to continue to smooth things over. So, after Frank had been patched up and returned to his wife with the deeply felt explanation that he had drunk too much and grazed his head when falling over in Tzarbinski's car par, Dimitri drove them all home and they sat in Boris's huge lounge discussing the integration of Project Cassandra with Project Haystack, (Loretta had insisted that her singing career be elevated to project proportions). Boris had little time for naming things but if it kept her happy, then so be it; in the end, everything would be done *his* way so there was no point in splitting hairs. If there was an agreed plan, it had become somewhat hazy after several litres of vodka and the definite inhalation of bumper sized spliffs. Eventually, Loretta crashed out in the guest bedroom while Boris and Dimitri admired the rising sun as it glistened on the bald head of Prince Albert, just like it used to on the golden dome of St Basil's in Red Square.

"This reminds me of Moscow," said Boris.

"I know what you mean," replied Dimitri.

"And I've been thinking about your Anita too."

"Yeah?"

"Yah. I've been thinking that when Loretta's Haystack cabaret takes off, we'll need to expand the programme a bit to attract the bums on seats, a stripper in the early hours of the morning should do the trick."

"Anita wouldn't want to be parted from her mother."

"Maybe, but I know a certain warehouse not a million miles away whose owner could be persuaded to like dogs Svetlana's way."

Dimitri gurgled as the penny dropped.

"Life offers so many opportunities," said Boris, "you just gotta be open to them."

"Yeah, we put this one on the front burner, huh?"

"And why not?"

Later on they enjoyed a good humoured breakfast and this time Boris didn't reprimand Dimitri for wiping his plate with his bread. When all was said and done, Dimitri was a family man who was in denial, one had to make allowances. So they chatted amiably about their next move, that being their imminent visit to Effie. When Loretta showed no signs of stirring they decided to head for Fropsham in Surrey, Boris in the Bentley, Dimitri in the Cascade delivery van.

"First stop Frank's warehouse, okay?" said Boris.

"D'you think he'll be suffering from a Monday morning headache, boss?"

There was more sniggering and gurgling.

"Well, he sure will if he hasn't started to organise things," said Boris curtly, he'd had enough of Frank's insolence and was determined to get things moving, "ring Effie first and remind her lunch is on us."

"What about toy boy?"

"Sure, he can come too."

Dimitri tried not to show his displeasure and made a mental note to watch Dale closely, "and what about Gaspard?"

"He's in for a surprise," chuckled Boris, "our man in MI5 is going to come in very handy."

Dimitri didn't enquire any further, strategy wasn't his bag, he was content to take care of the day to day activities and leave the thinking to Boris.

Boris headed off first in the Bentley leaving Dimitri to make the telephone call. It was a crucial day ahead, there could be some tricky moments but he would keep such thoughts to himself. He swung the big car past the Serpentine and assessed his tactics. Frank was no longer a problem, there had been real terror in the whites of his eyes. Effie was ambitious and a shrewd cookie, she needed to be watched carefully. As for Dale, he was a pushover, just give him money, end of story. And Gaspard? Boris played the tape of Gaspard's bugged telephone conversation with MI5 - "... the CIA are involved.. . I have photographs . . ." He chuckled to himself. What a prat. How was he going to dig himself out of that? Dimitri was right, they were dealing with an amateur. Gaspard needed help and soon it would be closer to hand than he realised. With certain conditions, of course.

The traffic was stop and start approaching the Chiswick roundabout. Boris checked the rear view mirror for signs of Dimitri. Nothing yet. It would be different on the motorway. Sure enough, it was. Along came Dimitri, headlights blazing, engine screaming, Capital Radio full blast, driving like a Jamaican. Boris waived as he sailed by. The Bentley was turbo charged but he didn't have to prove anything, besides, Dimitri needed to have his little bit of fun now and again. He could be a handful when morose but things would be different if he could persuade Anita and Svetlanov to move from East to West. And that was something else that needed to be sorted. A family home in Fropsham would be very civilised. It wasn't that he didn't mind Dimitri staying over a couple of nights a week, he just wished he would flush the toilet now and again and stop blowing his nose in the sink. Anyone would think that the Albert Hall Mansions was a youth hostel for itinerant Arabs.

As he approached the motorway turn-off, Boris put on a CD. Huge waves of sound engulfed him, the Bentley had state of the art stereo. It was Puccini's Tosca and Boris sang along with Scarpia. He loved to model himself on operatic evilness. If only Loretta could develop a taste for the classics. With her sultry sexiness and deep throated mezzo she would make a fabulous Carmen. He mused for a while and then rejected the thought. The lady just wanna sing the blues. Puccini took over again. Boris decided to pull over into a lay-by to concentrate on the end of Act Two, there was no need to hurry, Dimitri could handle things.

Eventually, when the drama ended, he arrived at Frank's warehouse in Farnborough. Dimitri was there to greet him. Poor Frank was still as white as a sheet, a sort of greyish white actually. He was directing the loading of desks and filing cabinets into a Luton pick-up van as harassed clerical staff rushed about marking up various cardboard boxes.

"Good morning, Frank."

"Good morning, Boris."

"A hive of industry, I see."

"We're transferring our administration to Aldershot, it's phase one of our expansion programme."

"My congratulations, I like to see a company thrive and prosper, now what had you in mind for phase two?"

"Follow me," said Frank.

Dimitri was gurgling with delight, hopping from one foot to the other like a primate who knew where the world's supply of bananas were stashed.

Frank led them through the main warehouse to a small building attached to the back. When they arrived, a team of fork lift truck drivers were putting the finishing touches to a huge stack of wooden palettes. There was a narrow gangway in one corner, not wide enough for two abreast but okay for one plus dog. It ran in a crooked corridor for about twenty metres and then opened out into a ragged arena with palettes stacked in terraces like a Roman amphitheatre.

"Very atmospheric," said Boris, smiling.

"I like to help," said Frank, with a nervous facial tic that was clocking up overtime, "can I get you a coffee?"

"No thanks Frank, I can see you've got a lot to do and so have we, just make sure none of your employees start flapping their mouths about any of this."

Frank's nervous tic broke out into a tarantella, "Dimitri has already spoken to me about the security situation and I can assure you that everyone's been briefed accordingly."

Boris smiled and placed a fresh Gauloise in his cigarette holder with exaggerated ceremony, Frank immediately whipped out a lighter and held his shaking hand in place as Boris took a long hard drag and blew a funnel of smoke into the air with theatrical nonchalance.

"Well, in that case we'll be on our way."

Frank said nothing as his whole body began shaking and beads of sweat broke out on his forehead. Boris turned and headed back to the Bentley. Dimitri followed suit, pausing only to take Frank's gibbering cheeks in his big hands and, with their faces only inches apart, emitted a big woof woof, followed by a deep throated gurgle.

He could be very playful when things hotted up.

17

In the Haystack theatre, Dale was at the top of the stairs tending to the Yum Bum tree. Gaspard wasn't too happy about this having already pointed out that, in his opinion, there were more important things to do than muck around with a plant that wasn't part of the Cascade stock in the strict sense of the word. Dale, being mindful of Effie's wish for secrecy, was in a bit of a dilemma. The Yum Bum's growth rate had accelerated even more and yet again it needed to be moved down another floor because the branches were pushing against the ceiling once more. The trouble was, it had definitely become a two-handed job and for some strange reason (other than bloody minded petulance), Gaspard refused to climb the stairs even to have a look.

Dale decided to remain out of sight for a while. Gaspard was always testy on a Monday and he would probably become even more so when Boris made his visit. As yet, Dale had not said anything about it. That was Effie's responsibility. She was the boss. This morning she had come in with one hell of a hangover and didn't seem inclined to chat about last night's party. The only thing she mentioned was that she and Freddie had had another blazing row, but that was par for the course, so Dale chose to sit happily in the middle of the Yum Bum. He liked it there. It was strangely soothing. The lower leaves had filled out to become much thicker and luxuriant. The biggest of them had developed a kind of fleshy texture covered with a fine soft down like a peach. It was almost as if they were forming into some kind of fruit because some of them had the beginnings of a horizontal seam, like a pod. There was a fine crimson line which contrasted beautifully with the overall colour of deep, velvety green. Dale was utterly fascinated by all of this, in fact, he had already been up to have a look earlier that morning. No matter what else was going on, he had developed a close attachment to the Yum Bum and was concerned for its welfare.

He couldn't remember much about last night except for a very strange homeward journey on Oil Slick, his old motorbike. All the street lights were purple and every so often Roz would say 'yeah' or 'wow'. At one point, as he was about to turn left, he glanced across the side-car and there was Cheryl, sitting astride it like a horse and she was stark naked except for a baby's nappy on her head. 'Don't mind me, you useless prat,' she had said, 'I'm only fucking freezing,' and then she had disappeared - poof! - just like that. He had not said anything to Roz about it. Surprisingly, he had not suffered a hangover, and in the morning, there he was, climbing the steps to the lighthouse to sit with the Yum Bum. It was just something he had this irresistible urge to do. It was very comforting. He had started to bathe the leaves in sour milk because apparently, according to Effie, that's what you were supposed to do with plants like that. Before applying the milk, he had gently dusted the leaves with one of Gaspard's pure sable hair paint brushes. The Yum Bum was very much his plant. He enjoyed its company. If Gaspard wasn't prepared to help him re-position it, then he would ask Roz to help him again.

"Don't worry mate," said Dale to the Yum Bum, "I'll get yer sorted," and then added, with great tenderness, "I may even read you a bit of poetry, 'ow about that?"

If trees could speak, now would be the time for conversation. Dale was into some conspicuous tender loving care and was not in the least bit embarrassed about it. The fact was, he may only have been a carpenter and occasional stage hand but his talents were growing daily. Effie had already told him he was fast becoming a promising horti-something-or-other, and clearly everything was on the up and up. Including the Yum Bum.

"Dale!" Gaspard's vexatious voice rose from below, "if it's not an invasion of your privacy, your services are required by your employer downstairs."

"Oh righto, coming."

Dale disengaged himself from within the arms of the Yum Bum, as arms they now seemed to be, and quickly dropped down the stairs and loped casually through the scene dock.

"I gather some visitors have arrived and you are required to chaperone them from one end of the building to the other," said Gaspard truculently, "needless to say, I know nothing about this."

"No probs, I'll handle it."

"Will they be traipsing through here by any chance?"

"Dunno, Gasp, I'll 'ave to ask Effie, won't I?"

Dale disappeared downstairs leaving Gaspard speechless at his drawing board. He hated being left out of things.

Boris and Dimitri were in the foyer of the theatre. Boris was on full charm and Dimitri was doing his best.

"Such a delight to see you again, Mrs Bannister," said Boris, in his best, beaming, genial basso profundo.

"Oh thank so much," said Effie, with more than a frisson of delight, "and please do call me Effie."

"Of course, and may I introduce my associate, Mr Pyshnyi, who I don't think you met last time?"

"I believe not, how do you Mr Pyshnyi?"

"I do fine."

"Please call him Dimitri, it's easier that way."

"Thank you, it's a lovely surname though."

"Yah, Dimitri Pyshnyi," said Dimitri, with a surprise flush of Russian pride.

Effie repeated his full name flawlessly and Dimitri was tickled pink.

"And of course, we all know Dale, don't we?" said Effie.

"Morning," said Dale, mooching in, "everything alright then?"

Everything was clearly alright. Yet again, Effie was bowled over in the presence of Boris in his Savile Row suit and gleaming Bentley parked outside. She wasn't quite sure what to make of Dimitri though, she'd never seen a great ape in a silver mohair suit before and there was something rather menacing about his colossal head with those funny little close set eyes which bore into her like bits of grit in a dumper truck.

"Dale, would you be good enough to keep an eye on the shop while I show our guests around?"

"Sure, no probs," said Dale, showing no signs of confusion at Effie's spontaneous change of plan, he was used to her being excited, "er, will you be covering the lighthouse?" he tried to wink inconspicuously but ended up flicking like a Belisha beacon.

"Of course, I want Boris and Dimitri to see everything, after all, the Haystack is a unique building."

Now Dale was confused, he thought the Yum Bum was supposed to be a secret or something.

"Four people on them narrow stairs is a bit dodgy isn't it?" he avoided looking at Dimitri who was as broad as the staircase itself.

"Nonsense, we'll take it in turns if need be."
Oh well, never mind, just go with the flow, he thought. He couldn't see what all the fuss was about anyway. Dimitri had picked up on the vibes though.

"Boss, if you'd like I'll go to the lighthouse with Dale while you and Mrs Bannister discuss business."

"I'm sure no one will be offended," said Boris, wondering how Dimitri had managed to pick up on all these funny British politenesses so quickly, "and then perhaps we can all meet up for lunch?"

"What a splendid idea," said Effie, her hangover long gone. And so that was that. They paired off and prepared to perambulate.

"What's this lighthouse?" said Dimitri bluntly, trying to force a note of friendliness.

"Well, it's not actually a lighthouse, we just think it looks like one," said Dale, wondering what Gaspard's reaction would be to Dimitri's silver mohair suit with rattlesnake tie, "come and see for yourself."

They entered the Seventh Cavalry assembly area. Dale took Dimitri to the centre where the milling gear used to be and they peered upward through the column of light. The leaves of the Yum Bum were visible many floors above.

"Where's the lighthouse?" said Dimitri gruffly.

"Oh that's right at the top, it's just a funny little room with windows all round, fantastic view. The first floor is the work shops and scene dock, that's where me and Gaspard hang out, he's the stage designer."

"Let's say hello."

"Okay."

Up the stairs they went and crossed the floor to Gaspard's office. Gaspard flinched on seeing Dimitri, not because he remembered him (after the pink champagne at the Trappist's Tool, everything had been a mystery), but because of Dimitri's general dress sense and demeanour. It was Neanderthal, ruder than gothic, beyond the more than tasteless. Dimitri seized Gaspard's hand and crushed it.

"Dimitri Pyshnyi."

"Gaspard Grant."

"What's upstairs?" said Dimitri, dismissing any attempt at small talk.

Gaspard was aghast. Clearly, this man was a peasant.

"I've no idea," he replied tartly, "it is no concern of mine, I believe it has become an annexe to Mrs Bannister's horticultural business, Dale may be able to elucidate further."

97

But Dale was non-plussed. He was about to tell Gaspard to stop being so bleedin' snooty but relented because, on second thoughts, it was probably just part of his insecurity.

"We go up," said Dimitri, command-like.

"Yeah, okay," said Dale, relieved to be moving on.

When they reached the Yum Bum, Dale made an executive decision.

"You couldn't give me an 'and re-siting this could you? it's growing so fast I keep running out of space."

"Yah, what is it?"

"I dunno exactly, it come from Tunisia, I can't say its proper name, I just call it Yum Bum. Effie's ol' man give 'er the seeds like, as a present, but she got a bit pissed off wiv 'im so I planted them like and they've gone bananas ever since."

"I can't see any bananas."

"No, I mean it just growed like there was no tomorrow and it keep going up and up and sprouting more leaves and stuff."

"What stuff?"

"I mean it just get bigger by the hour."

"By the hour?"

"Well, I ain't kidding Dimitri, but at seven o'clock this morning them branches wasn't touching the ceiling, now look at them, bent over by six inches."

Dimitri was suspicious. There was something funny going on here. What was the Tunisian connection? Boris had said Dale was on the inside, he could be useful, but how? He looked at the tree. It was huge, definitely a two-handed job and probably a crane after that. It was best to co-operate and find out more.

"Okay, I lift, you hold."

"Oh cheers Dimitri, I'd hate to see it all squashed up."

"We put it on the ground floor."

"You reckon?"

"Yah, no more moves after this, give it the biggest possible space, see what happens."

"Yeah let's go for it."

Dale began to gather the branches together in great swathes while Dimitri picked up the tub. It was no problem for him, he

98

could lift a man clean off the ground and throw him twenty feet without pausing. And that was with one hand.

Down the creaky stairs they went. Gaspard stared in amazement as they walked by. When they reached the ground floor Dale asked Dimitri if he was alright but he just grunted and carried straight on to the centre where the milling gear shaft used to be.

"This is best place," he said.

"Yeah, I reckon so," agreed Dale, "but I fink I may 'ave to re-pot it."

"No, straight into the ground is best."

"But there's a concrete floor."

"Break it up."

"I'd better ask first."

Dimitri shrugged. He understood what is what like not being the number one.

As they stood there catching their breath, the long gangling branches of the Yum Bum picked themselves off the floor and swung upwards towards the light. It was a single discernible movement, no question about it. Gaspard had seen it too. Unable to contain his curiosity, he had sneaked across the floor upstairs and was peering down the centre of the milling gear shaft directly above the Yum Bum. All three of them remained spellbound. What happened next was beyond all human experience.

The Yum Bum emitted a kind of low hissing sound, which was deeply powerful, almost hydraulic in nature, like a long, strange yawn. The sides of the tub split open and strong, luscious, tendril-like roots began to spread across the concrete floor. There was nothing alien or yukky about their appearance, just pure, natural, earthy fecundity. The leading tendril found a crack in the concrete and disappeared inside it. The Yum Bum yawned again, a happy appreciative sound like someone who has just woken up to a morning cup of tea. Other tendrils began to spread across the concrete where they too found other cracks which their tips explored and gradually entered with more happy yawns. Soon there was a large circular network about twenty foot in diameter, seeking and thrusting into every little fissure in the concrete. And now the

99

Yum Bum was wheezing and groaning, like someone who knew it was time to get out of bed. The tendrils dug deeper and began to break up the concrete as the thicker section of their body slid earthwards. Little bits at first and then bigger lumps until an inexorable excavation was in full swing. And then the tendrils struck earth. Rich, dark, fertile soil spewed upwards and outwards to form a huge base several feet deep like a gigantic pizza. It huffed and puffed and groaned and grumbled good naturedly until eventually everything came to a rest with a deep contented sigh.

Dale, Dimitri and Gaspard were stunned into silence. They knew they had just witnessed something mind-bogglingly mysterious and ring-piece twitteringly spooky. In short, it was beyond the foundations of rational experience.

Gaspard sank out of sight, trembling and confused. Peering over the edge of a fifty foot drop had made him nervous to begin with but now he was visibly shaking. He had been feeling rather peculiar all weekend but now he was beginning to doubt his sanity. What he had just witnessed did not happen on dear old Mother Earth, so where was he?

He crept back to his office, unplugged the Sweet Martini and starting gulping straight from the bottle. Downstairs, on the ground floor, Dale and Dimitri were gaping like goldfish. Eventually Dimitri broke the silence.

"I need vodka."

"Me too," gasped Dale.

Without saying another word, they headed for the Villain's Noose.

18

When Effie and Boris came bursting into the Villain's Noose a short while later, it was a bit like a reunion of the aliens from the Invasion of the Body Snatchers minus the screaming. Admittedly, only Dale and Dimitri had actually witnessed the Yum Bum's extraordinary self-rooting, but as soon as the first frantic vodkas had been downed (gin and tonic in Effie's case) she was feverishly recounting the sights and sounds of the Yum Bum as she and Boris had experienced them.

Having completed their tour of the Haystack they had walked round the outside of the building and entered the Seventh Cavalry assembly area through the main doors. The sight that greeted them was the Yum Bum, still wheezing away and in the process of forming a kind of rubbery crust over its pizza-like base.

"I stuck my hand in it," said Effie breathlessly, "and when I tried to pull it free, this gooey stuff clung to me, stretching out like huge strands of melted Mozzarella cheese, it was really quite frightening."

"I had to cut her free with my knife," said Boris, producing a vicious looking twelve-inch stiletto wrapped in pink toilet paper and covered in coagulated goo right up to the hilt. Everyone was too shocked to enquire as to why anybody would need to be carrying such a lethal weapon in the first place, although Dimitri knew that Boris loved to stab people in the hand with it and had once pinned a man's foot to the ground to stop him running away. (Those were the heady days in Moscow since when he had shown remarkable restraint).

They continued to knock back their drinks until Dale suggested that perhaps they ought to go back and check things out, just in case something else had happened.

"Is that really a good idea?" said Effie, clearly shaken by the event.

"Well, what else do we do, call the Police?"

"That's definitely not a good idea," said Boris quickly, "I'm sure we can handle it, after all, it's only a plant."

This was true, however, since it was a plant with characteristics that defied normal comprehension they continued drinking until eventually Dale said, "well it ain't done nothing wrong has it? and I was cleaning the leaves this morning, giving it a bit of the old TLC like and there was good vibrations if you know what I mean, and let's face it, me and Dimitri done it a favour 'cos it would never have got to where it is today by sitting upstairs, I mean it just sort of saw an opening and went for it."

There was a vague nodding of heads in agreement followed by more consumption of alcohol when it dawned on them that they had just attributed it with human behaviour.

"I wonder if Gaspard has seen it yet?" said Dale, "he don't usually miss a trick."

Five minutes later they were all crowded into Gaspard's office, offering consolation and support as he clung to his Sweet Martini bottle, rigid with fear. To everyone's amazement, (or perhaps not so, given what had actually happened) the Yum Bum had continued to grow and its main stem had eased its way past the level of the scene dock and was heading upwards towards the lighthouse. Its progress was accompanied by a series of soft, gentle hissing sounds that

102

were more soothing than threatening. In spite of that, Dale was the only one inclined to touch it. As he did so, its tendrils caressed him tenderly, forming a sort of lazy curve that slid across his arm and nudged his cheek before climbing upwards in its never ending quest for height. Dale was enraptured and just wished that Roz was there to see it all happening. He wondered how long it would be before she did? There was no denying it, you could actually see it growing.

Poor Gaspard appeared to be slipping in and out of some kind of catatonic trance. In one of his more lucid moments he asked Boris if they hadn't met before, but Boris, having had to adjust his strategy somewhat fundamentally since his arrival, said no, he didn't think so. He reckoned that the revelation that he frequented the Trappist's Tool was not something likely to impress Effie and without actually knowing what was going on it hadn't taken him long to come to the conclusion that a flowering opportunity was opening up before his very eyes, even though he didn't know what it was. It was obvious that Gaspard had been more affected than the others and Effie agreed to Boris's suggestion that Dimitri drove him home so that he could rest in a more comforting environment. Before their departure, Dale went back to the Villain's Noose and returned with rounds of sandwiches which they all devoured hungrily (except Gaspard) as they tried to take stock of the situation. Dale said he was quite happy to keep an eye on the Yum Bum while Effie and Boris concluded their business discussion. Effie was concerned about Gaspard but Boris managed to assure her that Dimitri would take good care of him and report back on his mobile as necessary. Boris's calm and authoritative manner won her over and they resumed their discussions in the Haystack's administration room behind the main foyer, with a bottle of chilled champagne that Dimitri had whistled up from the Bentley's mini-bar.

During their walk-about they had chatted freely and both had been impressed with the other's entrepreneurial flair. Boris had lost no time in plying Effie with several versions of his opulent business card, each one declaring an organisation of international stature, be it opera, cabaret, property development, and the import and export of fine art. Having laid on a charm offensive of Oscar winning proportions, Effie had swallowed the bait hook, line and sinker and, as a consequence, Boris had little difficulty in outlining his funding proposition for the Haystack on condition that Effie grant Loretta an audition.

"I'd absolutely love to meet her," said Effie, enjoying a mutual cloud of Gauloise smoke, "when I tell the Board about your two hundred and fifty thousand pound donation everything will be passed on the nod, believe me."

"I do Effie, I do, and perhaps you and Freddie would care to join Loretta and me for dinner one night this week?"

"Ooh that would be marvellous, but I have to tell you that Freddie isn't one for socialising, he has no capacity for small talk, he's too wrapped up in his work and unfortunately it's not the sort of thing he's allowed to talk about freely anyway."

"I understand, but please ask him all the same."

"Of course I will, had you a particular day in mind?"

"Shall we pencil in this Friday?"

"Yes, let's ink it in and go for it, come what may."
With that, they clinked glasses and toasted the future. Effie was aglow with bubbles. Boris was cementing his plans.

Meanwhile, back at Gaspard's house, Dimitri was slipping Gaspard a Dandelion Dacha. He was getting a bit fed up with Gaspard swooning all over the place and had decided to take matters into his own hands. Needless to say, before very long, Gaspard was slandering everyone and everybody in MI5 and MI6, including Sir Rodney Snodder and Gloria Fitzbagley.

"No wonder the country's going to the dogs when the two Heads of the Intelligence Services are sleeping together."

"A couple of alley cats," said Dimitri, not really caring much about it one way or the other.

"There's no morality these days," added Gaspard, believing himself to be beyond reproach.

"Some of us have got standards."
Gaspard peered at him quizzically, "it was good of you to bring me home."

"Think nothing of it," said Dimitri, knowing how pleased Boris would be with the information he had captured on tape. The telephone rang.

"Shall I get it for you Gaspard?"

"No thank you, I'm feeling better now, if you would excuse me one moment."

Dimitri settled back into the armchair while Gaspard answered the phone in the hallway.

"Hello?"

"We're still waiting for those photographs number six."

"I'm not at liberty to discuss that right now."

"We cannot wait indefinitely, political issues are brewing."

"I have a visitor, please stop pestering me."

"You pathetic poofter."

And then the line went dead. Narrow minded bigots, muttered Gaspard to himself and, for a fleeting second, the notion of revenge flitted across his mind. If that was what they thought of him, why should he bother any further?

As far as he was concerned they were all a bunch of amoral plebes, anyway.

19

"I'm not feeling very well," said Freddie, "I'm going home."

Ian Trubshaw started to twitter. Freddie had never had a single day off sick for as long as they had been working together, and since he didn't look ill, what was the nature of his malaise? As soon as Freddie had made his exit, Ian telephoned The Sprout.

"Just keep an eye on him," said The Sprout casually.

"Yes Sir," replied Ian, working himself up into a major twitter.

Just because his late father had been a close friend of Freddie's didn't imbue him with exceptional surveillance abilities. Who on earth did The Sprout think he was? His expectations of him were so unfair. He had gained a double first in physics at Oxford and his PhD had been a fifty-thousand word dissertation on compound strato-ionic mathematics as an application tool in the development of molecular structure in rocket fuel. In short, he was a scientist, not a one man detective agency. If Melissa got wind of his diversification, she would become highly critical. Notwithstanding the current situation, when little Sebastian had been born, she had said 'we have a son to bring up, please don't put yourself in any danger,' Too much responsibility made Ian nervous and prolonged bouts of stress caused eczema.

He was itching now. Was he supposed to follow Freddie in his car? Probably yes but that would mean losing his parking space twenty-three bays down from The Sprout in the DERA Central Laboratories (Propulsion Department) - Block A. At least when his father was alive other people would acknowledge his existence by not letting doors slam in his face too much. But now all that had changed. As a consequence of Professor Ted Trubshaw (New Year's Honours List nominee) conking out with a massive heart attack, the expectations of friends and family towards his son Ian were as intense as the poisonous jealousy emanating from other young scientists about him. Things were so crushingly competitive these days that it was all any decent young man could do just to avoid the paths of perversity and rough justice. Ian Trubshaw wanted peace, quiet, and solitude, plus the occasional cosmic bang to signify a certain level of progress in matters ballistical. And instead of that, he had been given responsibility for minding a distracted, taciturn, brilliant, deep-thinking lunatic who had just been publicly humiliated right the way down from the very top. It just wasn't fair.

And to make matters worse, ever since little Sebastian had declared himself open for life's mystical experiences, Melissa had become totally frigid. No wonder he had started fantasising about Effie Bannister. He had known her ever since he was a kid but the thing was, in spite of him being nervous, frustrated and confused, Effie's fabulous legs and beautiful poise were no longer lost on him. In fact, if he wasn't so knackered, he'd probably be masturbating. And to add one more fact, it was becoming increasingly difficult to avoid a wet dream The last thing he wanted with anyone was a big emotional scene, but the point was, his mother's party last Sunday was the third time in a month that Effie Bannister had invaded his personal space on one pretext or another and he was finding it difficult to maintain an appropriately humanistic distance without causing offence.

After Freddie had left the office, Ian picked up a pair of birdwatching binoculars that he had acquired as a result of redeeming a surprisingly high number of Barclaycard points. He focused on Freddie's car as it turned right into the perimeter road. A mini-roundabout some way along offered the choice of branching left for the main line station or right for the town centre. He saw Freddie swing left.

"He went to Waterloo station," he reported to The Sprout a little while later, "I was unable to follow him because my car wouldn't start."

"That is understandable, perhaps you should renew it?"

"I'm afraid I can't afford it at the present moment."

"There is a Focus Group proposal for more promotional posts currently awaiting my attention, although I cannot say in what direction my thoughts lie at the present moment."

Ian retreated from The Sprout's presence with just the right amount of humbleness. Material things like money and cars were of no interest to him even though he was aware of the need to be grateful for the relative ease with which both those comforts had been made available to him. He revered his father, couldn't understand his mother, and was backed up in a rather frightening corner as far as Melissa was concerned.

All any young scientist could do today was decide whether they wanted to preserve life or blow it away and then get on with their chosen decision. Nazi or Buddhist or something in between, it was as easy as that, wasn't it? Perhaps not. Sometimes people got in your way and if you couldn't nip aside courteously on the pretext that your jock-strap elastic had just snared your right testicle, then the alternative of removing their life from off the face of this earth became a considerable burden.

Ian didn't hate Dale but he knew of his existence (he had met him once or twice before). Effie sang his praises all the time. When she and Dale were together, everyone agreed that there really was a zangy twang in the air. They buzzed together and, as a consequence, others were drawn towards their honey-pot of fun. Rumours about their relationship were beginning to circulate but Ian knew that this was just idle gossip. At least he hoped it was, for Freddie's sake as well as his!

"Don't worry Freddie, trust me and everything will be alright," said Boris, looking wistfully at the dome of Prince Albert and wondering why it was that Freddie was saying how difficult he would find it to pretend in front of Effie and Loretta and himself, that he did not know either of them until now, when now was going to be a full blast beano at Tzarbinski's, with nobody querying the excesses afterwards. This was an aspect of the British, or perhaps a certain Chechnyut chapter of the English, that he just couldn't understand. You offered them a feast and the prospect of a knees-up, Cossack or otherwise, and their immediate reaction was to look at you superciliously whilst retreating in polite panic. A night out was a night out was a night out. What in Gagarin's name was the problem?

So, Freddie, a little white lie to Mrs B, who, as we all know has just stopped shagging Dale because she suspects that he is shagging Roslyn de Winter and, let's face it, you've been lying to each other for nearly forty years or more, so who's to blame? and then we can all carry on pretending to be friends as before except in those instances where we actually are. What's the problem?

Well, yes, Boris knew that Gaspard was going to be a problem. A snooty, uptight, frustrated, utterly repressed, nanny-bred cultural sodomite whom he had actually fancied now and again in a moment of anguished sterility. But none of the others knew that. Effie was the key to his operatic aspirations and Gaspard could be the vessel into which he, Boris Blodvrinsky, would conduit his grandest production. He knew that Gaspard would argue at every artistic juncture in the manner as befits the queen he was and, prat that he may be also, he needed to understand that he could only become Gaspard de la Grant, Stage Designer under exclusive contract to Blodvrinsky International Artists, if he kept his trap shut and fed them with all the MI5 and MI6 junk. Freddie and Effie need not know about that. Loretta would because Loretta always did. He didn't want to upset her any more. He

109

had heard her sing night, after night, after night, in all kinds of hotels, from the still-drying breeze blocks to the polished granite marble, and she was marvellous. And he loved her. An electric babe who turned the boys on every time. Carmen. Queen Dido. Diana Ross. How the hell Freddie had managed to stay on two feet the day after what he had seen the two of them doing together in the Tunisian hotel bedroom video, must have been a case of what they call, the English stubbornness. She was just fantastic. An entire one-stop, instant sexual service provider who could also pluck your heart out when she sang the blues and then box you in later with her cynical but wonderfully incisive thinking. Gaspard had already seen her, albeit with Freddie, in the foyer of the Great Cumberland Hotel, and that was a connection that Gaspard would have to lie about. And who would receive those lies?

Boris's Godfathers were a treacherous lot. They came from the same line who had caused his grandfather Yevgeny Blodvrinsky to end up in front of a Bolshevic firing squad for the sake of political expediency. And a generation later, when somebody blew the whistle on his son Vladimir, they pretended not to notice as he sank to the bottom of the Volga like a trussed up cat. And that was after Stalingrad too! Those were in the days when the Blodvrinsky's were not hooligans but actually controlled every inch of the streets, both in Moscow and Kiev. They took the organisation seriously and trained in Chechnya. Not surprisingly, a few of the locals came on board at the same time. But now it was a mess. Every Ivan with a bazooka was making off with the latest bit of computer hardware and shouting that he would change the world by force if necessary. There was no dialogue any more. Be angry if you want to, sure, but leave the violence until the end and then only as a last ditch necessity following prayer.

Dimitri had a second uncle who was Chechen. Dimitri's dad was a Tartar and his mother was Mongolian with a fair bit of Chinese in her make up. Another gene must have infiltrated from somewhere else to account for those funny little closely-set eyes, but whatever the case, he couldn't be slapped around. He was quite happy with the orders thing and, better still, if you cocked up on the strategy thing, he would get you a vodka and say drink this first then tell me what to do next. If he could just get Anita and Svetlana over and have them all live together in one of those big mock-Tudor mansions that they were building just outside Fropsham, they really would be firing on all cylinders.

Boris knew that Dale would have to be watched but everyone was bribable. As far as he could see, the only problem he didn't know how to tackle was the Yum Bum itself. But Effie knew people. She had the horticultural contacts. If they started playing up, he'd get Dimitri to lean on them. As of today, everything was as under control as it could be. His mother would be proud of him. So would his step-father, even though he may have taken a leather belt to him first and then insisted that they got drunk afterwards to celebrate their manhood.

"So Freddie, just remember what you want out of all this."

"I want to realise Project Cassandra."

"And who's doing the most to help you get there?"

"You are."

"Okay, so now we understand each other, this it what happens next. Loretta's gonna give you a bit of home entertainment at her place, and Dimitri's going to run you both there in the Bentley and take you back to Waterloo station afterwards. Normally, I'd be happy to have him drive you all the way home to Fropsham but I'm having the Third Secretary of the Russian Embassy round for a spot of informal tea so the protocol is that I have to pick him up in my car. So let's say adios for now and see you at Tzarbinski's on Saturday."

Nobody bothered to try and get the last word in.

20

There were so many unanswered questions shimmying across Freddie's mind as he nuzzled between the soft erotic seas of Loretta's breasts that he didn't know which one to deal with first. After a while, the cushion on which his thoughts bounced back and forth had such a soothing effect that it hardly seemed worthwhile bothering about any of them. Perhaps he really should try and relax and adopt a different mind-set than hitherto applied to the unfolding events of his life? Boris appeared to be on top of the situation and had not expressed any doubts about his role in helping him bring Project Cassandra into reality. So why not just go with the flow and enjoy each moment for what it was? When all was said and done, this was hedonism, this was Effie's way and he had been tolerating the fall-out for most of his adult life. Now it was his turn to get some in. A five-course dinner sitting opposite Loretta, knowing all the while that Effie would be thinking that only she was capable of an extra-marital fling would be rather satisfying in a moralistically spongy sort of way. Boris was clearly a maniac, a dangerous mega-hooligan with a back-up organisation that seemed to have tentacles everywhere, and no doubt malevolent ones at that. But he was no longer bothered by this. The top brass in the UK Ministry of Defence were no better and their political masters were merely the self-serving malignant tumours that instigated the fatal rot in the first place. No, far from it, Boris was a blessing in disguise and Loretta was a living dream who took him there and back to oblivion whenever they made love.

Loretta gasped as Freddie erupted inside her. Mutual orgasm again! Much more of this and it would fast become a habit. Not that she was complaining. Things seemed to be moving in the right direction. Boris had clearly got the message about doing things without telling her but then he was, and always would be, a control freak, so she would continue to keep an eye on him, humour him a bit and try not to be so strident with her criticism. The truth was, he would crumble if he couldn't cry on her shoulder now and again. Dimitri was okay. She could handle Dimitri. They respected each other for the tough cookie that each of them was. For her, the unknowns at the present were Effie, Dale and Gaspard. She would assess all of them in her own good time but her gut instinct told her that linking up with a secret service agent was asking for trouble. Well, when she finally got to the Haystack she would no doubt meet Gaspard then.

She eased herself off Freddie. It was rather endearing the way he liked her to come on top of him. What was it he had said when they were rolling about in search of a mutually satisfying position? 'I always enjoy watching the blast off'. He was a sweet man. Right now he was falling asleep. Well, let him rest. The ideas in his head were enough to send the civilised world into leap-frogging an entire millennium. She didn't know much about rocket science but when you started to play with people's minds by way of a complex mathematical equation, then maybe it was better to look, listen and learn and not let on too much to anybody, especially a megalomaniac like Boris.

"You look absolutely fabulous under here," said Dale to Roslyn, "them Yum Bum leaves sort of give you a look of quiet contemplation like."

Things between Roz and Dale were such that he had no need of any assistance from the likes of Cyrano de Bergerac, ta very much. He reckoned that Effie had got the hots for Boris and, judging by the way she had suddenly come over all friendly when she had caught him and Roz mucking about like, she had known, from that moment on that he had two-timed her. So he had been grateful for the absence of instant aggro. He had seen enough of that in his short life to know that it never paid off. Even a few seconds helped. Those few desperately exposed moments before committing to a deeply held pattern of behaviour. Call it karmic if you like but two geezers, or one geezer and his wife, or two wives and their geezers, kicking the shit out of each other, first verbally and then almost certainly physically, was definitely out of order and didn't make sense towards the cause of harmonious living like.

He and Cheryl had existed in discord every bleedin' day of their married life. She had not been averse to punching him in the face, nor had she paused for a second before kicking him in the stomach, if she thought she was in the right. He would slap her back on a few occasions and she hadn't liked it because he was strong and did not have a temper. So there was more slagging off in their household than the average number of cat fleas in a sofa.

By the way, their cat, Miss Jizzum, had long since picked up the bad vibes and slung her hook. By all accounts she was terrorising the neighbourhood after dark and licking the blood off her paws during daylight. He had tried to coax her back but to no avail. In a moment of quite gut-wrenching tenderness, Miss Jizzum had nuzzled his cheek and whispered something in his ear. Being human, he couldn't understand exactly what she was saying, however, there was something almost spiritual in her embrace and some kind of wisdom had been transmitted instantaneously. She was grateful for the basic home that he and Cheryl had provided for her thus far. However, in life, you had a choice. You could either be happy or you could not. She had taken a break to allow them to

114

resolve their difficulties. By herself for a while, she had become happy again, although she would be the first to admit that a period of extreme violence that she had felt necessary to use in order to establish her street cred, was, in retrospect, a highly disturbing experience. She wasn't actively seeking a new partner right now because she was convinced that the universal Law of life would reveal somebody else in the natural unfolding of day to day events. In short, she had whispered in his ear, find the middle way mate. All this from a moggie!

So, he had backed off from confrontations with Cheryl. Endured the insults. Got a handle on the finances. Decided what he could afford to pay and what he could survive the loss of, then made her an offer he was relieved to find out she was happy not to refuse. 'You must respect one another', his old queen had said, only a few months before her fatal moped accident. He could see what she meant. The old king and queen sure had their slanging matches but they never actually slagged each other off. After a heavy session the old king would say to Dale, 'well where else would I go to find a woman like that?" meaning loyal, trustworthy and cheeky. The old queen would catch him maybe ten minutes later and say, 'your ol man's a nice bloke but he don't 'alf get worked up abart fings and I ain't 'aving 'im shout 'is mouth off for the rest of me life'. And they never struck each other.

Dale was now pottering along with this oily but rugged old motorbike and side car and it was proving to be quite fun. Oil Slick had grown on him. Better still, when Roz was riding pillion, it was something of an erotic experience. In short, they had started to fall in love but hadn't quite realised it at that precise juncture.

"You look absolutely fabulous too," she replied, "and I've even got my glasses on."

The two of them fell about laughing. After a few minutes they calmed down and began to soak up the loving ambience that they had discovered in between the verdant leaves of the Yum Bum. Then they kissed and fell silent again. It was a silence only in the sense that they did not speak to one another because their actual communication was on a spiritual level. They revelled in each other's existence and, granted that this included the full circle of the sex thing, their biggest joy was being together in perfect harmony.

The Yum Bum sighed with the most subtle, almost inaudible, gentle hissing.

It had got where it wanted to for today.

21

"They're squeezing Gaspard for the CIA photographs," said Dimitri, "what are you going to do about it?"

"Simple," said Boris, "we'll fake something with Loretta, she's good at role playing, and he can give them that."

"What if he doesn't play ball?"

"I'll tell him he's never gonna design for grand opera in his life and may not even make it to the next Haystack production."

Dimitri chuckled. Boris was getting into the swing of things again. He didn't like it when Boris had excluded him from the Tunisian trip because he reckoned Boris and Loretta were heading for some kind of showdown and he was the right hand man whereas she was only the left hand woman. Boris needed him in order to see both sides of any situation and, thankfully, since his return, that had started to happen again. They had even had another chat about Anita and Svetlana.

"Go look at Cedar Park Mansions at the top of Fropsham Heights and tell me what you think," said Boris, "they've got five bedrooms, two receptions, lots of those little leaded windows and a three bay garage with electronic doors."

Dimitri had duly reported back that as a potential home for Mr and Mrs Pryshnyi and daughter, it was a definite goer.

"What should I do next? he asked.

"Ring the estate agents and tell them I'm buying it," said Boris.

At first the estate agent couldn't do enough for them but a few days later he had started to get a bit snooty.

"Has Mr Blodvrinsky ever been excluded from an electoral register?" he asked Dimitri.

"Hold on, I'll ask him."

"Tell him I'll pop in tomorrow in person with all the appropriate references," replied Boris.

By Thursday afternoon, Boris had issued a banker's cheque from the Bank of Dubai and, as a consequence, by midnight London time, the entire Cedar Park Mansions estate, consisting of seven identical mock-Tudor mansions each standing in half an acre of ground, was his. Additionally, the estate agent had promised to keep an eye out for an English castle with a working portcullis and a moat that was not under the jurisdiction of the National Rivers Authority and, the minute one came onto the market, would fly him there in a helicopter, courtesy of Pendred, Nutting and Holland.

Dimitri was very encouraged by all this. It meant that he would be close to Svetlana's dog arena which would be dead handy because he'd had this idea of linking the fights with a strip show afterwards, or maybe in between. He would run it past Boris first, of course, even though he knew that both of them were going to have their hands full with the Haystack and the Yum Bum and everything else that came with it.

"You can start moving in next week," said Boris.

"What do I use for furniture?"

"We'll go to Harrods."

"What about the other six houses, who's gonna live there?"

"I'm sure we can attract investors with the right attitude," said Boris, obviously delighted with the possibilities that his purchase had now opened, "I could have a quiet word with Mr Al Fayed while you and Svetlana are choosing bed covers, have you told her by the way?"

"Not yet."

"Well give her a ring now and we'll sort out the travel arrangements."

Dimitri couldn't wait to get started and was really annoyed when he couldn't get through to Moscow.

"We should've fixed telecommunications before we left Moscow," he growled.

"Believe me Dimitri, when I get my hands on Freddie's ballistic missile system, including the rocket, we'll be fixing so many things around the world that everyone will be ringing us, not the other way round."

Dimitri tried to put his boss's statement into some kind of perspective. Okay, it was big. It was global. Secret intelligence agencies from every government in the world would be watching them. It might make his dog fighting cabaret idea a bit difficult to establish but when you'd got the strongest fire power, most sensible people backed off. He put his mind back on the job again.

"Okay, so what about Gaspard and the photo-shoot with Loretta?"

Boris was leaning back in his chair and beginning to trip off on Prince Albert's head again. He had a master plan outlined in his mind and he knew that the time had come to start knitting the detail together. He could prioritise, sure, and maybe that would kick a few diversions into touch. But the thing was, life had a devilish habit or rearranging your daily menu just when you thought you knew what you wanted. As for getting nervous about what decisions to take in the context of long term destinations, well, forget it. His success resulted from dealing absolutely with the thing that was right there in front of him, duck that and he knew that you were in all sorts of shit which, surprise, surprise, created more unresolved issues that piled up until they practically obscured normal eyesight. So, he would flush everyone out in one go. He would start with this Saturday night's dinner at Tzarbinski's. He intended to include Gaspard and Dale on the guest list. He swung round to face Dimitri. Whatever look he must have had on his face it certainly put Dimitri on green alert. He still didn't know what he was going to do about the Yum Bum, but he sure as hell knew what he was going to do now.

"Dimitri."

"Yes boss?"

"Get the Bentley, we're going to see Gaspard."

"Yes boss."

"Use the car phone to try Svetlana again."

"Thanks boss."

"I'm gonna talk to Loretta about becoming a CIA agent."

The two of them laughed. And then laughed some more. And then had a quick slug of Armenian vodka and laughed again. Life was a game. Win or lose. Just enjoy it day by day.

"That was a good vodka, boss."

"Yah, it had better be, the Third Secretary of the Russian Embassy gave me ten crates of it."

They both fell about laughing again.

Dimitri staggered off through the doorway and Boris lit up a Havana cigar. He had decided to play some more Glinka on the CD before ringing Loretta. Unusually for him, the slug of vodka had bounced off an empty stomach and he missed the CD button and pressed the tuner amplifier instead. Straight into Classic FM on full volume and the opening bars of Glinka's Ruslan and Ludmilla overture. He'd only just got time to grab the rat-tailed mop and steady himself for a knees-bend jump before the violins raced dizzyingly downwards on the other side of their first scintillating up and down roller coaster run. Vomp! He hit the deck bang on with the bass trombone but couldn't keep up with the horns which were trampolining away like greyhounds out of a trap. The music may have been too fast for him but he was right in there with the elation.

"I got everything moving, mummy."

'Just watch your back, I don't trust that Effie Bannister.'

"I find her most charming."

'They're the dangerous ones, take a look at Loretta.'

"What about her?"

'She's got you all sown up, you're dancing to her tune now and the same will happen with Effie Bannister. Before long, between the two of them, they'll cut your legs from under you.'

Boris screamed and ejected the rat-tailed mop like an Olympic javelin through the open window. It plummeted to the ground, almost impaling a Norwegian back-packer eating an orange on a bench along Kensington Gore. Dimitri witnessed the trajectory and chuckled to himself. The boss liked to let his hair down now and again. He'd buy another mop in due course, as he always did, and carry on as if nothing had happened. Well, if you didn't let off steam you weren't in business.

Dale was tending the Yum Bum several floors up when he heard Effie answer the phone in the back of the shop.

"Boris, hello, how are you? how lovely to hear from you."
He could tell from the tone of her voice that she was genuinely delighted and it confirmed his opinion that she was no longer angry about him and Roz because Boris was now the man who was digging the beans, so to speak. This made him happy.

"Boris, that's absolutely wonderful, what a good idea, I'm sure they would both be delighted to accept. Now listen, far be it for me to take advantage of your hospitality but I've just thought of something that will liven things up."

This was an occasion when Dale wished he was on the other end of the line. Effie sounded in remarkably high spirits and she hadn't stopped nattering all week about her dinner date with Boris. Her and Freddie's date, that was. He reckoned that Freddie wouldn't go a bomb on the invitation and Effie would rather he piss off and play with his missiles leaving her creamy free to flirt with Boris. What he heard her say next was definitely an ear's prick situation.

"If Dale and Gaspard are also going to be there, and I can't think for one minute that they will not, and so is Dimitri, which naturally I'm glad about, the numbers will be uneven, so why don't I invite Roslyn, Dale's new girlfriend? She'd absolutely love it and it would make the numbers up to eight."
There was a short silence while Boris replied and then Effie let rip with one of her great, guffawing, tobacco fragranced laughs. There were further conversational exchanges until eventually Effie rang off and burst through the rear doors of the shop honking and wracking in phlegm spluttered wheezes. She climbed the stairs to where he was and semi-collapsed on the nearest tread.

121

"I can't tell you what a fabulous conversation I've just had with Boris."

Dale wasn't going to let on that he had caught the tale end of it, so he allowed Effie to relay the details with maximum enthusiasm and then addressed her directly.

"So you ain't angry wiv me?"

"No, I'm hurt but I've been expecting it."

"I'm sorry, but it just happened like, I couldn't 'old back any longer."

"You don't have to explain, I was like that at your age too."

"I still fink you're great Eff."

"And so are you Dale, I haven't had such a laugh in years, so let's stay friends and keep the bandwagon rolling."

"Right. Sorted."

Dale nearly fell out of the Yum Bum in surprise. He had really thought that Effie might turn nasty and had envisaged all manner of bloodshed flying around. But no, here she was saying, I can take it and let's get on with the rest of it and not fuck things up. He reckoned that took some doing.

"I'll be honest Eff, I'm gobsmacked. 'ow you can manage to say that you can take it after I'd been wiv' Roz in the middle of it and 'adn't got round to telling you that I'd been and took it first like, I just don't know."

"Well, there you go," she said, struggling with her emotions as well as his explanation, "put it down to experience."

She didn't want to get rid of him because he was so involved with everything and so popular with everyone, including her customers, and if she started to cut Roz into little pieces it would affect her acting, and she had to admit that Roslyn de Winter had an extraordinary talent. It was best to look forwards not back, and let's face it, the future looked promising, "now I'll leave it to you to speak to Roz and we can discuss the transport arrangements for Saturday night later on, meanwhile, what do make of this, isn't it fascinating?"

Effie was of course referring to the Yum Bum which had finally stopped growing. Nevertheless, it had spread across every ceiling, infiltrated every corner and spiralled upwards round every vertical until it had reached the thatch roof at the very very top. There it had paused. Then quietly, almost unobtrusively, it had set about consolidating itself in the beauty stakes. And it was beautiful beyond any whispered notion of a doubt.

The Yum Bum had now revealed itself to be something rather vine-like in overall structure. Its mozzarella pizza base had dried out to become a massively close-knit tentacled circle, like a plate of gigantic spaghetti. The main trunk, which was easily the circumference of a size twenty woman, was like a children's painting in nursery school. The predominant colour was ruddy brown with generous slappings of mustard yellow. It rose in a magnificent arc, like a rainbow turned on its side, and swept through the high ceiling of the Seventh Cavalry assembly area as if it were General Custer cantering towards heaven. The huge, strong, sinewy branches changed colour from their base to their tip. It was a startling kaleidoscopic journey from burnt sienna to cobalt blue. The vine-like branches meandered in random, lazy loops and where the light from the windows struck it directly, it twinkled like a thousand tiny mirrors. From the branches drooped the most fabulously succulent leaves. Each one was as big as a pillow, and in some cases, almost as full as one too. They were the deepest of sea green with a soft, translucent purple aura spread across their surface. When one dared to go closer, one could see a billion, trillion, tiny hairs gently sensing the atmosphere. A single, brilliant, red hair-line defined the seam on each side of a pillowy leaf. On the most mature leaves, tiny little nodules had begun to sprout. There was evidence of some kind of shimmering order as in a peacock's tail. Each nodule had a sticky tip which glistened as brilliantly as mercury. The central trunk, at this point more like a stem, curved upwards through the scene dock in a graceful, languorous curve. More insinuating branches, tendril-thin at their extremities, spread everywhere in a loose, haphazard, unearthly pattern. The pattern was repeated on every floor, becoming ever more delicate the higher it reached.

And then there was its scent. It was more than a scent, more than an aroma. It had created a pure atmosphere of its own, fresh and clean as if it had just rained and washed all the toxins out of the air. Everything was so clear and brilliantly defined that it lent clarity to the mind as well. Within its vaulting fronds there was a sense, not of ensconcement, but of freedom. It was as if the limitations of one's consciousness had disappeared and as far as the eye could see was merely the beginning. There was always a beyond.

Dale and Effie both experienced it sitting there but they were unable to articulate it. It just was. A moment of simultaneous arrival and departure. Stillness and movement. Opening and returning. The mystical Law of cause and effect. Effie smiled at Dale. Even though they did not touch physically, their lives connected and from that moment on they knew they would always be friends.

"I'm going to see how Gaspard is and tell him about Boris's invitation," said Effie, setting off down the stairs, "that should cheer him up, he simply adores a good dinner party,"

"I don't fink he's in shock no more," replied Dale chirpily, "I just fink he's 'ad this terrible fright what he don't wanna talk about like."

Gaspard had indeed had a fright. The thought was not lost on Effie that he was the only one that had viewed the Yum Bum's self-rooting phenomenon from an entirely exclusive perspective. She wondered if he had seen something particularly significant from his vantage point directly above the eruption that was the cause of his thankfully, only temporary, catatonic trance? He did not seem to have experienced any joy in the event and yet he was clearly in awe of its form and beauty.

"I would love to attend a dinner party Effie, thank you very much, Tzarbinski's sounds just the sort of place that Dale would love and I don't suppose it would matter which knife and fork he was using."

"I've also invited Roslyn de Winter, his latest girlfriend, and I'm not sure whether there's a seating plan, Boris seems to favour a free-for-all."

Gaspard's face dropped like a ton of beetle dung. Effie had decided that catatonically in recovery or not, Gaspard would have to understand who was calling the shots. She was.

"Is dress optional?" was all Gaspard could manage.

"Yes, but I suspect that not even Mr Pryshnyi will be wearing trainers."

Gaspard wasn't quite sure who Mr Pryshnyi was nor, if he was brutally honest with himself, this man called Boris. He knew, because having looked at it this morning, that he had acquired an opulent looking business card from an international opera producer called Boris Blodvrinsky, but he couldn't remember how. Nor was he about to ask anyone how he had ended up naked in bed recently, with his dressing gown tassels in the most inappropriate of places. He knew that he had received a telephone call from the section and they were becoming extremely persistent about photographs that he had not got. That did not even exist. He also knew, but was too afraid to admit it, that when he had seen the Yum Bum break out of its pot and perform its fantastic transmogrification, he thought he had heard somebody whispering - I can help you. So much was blank after that that he wasn't quite sure when he was in touch with reality or when he was dreaming.

So Roslyn and Dale had gone public.

It was a nightmare.

22

Tzarbinski's Restaurant was not the kind of place you would take your grandmother to, although plenty of people did without knowing it. Tzarbinski's was the front for the UK Operational Centre of the Blodvrinsky International Corporation whose HQ was in South Kensington only thirty-eight miles away as an old Sputnik might fly. Boris had determined that Freddie's missile research centre, which would include a fully operational launch pad, would be within a five mile radius of Tzarbinski's. This had been achieved. Dimitri was about to move into a permanent residence overlooking the Haystack theatre which also, very conveniently, was itself only two miles outside the Tzarbinski five mile radius and a mere twelve overall to the missile site. The UK Ministry of Defence had a number of properties within the general area which served the activities of the various Defence, Evaluation and Research Agencies. Security at their sites was as tight as to be expected and you couldn't do anything too silly on the surrounding roads without attracting some kind of authoritative attention between the hours of ten to four p.m. It was certainly no push-over after then and most people paid their Road Fund Tax and carried their Insurance Certificate and Driving Licence just in case they were stopped by the police. Boris had set up an infrastructure of service contracts with the DERA bases and, as a consequence, seven out of ten commercial vehicles belonged, eventually, and very circuitously, to him.

All the cabling for Freddie's computer suite, which was situated in the biggest top floor office of Frank Files' vacated warehouse, was delivered last night in a Mercedes diesel van. Nobody batted an eyelid as the white van with a pink flash down the side advertising Cistern Chapel Sanitary Services came in and out of the building as it had done on so many occasions before. Someone's fingers had scrawled 'Investors in Pissers' across the mud splattered rear panels but nobody could be bothered to wash it off.

Tzarbinski's itself used to be a huge, draughty Anglican church, probably built in the 1920's. It wasn't particularly attractive but it did have enormous expanses of high block walls held in place by square solid buttresses. Before Boris had bought it, a surveyor had suggested that he rebuild the north transept because the great stained glass window fifty feet up was beginning to crack and this he attributed to subsidence. When Boris took one look at the massive wall with its big solid blocks all sitting comfortably like a child's game that had never been unpacked, he decided that the surveyor was trying to pull a lucrative flanker, so he had Dimitri ram his BMW Seven Series against the crash barriers along the Guildford by-pass and a few days after the accident, the surveyor amended his report. After that, the builders moved in. They left the vast superstructure in place and built the Tzarbinski restaurant inside it.

The seating plan was circular not square. There were ten levels each stacked one on top of the other like tiers on a wedding cake. The lowest level, which was effectively the ground floor, had a continuous bar running round the circumference. People could wander in and perch themselves on a high-legged bar stool and not be bothered from one end of the day to the other, provided they didn't fall asleep or get drunk. The remainder of the floor space was set aside with

127

small tables for one or two people to enjoy a smoke and a chat. Those who favoured tea and coffee and chocolate milk-shakes with a slice of some sweet tasting patisserie, had to go up a floor. Again, it was a big area and there were combinations of seats and tables for two or four. There was no square furniture anywhere, it was all round. Level three offered slightly more in the way of tasty pasta dishes or bowls of French onion soup with chunks of poppy seeded bread and basic dishes of a bistro inclination. If your desire was for something different then you went up a level each time.

And this was how it worked and it worked very well. The more you wanted, or the longer you had to eat, or the more sophisticated the cuisine and level of service required, or the importance of ambience for the occasion, you simply made a reservation at the appropriate level. The higher the level the greater the cost and the less availability because, like every wedding cake, it got smaller towards the top.

Positioned at the very pinnacle, right under the roof, as if to resonate with a pastry chefs' most elaborate marzipan twirl, was Boris's private table. A huge round affair made of Burmese Teak with matching high backed chairs inlaid with black and gold leather. It could seat twelve people comfortably. The entire podium was surrounded by pillars and arches, with heavy pelmeted curtains and drapes that could be adjusted according to the degree of privacy required. It was like entering a mini-Royal Albert Hall, which was not surprising, since it was amongst the loggia and boxes within that vast Victorian edifice that Boris had gained his inspiration. His interior designer had very little choice although Boris was delighted when he saw the whimsical art nouveau statues clasping the pillars in Mucha-like adoration.

Igor Tzarbinski himself was a Russian, and a genuine one at that. But he was not a chef or even a restauranteur. He was an actor. Boris had met him at a party in Moscow following an end of season performance by the Bolshoi Ballet of Les Sylphides. Igor had declared his love shortly afterwards but Boris was made of sterner stuff and would have none of it. When the time came to shift his operation to the West, Boris offered him the job and Igor had jumped at it. So utterly besotted was he that he continued jumping at the mere twitch of Boris's fingers.

"Everything's ready for Saturday night," he said breathlessly.

Boris smiled at him. Igor was tall and blonde and very good looking.

"I knew it would be Igor, how about the interview room?"

"Yes, the carpet was hoovered this morning and I put fresh tulips and jonquils in your favourite cut-glass vase."

The interview room was down in the cellars alongside the wine racks. It was bugged in every conceivable way and apart from that, it was, to all intents and purposes, a rather classy rest room. Like everywhere else in the building the rooms were square, but it did not prevent Boris from indulging his obsession for anything round or spherical. One exception was the twelve-inch stiletto dagger which was now covered in Yum Bum gunge. It was a present from Igor. Boris unsheathed it from a cardboard scabbard which Dimitri had quickly rolled together from the inserts of the vodka crates presented as a gift to Boris by the Third Secretary of the Russian Embassy. Most of the pink loo paper was emasculated into the blade and the Yum Bum gunge had dried like blood.

"Sorry about this Igor," said Boris, handing him the dagger, "I had to get a lady out of a spot of bother, can you clean it up for me?"

"Of course, I'm so glad it came in handy, I'll have it ready for you by Saturday night."

"Good lad."

Igor would be twenty-six on October 4th. Only another six months to go. Would Boris then call him a good man?

He would do his bidding nonetheless.

"What time do you want tea and coffee in the interview room?"

"As soon as Dimitri arrives with Mr Grant."

"Is he somebody special?"

"Yes, very, and he's in show business."

"How wonderful," exclaimed Igor genuinely, "things *are* looking up."

Boris grinned like Yeltsin, clenched his fist and hit Igor playfully on the right shoulder.

"Yah Igor, for *both* of us."

Igor made his exit feeling great. He would keep an eye out for Dimitri and set about cleaning up the dagger. By the look of it, he would probably have to immerse it in cellulose thinner which nearly always gave him a headache.

"Let's put it this way," said Boris to Gaspard, as they sat in easy chairs round a highly polished circular coffee table hand crafted from Siamese Paduk, "we also know that Sir Rodney Snodder and Gloria Fitzbagley are taking tango lessons together at least once a fortnight."

Gaspard's face froze like the Tundra. His worst fears had come to light. The other side had got hold of him. All the training in the world did not alter the fact that capture was his greatest fear.

"What do you want me to do?" he said, without hesitating.

"Everything I ask."

Gaspard broke into a cold sweat, he could feel a clammy trickle making its way over the first of the many furrows in his brow. He was ageing by the second.

"Would you like another cup of Mango tea?" asked Dimitri.

"Yes please."

"We can help you," said Boris, almost avuncularly, "we know you need some photographs."

"Yes," replied Gaspard, realising the futility of side-tracking.

"So let's start with that and see where we go from there, yah?"

"Thank you."

"Would you prefer a sweet Martini?" offered Dimitri politely. Gaspard nodded and Dimitri poured him a generous slug. He then added three exquisitely cut triangles of lemon and dropped in a cylindrical bullet of ice.

"Boss?"

"Just stick a Grand Marnier in the coffee and help yourself. Would you like a cigar, Gaspard?"

"I don't smoke thank you."

"Do you mind if I do?"

"Good gracious no, it's a free world."

"Sometimes," quipped Boris, and all three of them laughed. Gaspard admired the composition of his drink before taking a liberal swallow. It made him feel better.

"Mr Blodvrinsky -"

"Boris, please -"

"Thank you, er Boris, I don't wish to sound presumptuous but do you by any chance have any business interests related even remotely to opera?"

"Why, have you lost my card already?" smiled Boris, handing him another.

Gaspard nearly lost his nerve. The dream or reality syndrome was still kicking in. He scrambled for words.

"I'm sorry, I've been rather confused lately."

"It's quite alright, don't worry about a thing, everything will fall into place eventually, meanwhile, just relax, enjoy yourself, I trust you are looking forward to our dinner party tomorrow night?"

"Yes, very much so, I'm most grateful for the invitation."

"The pleasure's all mine," Boris pressed a button hidden in the carpet which would summon Igor to the room in a couple of seconds, then continued, "why not finish your drink, then I'll have somebody drive you home, we can always talk about opera tomorrow night."

Gaspard was still thanking him profusely when Igor entered the room.

"This is Igor," said Boris, "he has yet to play Hamlet but he knows how to drive on the left hand side of the road."

Gaspard fell instantly in love with Igor. He was much taller than Dale and his features were more aquiline, more aesthetic. Big high cheek bones above which were set the palest of blue eyes whose radiance bewitched like an icon. Gaspard was so captivated that by the time they pulled up outside his house, he had hardly uttered a word. He managed a nervous smile instead.

"See you Saturday night," said Igor, his eyes as steady as Jesus on the cross.

Gaspard's heart was still palpitating when the telephone rang. Concentrating would be difficult but he lifted the receiver nonetheless.

"Hello?"

"We are still waiting for the photographs, number six."

"I am about to process them."

"That will not be necessary, you know we always do that ourselves."

"I am aware of that, however, on this occasion I wish to retain a copy for my personal file."

"Don't hide your inadequacies behind the grievance procedure, number six, the section needs a success."

And then the line went dead. Gaspard put two fingers up as he replaced the receiver.

It was a pity that Igor could never resemble a CIA agent.

23

A Saturday night at Tzarbinski's was like Aladdin's Cave and Scheherazade rolled into one. On the ground floor, amongst the bottled beers and big black ashtrays, all sorts of illicit deals and peculiar friendships were struck. Above the ground floor on each level, the social mix was subtly different. Nevertheless, Tzarbinski's was clearly the place where people liked to string out their story no matter what level they were on, or who they were, or where their lives were going. It was fast becoming a cult-eating house that most of its diners secretly hoped would never attract punters from outside the county boundary. Okay, Surrey at a push but Sussex probably no, and as for East Sussex, well forget it. One table of Brighton transvestites sharing their hormonal trauma was enough. And yet it was almost common knowledge that all the waitresses at Tzarbinski's were transvestites too. Igor had employed them as an act of compassion. Boris had found out about it by accident after Dimitri complained to him that there was a 'sharp Rasputy in our executive piss tray'. Boris looked, and saw and came away again, having first said to Mitzi from Bistro Soups, "if I see you pissing in here again I'll cut your prick off with this dagger." Everything was just fine from then on.

Given the total Tzarbinski Experience, the huge choice and palpable love of customers, the entire wedding cake arena had developed its own peculiar cultural environment. There was rarely any bovver and people with no table manners rarely got seated. As a consequence, the entire restaurant, all ten levels of it, had one of the easiest-going and friendly ambiences that you were likely to find in any kind of eating hemisphere the world over. It was a real kick to book a table on floor seven or above and then walk casually all the way through the aisles and stairways past hundreds of other diners who pretended not to notice you but were inwardly making notes. And there were minor variations of that as each floor of regular diners inter-acted with those above and below.

The cultural environment at Tzarbinski's that Saturday night was definitely aglow. The real spring weather, those fabulous darts of sunshine that are like intravenous injections of happiness, had lifted everyone's spirits and a sense of pure enjoyment was in the air. Also, Mitzi from Bistro soups, having been successfully counselled by Igor, had become quite a little middle management gossip and the word was out on all floors that the big Russian who owned the place and had connections in very high places, was hosting a private dinner party tonight. All eyes, including the dilated-pupils-brigade who were idly practising their pipes-of-Pan embouchures across the tops of their Miller Lites, were peeled for the first sighting of the ultimate favoured guests. The biggest frustration was that the one and only table on the top level, the Albert as it was generally known, had special entry arrangements. It was the only table in Tzarbinski's that could be approached without having to walk past all the other tables on all the other floors. Boris was no fool. Even so, he had made a right show of it.

The entrance to the Albert was via a long steel gantry suspended horizontally from the roof of the church. Left as it was, guests could be forgiven for thinking that they were astronauts about to walk across the final launch ramp into their space shuttle. But Boris had softened things up a bit. In

134

fact he'd got carried away by the Royal Albert Hall cream red and gold touch and covered the entire structure with yet more pillars and drapes and tasselled alcoves. His designer, Lotte Polanski, who got kicked off the Dome project, had seized her opportunity. Boris agreed to her request to position more Mucha models but overlooked the need to discuss where. He had naturally assumed, in the interests of those who admired the awesome passivity of Roman statues, that Lotte would erect lots of little Muchas on the main vertical struts, or maybe every ten metres, and leave it at that. But no, the lady went flipside and slung a vast naked body horizontally underneath the entire span of the gantry. There was something haunting and beautiful about the marble hermaphrodite with its enigmatic smile that said so many things to so many people. Boris had wept when he first saw it and gave Lotte a five hundred pound bonus on the spot.

At the dinner table, Gaspard, thinking that he was now in a much better position to enjoy life a bit more, was surprisingly smug about everyone else wanting to know what the inside of the Yum Bum looked like from fifty feet above. It was almost a macho smugness.

Dale was Dale and even more so now that everything had been sorted about him being with Roslyn like. Roz, being an actress, naturally went all out to display her talent for oral communication and this certainly gave the night a few buzzes. But it was Loretta who stunned all with her sheer sensuality.

As for Effie, she was on top form too, laughing, drinking, smoking and convulsing all night long. And Freddie was Freddie. Not quite as open as Dale but nevertheless, he too was having a good time.

Boris had promised him that his missile research centre, including one or two special security measures that he hadn't even asked for, would be fully completed by the end of next week. Freddie thought that was an impossibility and had politely expressed that point of view. Boris had just gripped him on both shoulders and with bear hugging friendliness had said 'just you watch me'. So that's just what Freddie did every spare moment he had. And it was quite an experience. Everything Boris set out to do he seemed to achieve.

Freddie, being a scientist, chose to examine the small things. He noticed Boris's habit of tapping and playing with his fingers. Effie noticed it too. Were they the hands of a frustrated pianist? Closer inspection at the dinner table revealed that they were too callused to be musician's hands, in fact, they were weapons of muscle and bone. So were Dimitri's come to think of it.

"Yeah, me and Dimitri pick it up like," said Dale.

"Nyet, I picked it up," said Dimitri.

"Oh yeah, that's right and I 'eld all them branches, they was dead springy like, but we got it downstairs, didn't we?"

"Yah, and then it start happening."

Dimitri slapped his hand on the dinner table and took another slug of vodka. By now, everyone had heard his experience several times over and yet each time Roz wished how much she too could have been there to witness it.

"It has such amazing fecundity," said Roz, making her vowels float like a bag of Golden Delicious.

"I can't wait to get turned on," said Loretta dryly towards the end of the evening. Being the only one who hadn't known what the Yum Bum was, let alone seen it, she was a bit pissed off but wasn't going to admit it.

"Let's fix something up soon then," said Effie, coming to the rescue.

"Yah, how about Monday?" said Boris.

"Anybody want to include me too?" said Loretta.

It bing banged around the table but eventually got sorted. Wednesday it was.

"I'd love to have one of your water gardens up at Cedar Park Mansions, Effie," said Dimitri later on.

"I've got fifty, I'll lend you one," said Boris.

"Oo's gonna fix it then?" said Dale.

"I'm sure Gaspard isn't," said Loretta snidely.

"I agree, it would be a perfect waste of my talents," nipped Gaspard, "however, if any consultation were sought on matters of interior design, I would be only too happy to oblige."

"Good of you to say so," said Dimitri heartily, "but I got Lotte Polanski working on the porch at the moment so let's see how it goes."

"Hey Dimitri, how did you sign her up?" asked Loretta in a cloud blue smoky corner, knowing that he had still to master the Cyrillic alphabet.

"I took care of the contractual arrangements," said Igor, appearing at the tableside with a plate of rum truffles. He flashed his icon eyes at Boris for approval.

"I just love rum truffles," said Boris, "and Igor goes especially to Harrods on my behalf."

There was a frisson around the table that not every one of them noticed. As Igor passed among them to offer the rum truffles, Gaspard became ever more pulpitacious the closer he got. By now the question was familiar so Igor simply inclined his body politely and smiled.

"Thank you, these look gorgeous," said Gaspard.

"I have only seen them in Knightsbridge," replied Igor.

"Actually, you can also get them in Debenhams, Oxford Street," said Roz, fizzing with champagne.

"Let's all go to Oxford Street," yelled Dale, "we got enough cars."

In the end that never happened but everyone was feeling so friendly that it was openly agreed as a future option.

Across the other side of the gantry was a brick-lined antechamber where dinner guests could attend to their robes or stockings or whatever. Igor was on hand to assist in any matter pertinent to their leaving. As Ros took her silver gossamer evening jacket off the hook, the neck tag broke.

"It happens to all of us," said Igor, smiling the blue sky stuff.

"Yeah, know what you mean," said Dale, "'ave a match" and he tossed a box of Swan Vestas towards him, but it was Boris that caught them.

"Look at me, I'm an arsonist!" grinned Boris.

Gaspard was consumed with fire.

24

"I'm off home," said Freddie.

"But it's only four o'clock," said Ian Trubshaw.

"So what?" said Freddie and let go the door.

This was clearly his new established pattern. Ian no longer bothered to tell The Sprout about it. When it had first begun, The Sprout said to him that it was a natural reaction to the disappointment of his new position. Ian had backed off politely. The powers that be had everything monitored. As he watched Freddie get into his car, the office telephone rang. He answered it, not a little bit hot under the collar.

"Ponsonby-Spratt here, Trubshaw."

"Yes Sir,"

"There is a Vauxhall Nova staff car at Gate 17, the keys are in the ignition, just follow Freddie and let us know what he's up to, okay?"

"- Er yes, sir."

And that's how it had begun. The Sprout had specifically assured him that appropriate security measures were active and it would be unlikely that he would be called upon to execute responsibilities that might deliver him into an embarrassing dilemma. And here he was, a scientist cum private dick. By the time he found the Nova and got it started and found reverse, Freddie was long gone. So he decided to drive home and call it a day himself. On route to Farnborough however, he spotted Freddie and was obliged to follow orders. Freddie's car, which was an old yellow Triumph Toledo, turned into the entrance of a large warehouse. The sign outside said Frank Files Distribution Service (UK) Limited. And then underneath in smaller lettering, it added: Part of the Regina Group. Ian reckoned that sounded fairly innocuous and since there were quite a few other cars about, not to mention various trade vehicles plying their business, he followed Freddie in and watched him park. He positioned his own car on the far outside of the car park nearest the main exit and felt quite pleased with his strategic thinking at that point.

Freddie didn't go through the warehouse doors but chose instead to take a flight of stairs up the side. They led to a long row of lit windows each fitted with black vertical blinds. There was a large double door in front. Ian took out his bird-spotting binoculars and focused on Freddie as he went through the door. Ian surmised that there must have been some kind of security fob system in operation because Freddie usually dithered with that sort of thing. He wondered if there was another way in, or perhaps somewhere within the warehouse that would afford him a view of the room Freddie was in. He wasn't sure what to do, so he played with his pocket calculator in the hope that his astro-mathematics programme might stimulate some course of forward motion.

Freddie meanwhile went straight to his command module computer suite which Boris, true to his word, had completed on time. If only things could move as fast as that in DERA. He cast his eye around the room and felt immensely contented. Boris had even supplied him with a cold water dispenser and a small inset kitchenette, fully plumbed, included a microwave oven and hot air hand drier. There were various potted plants around that he recalled having seen in the courtyard outside Loretta's hotel suite in Tunisia. Nice touches here and there made for a most comforting environment. And yet, in spite of the discreet uplighters, when he booted up the central console the room was charged with images that put a zing into the atmosphere.

His original specifications had been quite moderate since he was conditioned to receiving only the bare minimum by way of equipment or any kind of technical back-up service. But Boris had urged him to think big, even told him that money was no problem. And so now, from a keyboard with three levels of keys and a bank of electronic signals, he could view Project Cassandra on three separate screens each two metres square. He could see the earth as a spherical globe and satellite co-ordinates could be identified and logged onto with the press of a single key. The view could be zoomed in and out with incredible ease and could identify separate countries, and their deserts or waterways, and their cities and bazaars, it was so powerful. Trajectory and strike data could be accessed immediately and would update in real time with verification checking and safe archival filing taking place simultaneously.

The range of symbology available was impressive and Freddie made quick checks to see what data was being offered on various sites. Nothing new on Defended Assets or Sensor sites. Troop concentrations in the Middle East and Africa changed quite a bit but that was only to be expected. Grozny was a mess. Military intelligence reckoned that the Chechen rebels had acquired a Surface to Air Weapon system. Freddie had told Boris he would be the first to know when they used it. He checked on certain tracks now. Suspect, Unknown, Friendly, Assumed Friendly, Neutral and Pending. No lunatics tonight. Good. He pressed a key that closed the programme and immediately bought up a blank screen with a silver grey background and columns of figures in black.

A cursor ran here and there with great speed and then highlighted subtotals, then totals, then macro-totals. There were only two colours in the programme and they were black and red. That was all the sophistication Freddie needed. Too much red and he knew instinctively that the figures weren't adding up to much. The subtractions and other abstract convolutions that were part and parcel of the overall project were taken care of by the Cassandra Main Bridge system and that had already been system tested for the last sixteen

140

months by his DERA team. A team he no longer had, except for a poisoned Nebelung called Ian Trubshaw. The Sprout was a bastard and he would have his revenge in the fullness of time. Right now, he needed to test the most astounding part of the programme. It was the bit that finally pushed the MoD over the edge to NO. The Ergonomic Psychology Factor.

When Freddie had first presented the paper to The Sprout, there was a mild form of panic in high places and eventually, the Queen's third psychiatrist, Sir Rumphal Agitsah, had been engaged to assess Freddie's mental condition. Following his first session with Freddie, Sir Rumphal had astounded the entire Defence Ministry Personnel Department by declaring Freddie certifiably sane but with a marked capacity to indulge randomly in the opposite direction. The Defence Minister had been consulted and had promptly issued orders for the entire programme to be obliterated. By then Freddie had already taken his own personal copy, plus two back-ups and nobody was any the wiser. Subsequently, the Minister had lunched with Gloria Fitzbagley and an entire section of MI5 was set up to provide round-the-clock surveillance on Freddie Bannister. They even filmed him at Ted Trubshaw's funeral. News that the CIA may have also been on the case had not yet reached ministerial levels but when Gloria Fitzbagley told Sir Rodney Snodder, he thumped the pillow and swore that he would let those mineral-water-sucking-dick-heads know just who was running the show.

The telephone rang and Freddie answered it.

"Hi, how's it going?" said Loretta.

"Very well, how about your audition?"

"Effie can't wait to get me started."

"I am delighted to hear that, she can be a very stern critic at times."

"Will I see you tonight? I'm still at the Haystack and Boris is joining us for drinks later on in the Villain's Noose."

"We can't go anywhere afterwards."

"You think I don't realise that?"

"No."

"Anyway, there are six mansions half a mile up the hill courtesy of Boris so it won't be a question of space, just time."

"Time is irrelevant. Nothing is fixed or immovable. I have the figures to calculate that."

"So what's your calculated answer to will I see you tonight?"

"Yes, and mine's a champagne."

Dimitri had borrowed the Bentley to pick up Svetlana and Anita from Heathrow Airport. He had not seen them for eight months so it was an emotional welcome. They both looked fabulous. Svetlana was in her forties and had a short, compact body with firm breasts and a flat stomach. She had cropped hair and arched eyebrows and there was a fierceness about her that was quite arresting. She was lithe and sexy and hugged Dimitri passionately. Anita was extraordinary. She had inherited her mother's striking good looks and her father's squat frame. She too was sexy but in a more gamine way. She had dyed her hair platinum blonde which made her large green eyes look exotic. She was very physical too and the three of them hugged and kissed each other unashamedly. They chatted incessantly amongst themselves and by the time Dimitri swung the Bentley into the main drive of Cedar Park Mansions, they were up to speed on the latest developments in Moscow, London and Fropsham.

"So when do I get to see the dog arena?" said Svetlana, looking at all the labour saving gadgets in the kitchen.

"Maybe tomorrow, we'll speak to Boris," said Dimitri.

"If Loretta's had her audition, when's mine?" asked Anita, pouring a brandy into her freshly percolated expresso.

"All in good time."

Boris had reminded Dimitri that he hadn't yet broached the subject of Anita to Effie and didn't want to push the issue any more at the present moment. If she could be persuaded to acclimatise gradually he would welcome that.

"A few more of these and a hot shower in the morning and I'll be as fully acclimatised as I need to be," said Anita confidently.

Her English was remarkably fluent and she spoke quickly with a hint of an American accent. She had spent a year in

Chicago with Dimitri when she was fourteen and had taken to the Western culture and language like a duck to water. Returning to Moscow was a real wrench for her but she knew how much her father loved her and she could be as patriotic as any Russian when the chips were down. When Dimitri had suggested they live in England she had been instrumental in talking her mother into it. She had travelled in Europe too and was pretty astute when it came to assessing which side of life's bread the butter was spread the thickest on. Russia was in a mess and Moscow had become the pits. You just didn't know when you were going to get beaten up, shot or raped. And it was no fun joining the bread queue when you had spent half the night with your clothes off and a cigar stuck up your fanny. She read the international press too and was politically aware. Okay, so what if the English *were* an historically duplicitous race? at least you could more or less say what you liked without being carted off to some whitewashed dungeon. And you could appeal against all sorts of things. Yup, England was a good bet and her mum would get the hang of it eventually.

She watched her mother and father as they cuddled up on the sofa in front of the telly and decided the time had come to listen to her Walkman in the jacuzzi. As she sank into the suds she thought that perhaps her father was right, every thing would happen in good time and meanwhile she would have a good time.

Ian Trubshaw was not having a good time although he had found an alternative route which led to the corridor outside the room that Freddie had entered. He had broken out in a nervous rash and was dying to scratch himself all over; it made keeping still extremely difficult. He did not know what to expect when he peered surreptitiously between a crack in the vertical blind in the far corner window. When he saw Project Cassandra on the screens in front of Freddie, he practically wet himself. What was he supposed to do now? Steal it back? Surely, this was MI5's responsibility?

He had a wife and baby son to contend with and his career had yet to take off.

25

"Jesus Christ, we've got to get rid of that prat!" said Gloria to Rodney.

"We?" he replied, easing his pillow.

Gloria turned over to grab a Silk Cut from the pack on top of the Art Deco plastic teas-made.

"I accept that, however I was not the one sucking up to the Minister by supporting that ridiculous paper on the cross-pollination of our agencies."

"Maybe not, but you did recommend Gaspard Grant in the first place."

"I don't deny that but I simply don't have the money and people to train intellectual pansies like that when your lot can do it so competently with a blunt instrument."

"Well what am I supposed to do, shoot him?" said Rodney, becoming irate, "already the local press are sniffing around over Blodvrinsky's quarter of a million pound donation, if they find out the CIA are on the case there'll be absolute mayhem."

"You don't know for a fact that they are."

"Well there's no mistaking that Freddie Bannister's in bed with another woman who's not his wife and she was spotted in

Rio when the CIA smashed up that Russian Colombian drugs deal."

"Oh really?

"Yes really, pass the tissues."

"Why?"

"Well is this your wet patch or mine?"

At the Haystack, the word was out on the street about all manner of things. News of the Blodvrinsky donation was bouncing from one room to another like a ping-pong ball on a trampoline. Was Blodvrinsky the guy with the British Racing Green Bentley and a minder that looked like an orang utan in a suit? Apparently he fancied Effie Bannister and some say vice versa.

Not surprisingly, the Yum Bum was now common knowledge too. The stage crew had seen it first, and after them, every actor had had this insatiable urge to wander through the back of the theatre and across the scene dock and up the stairs to the lighthouse to look at it. Everyone marvelled at the pure clear air and mysterious patina of its deep verdant leaves. You could almost tell who had seen it and who had not simply by looking at their faces. Their general countenance seemed to confirm that they were taking a sincere look at their life situation viz a viz change. It was all very positive and tremendously dynamic.

Roz seemed to know the most about it. She was sleeping with Dale and he had planted the Yum Bum seeds that Effie Bannister's husband had smuggled in from Libya or somewhere like that. Apparently, Dale had been given the go-ahead to re-build the rickety old steps to the lighthouse where Roz had shagged him when the Yum Bum was just a pot, as a preliminary stage before more substantial building works were undertaken. Dale was working on the plans but already Gaspard was bitching about him, saying that he should be paying more attention to *his* plans which were all about a grand opera that the big Russian was funding lock, stock and ten smoking barrels.

Two new production teams had been set up and one of them was for a late night cabaret. The buzz in the air was auditions. The hot gossip was that a Russian stripper might be taking part as well as this fantastic black jazz singer called Loretta. Some of the actors had sat in on her audition, at her request, and they hadn't stopped talking about her fabulous voice and amazing stage presence ever since.

A second production team, much larger than the first, or it would be when it got going, was headed by Gaspard and everyone wanted to know why. And what's more, who was the Russian heavy that kept buying him drinks in the Villain's Noose? Was he Blodvrinsky himself? And to what extent was the Haystack diversifying? Whatever the case, the fact of the matter was you could forget the Dome because the Haystack was fast becoming the millennium place to be. The actors were ringing their agents to say that they were very happy with the present situation and would certainly not object to approaches being made to negotiate for any possible extension to their existing contract. Admin were processing over one hundred audition enquiries a day received via the Spotlight offices who were pleading with them to put a box ad in The Stage to stem the flow. All Fropsham was humming with a kind of excited, expectant, magical, sub-throb.

"Guess what?" said Roz.

"What?" said Dale.

"Effie's asked me to write a press release for The Stage."

"Well don't ask me to read it, you know what I'm like."

"No, but I could speak it out loud and you could say what you think."

"Okay, give it a whirl then."

Roz cleared her throat and delivered her copy as clear as a newsreader.

"The Haystack Theatre Company is pleased to announce that it has received substantial funding from the Blodvrinsky Arts Foundation. This will enable redevelopment and restoration work to take place which, when completed, will facilitate an increase in the number and genre of its productions.......what d'you think so far?"

146

"To be honest, I don't know what you're talking about."

"Dale - "

"No, I mean I got the first bit about the money like, that's good, keep that bit in, but why not just say what you're going to do about the auditions?"

"Well I thought I'd give some useful background first."

"Why?"

"Because The Stage said I can have space for three hundred words."

"Well why not just write fewer words in bigger letters? I bet you there ain't an actor out there what cares a toss about 'oo's stumping up the money, they just wanna know 'ow to get a job – so tell 'em."

"Okay, so I keep the first bit and then what do I say?"

"Just give 'em a freephone number to register their name, address and telephone number, or their agent's, and say you'll be in touch like."

"I don't think we've got a freephone number."

"Well 'ave a word with Boris, he'll fix one up for you."

As things turned out, Roz spoke to Effie first and she agreed that a freephone number was a great idea and had a word with Boris immediately. In three hours Boris's boys on satellite installation had six numbers up and running and Roz was able to quote and confirm all of them by the copy deadline.

Meanwhile, Gaspard was becoming increasingly irate at the number of actors that were now strolling back and forth across his scene dock en route to the Yum Bum. They would often linger and chat to Dale who was now totally absorbed in rebuilding the staircase, a priority that had been applied by Effie which made it doubly exasperating. He mentioned it to Boris during one of their progress meetings in the lounge bar of the Villain's Noose.

"Look at it this way Gaspard," said Boris, over a bottle of champagne that Cedric had served himself, "when the staircase is done we'll be able to extend the floors and build the enlarged auditorium. Then we put the ramps over the orchestra pit and provide a three-dimensional flying space above an extended proscenium arch. Then after *that* comes the opera, okay?"

"I can't wait to get started," replied Gaspard.

"Me neither," said Boris, "we're gonna do Aida."

"I wasn't aware of that," said Gaspard, becoming petulant, "I rather favoured The Trojans."

Boris gave a bear-like chuckle and topped up Gaspard's glass.

"Well let's just say that nothing is set in tablets of stone just yet. I would certainly welcome your co-operation in providing MI6 and MI5 with various progress reports, particularly now that they're chasing all over the place trying to identify that CIA agent."

Gaspard returned his guffaw with a thin smile. It was the best he could manage. He knew that the nasty stuff was about to begin. Well, better get it over and done with.

"Was there anything particular you had in mind?"

"Yah, who looks after Gloria and Rodney's diaries?"

"I would imagine they do themselves."

"Imagination is not what I want Gaspard, I want facts. Mud in your eye, as they say."

Boris slapped back his champagne and summoned Dimitri on his mobile. Cedric, noticing the movement, began to fluctuate around the table like an albatross with a cash til in its beak.

"How much I owe you, Cedric?"

"About two hundred pounds."

Boris flicked a roll of fifties out of his pocket and gave Cedric two hundred and fifty.

"Maybe I can have some gravlux and rye bread next time?"

"The local fish farm is on standby and our bakers supply us daily," replied Cedric, fawning as if mid-day had been and gone.

Boris gave Gaspard a final big grin and walked out of the bar.

Gaspard finished his baked Camembert with cranberry sauce, drained his salted tequila and left shortly afterwards. He crossed the road and walked unhurriedly across the shingled car park towards the telephone kiosk. He was a little bit pissed. No one was watching as he dialled the number.

"You recognise my voice?"

148

"Of course number six, but not the photographs."

"What do you mean?"

"Where were they taken?"

"In Tunisia."

"We gave you no clearance to be there."

"I had to take the initiative, time was short."

"Don't bother to submit an expense account, we shall reject it."

"Quite possibly, but not, I doubt, Ms Gloria Fitzbagley."

And this time it was Gaspard who put the phone down first.

26

"You seem to be working very late these days," said Melissa.

Ian Trubshaw had started to log his overtime hours officially ever since The Sprout had indicated that remuneration in exchange for rumour suffocation would be favourably encountered. The truth was, The Sprout was furious at MI5. They had given him cast iron assurances that an entire section was monitoring Freddie's activities and the chances of Project Cassandra falling into enemy hands was zero. Now look what had happened. He had authorised a staff car allocation permit to Ian Trubshaw who wasn't exactly resourceful or dynamic. A clever-dick yes, a private dick no. How on earth a weak-hearted dreamer could hold onto a wife as delicious as young Melissa, he really did not know, although he had picked up on the net that she was totally frigid.

"Yes," said Ian, "things are somewhat hectic."

Melissa looked at her husband and made a few executive decisions. The first one arose from the acceptance that her husband was useless. Useless in bed and useless at work. So she would have to look elsewhere. Sebastian was a doddle provided she got enough domestic support. Not much from Ian there. He was physically awkward and the drawback extended way beyond misunderstood domestic appliances. Being the golden lackey for The Sprout wasn't exactly a career track move either. She admired his brain, yes, that had been a turn-on during their courtship but nowadays it seemed as if he had disconnected his brain and transported it to another planet. And then there was his rash. He would scratch at night under the bedclothes and mumble to himself. Last night he sat bolt upright and screamed Cassandra! Well, if her knowledge of classics was correct, they were in for a bumpy ride.

The Sprout was angry by the time he got through on the line to Gloria Fitzbagley's office.

"He has set up an entire project site outside of MoD authority!"

"We know that Reggie," said Gloria, trying to placate him.

"How?" he almost exploded.

"We've been working closely with MI6 on the Blodvrinsky man and they are connected."

"Are you aware that Effie Bannister has accepted a quarter of a million pounds from the Blodvrinsky Arts Foundation?"

"Yes, Rodney read about it in The Stage."

"Are you aware that Christopher Carrington has a dinner date with Blodvrinsky at Tzarbinski's? "

"No."

"Well I'll keep you posted. Please keep the lid on things, I would quite like to enjoy my retirement pension."

The Sprout tried not to slam down the telephone. He was wrestling with his next best move. The leak came from Muriel Carrington, Effie Bannister's best friend, so he needed to get closer to Effie if he was to stand any chance of finding out what that drunken buffoon of a duplicitous merchant banker Christopher Carrington was up to. Who better than Muriel's own son, Trubshaw junior. He picked up the phone and pressed 246.

"Hello," said Freddie Bannister.

151

Blast, wrong number thought The Sprout, but he knew he would have to keep talking.

"Morning Freddie, how goes it?"

"Everything is satisfactory thank you."

"Good, good, well if there's anything you need, just buzz me."

"Thank you....er, there was something that you might be able to help me with."

"Of course Freddie, fire away dear chap."

"Why has my assistant been granted a staff car?"

The Sprout nearly choked on his mid-morning Drambuie, he did not see that one coming. Blast. What was the matter with him? He was losing his edge. He would have to think of something.

"His own car was playing up and I thought with a highly strung wife like Melissa and a little baby, he would welcome it."

"I see, that's very thoughtful of you, perhaps I might have one too?"

"Is there a pressing domestic situation Freddie?"

"Yes, my wife is having an affair with an uneducated muscle-bound carpenter nearly thirty years her junior."

Again The Sprout nearly caught his breath mid-Drambuie. The word on the street was that she was making passes at Blodvrinsky, and who the hell was this carpenter? Rambo or Jesus Christ? If he gave Freddie a staff car he could have it bugged first and that would make up considerably for Ian Trubshaw's deficiencies.

"I'm terribly sorry to hear that Freddie, I had no idea, I quite understand how you must be feeling, I will arrange for a comfortable staff car to be made available as soon as possible."

"Thank you," said Freddie, and rang off.

Marcia Fairbarns stabbed the switches in Gloria Fitzbagley's office with practised polish.

"Yes?" said Gloria.

"Reginald Ponsonby-Spratt again."

"Okay."

"Gloria?"

"Reggie, so soon."

152

"I need your help."

"What do you want?"

"A Rover Seventy-Five fully bugged."

"Who for?"

"Freddie Bannister, he's become a weak link, his wife has a toy boy and I think he's liable to blow a safety valve any minute."

"Well, even allowing for your customary exaggeration, I'll still give you the car."

"Thanks Gloria, that's heaven sent."

"Well, I'll probably nick it from Rodney, he's got manpower problems so there could be a few leather upholstered seats going cold. By the way, has Freddie got a GP?"

"I imagine so, why?"

"P'raps he ought to be giving Freddie some valium?"

Marcia Fairbarns cut in before The Sprout could reply.

"I have the Defence Minister's secretary on the line."

"Okay – Reggie I have to go now, we'll speak soon."

Gloria took the call. "Hello Cindy."

"Hi, can you meet him this Friday for lunch, he's received a report from MI6 about Blodvrinsky being involved in some Balkan war lord's murder and the American Ambassador has complained to the Home Secretary about a consignment of AppleMacs destined for his embassy that was stolen at Heathrow recently."

"Okay what time?"

"Twelve forty-five."

"Got it. Bye"

As long as Reggie didn't find out that she was two-timing him with Rodney, she would be able to keep the lid on most things.

Dale was checking his drawing of the lighthouse staircase. It was a big job but it was going very well. Effie had allowed him to hire an extra team of ten chippies. Dale was surprisingly good at managing them and found that it gave him quite a bit of spare time. Gaspard had been incredibly bitchy while he was setting it all up but now that the Yum Bum had been ruled off-limits to the company he had become more agreeable. He had invited Dale back into his office and offered him a sweet martini. Dale reported back to Roz afterwards, he was becoming quite a gossip.

"He kept banging on abart Igor, I can tell you that much," said Dale to Roz, during a break in her rehearsal. They were sitting outside having a fag in the car park.

"I can certainly see why, he's like a Slavic version of Adonis."

"Oo's Adonis?"

"A beautiful Greek God."

"Is he gay?"

"Probably, most of them were."

"So, old Gasp's in wiv' a chance then."

"D'you think Igor's gay?"

"Dunno, ain't given 'im much thought to be honest although I saw 'im give you that pass when you put yer jacket on."

"Yeah, and then you threw your matches at him, I know."

"I was showing restraint, good weren't it?"

They kissed and cuddled in the spring sun. Across the street, Cedric observed them from the lounge bar window. He was a past master at noticing the coupling and de-couplings of the Haystack fraternity and he had seen, with his own eyes, Effie kissing Boris.

That was still a secret.

27

"Have you ever been to Tzarbinski's?" enquired Melissa, of her mother-in-law.

"No," replied Muriel Carrington, "but Christopher's got an invitation sometime next week and I think I'm included."

"I was going to suggest to Ian that we got a baby-sitter last week and tried it out but he was late back from work as usual."

"He's looking very pale these days, is Sebastian keeping you both up?"

"No, he sleeps right through, he's an absolute angel."

"I'll have a word with Chris, maybe you could join us, I don't think it's business, although what isn't where Chris is concerned? and perhaps Ian could give you a night off if you can't find a baby-sitter?"

This was music to Melissa's ears.

Dale put his T-shirt back on to soak up some of the sweat. The lads had got the first two levels of the staircase rebuilt and he had been right in there with them.

"Okay, that's it, you can all knock off, I'll sweep up like," he said. It was looking good, and they lingered for a while to admire their own handiwork. "I reckon if we carry on like this we'll be done by the end of the week and then we can start selling tickets."

They all laughed and strolled off. Little did they know that that was just what Boris had in mind for the near future. Whatever anybody else had spotted about the Yum Bum, as far as he was concerned, it was its sticky little tips that had most attracted his attention. He had already asked Dale to provide him with a small sample of the tacky secretions for scientific analysis and Dale had yet to supply.

Dale picked up his brush and began to clear the sawdust away. The Yum Bum was emitting a fine shower of perfumed vapour which doused things down nicely and soon Dale had finished his task. He sat down beside the Yum Bum, close to one of its big pillow leaves and wondered what Boris was up to. The sticky stuff on the nodules he had already tried. Like some kind of Fabbo cream it rejuvenated your hands bloody good like. Roz had tried some too and said it was great. They had also used it as a lubricant and it was just fantastic. So, what else could it do that Boris wanted? He hadn't a clue, but he saw no reason to obstruct him. The bloke was all right.
A bit dodgy here and there but nothing he could see that made him think he was seriously off his rocker like. Dimitri was the one to watch out for. So far they were good friends. Dale was pleased about that and hoped it would continue.

He turned towards the Yum Bum and passed his hands gently and delicately across the zyriad thronds that washed amid their purple leaf-top glow and felt a stickiness develop on his hands. It was moist and beautiful and he did not want to withdraw.

"Enjoying the view?"
He turned towards a not too familiar voice. It was Loretta.

"Ello, what's 'appening, much?"
He could be cheeky at times, she could see that and she didn't think he was as daft as he made out either. A barrel boy mentality? Yes. He dealt with people head on and didn't want any aggro. He was sort of cool without actually knowing it.

"I thought I'd wander on down to see this tree that everyone's talking about."

"So wodjafink?"

Loretta took a long hard look at the Yum Bum, twitched her nostrils and flexed her life senses and felt, for the first time in her life, that she was fantastic.

"It's cool, Dale, it's cool."

She joined him sitting on the newly laid stairs and they just sat there together for a while until she asked him "what's on your mind, Dale?"

"Nothing really, just like being 'ere and doin' this."

She could see he was genuine and understood why. He wasn't trying to make it because he already had. He'd got no front. He was happy. It might be that he was happy-go-lucky too but all the signs were that he had finally put down his marker.

"I like this place too," she said.

"Great, why don't yer 'ang around a bit more then?" he replied.

"I think I will," she said.

They sat there on the stairs together and shared a fag. Dale had got into the occasional habit with Effie who was now smoking her way through sixty a day. They smoked Loretta's Brazilian Agio cigars.

"I've been promised a show here," she said with surprising candidness.

"I know," he said, "and I've been promised to make the scenery, so we'll see 'ow we're going to get on like."

"I don't know Effie Bannister as well as you."

Dale wondered how well he knew her himself. She was blue touch paper stuff, no denying it. Bloody clever too. Kept everyone on their toes like. The Board of Directors, the Management Committee, the Patrons Association, the Haystack Arts Policy Steering Committee of which she was Chair. She wasn't about to see two hundred and fifty-thousand quid go down the drain for nothing. It was her meal ticket and she was going for as many courses as possible. Including those at Tzarbinski's.

"Eff's all right," he said, "as long as no-one don't upset 'er."

"I'm not about to upset anyone," said Loretta.

157

He was about to say how much he agreed with doing things without upsetting people when Gaspard's voice rode clear and stridently across the air. The scene dock was superb for voice projection exercises because the wood and hessian stopped the sound bouncing around too much. His words were clearly nearing a state where mounting apprehension began to consider a higher level called panic.

"Excuse me, that is private theatre property, you cannot go there!"

"It's okay, I can, my adopted Uncle owns the place."

It was Anita Pryshnyi, and she was utterly confident. She was up the stairs and looking around in a trice. Dale smiled and said hi to her.

"Hi, my name's Anita Pryshnyi, I'm from Russia and I'm soon going to be doing a show here so I thought I'd have a look around first."

Dale thought she was right on the mark. You knew exactly where you stood with a girl like Anita.

"Great. My name's Dale, this is Loretta who's also doing a show here soon, and I'm building it."

"Oh wow that's great," said Anita, and shooting a look at Loretta said, "I'm a stripper, I bet you're a singer."

"Got it in one," said Loretta

"Say can I be in your show too?"

"Everything's possible if you put your mind to it."

"Yeah sure, it's finding the right mind that's my problem."

"Well, problems come an' go don't they?" said Dale.

"Yeah," said Anita, "I get over most things, can I have a light?"

He lit up her Rothmans and she puffed away and told them her life story.

"I'm not happy about mum and the dogs," she finally concluded, "but what can you do? We are from Moscow in the year two thousand."

"Vladimir Putin will sort it all out," said Loretta rather drily.

"Vladimir Putin will put everyone's defence budgets up,' said Anita without hesitating, "did you know the first thing he did in office was to threaten the munitions bosses that he would block their expense accounts unless they tripled their out-put. He's got NATO really worried. He's pals with Saudi Arabia as well as Iraq, and Gaddafi lends him his private jet."

"How do you know that?" said Loretta.

"I spoke to a girlfriend of mine who I met in Chicago when I was fourteen and have kept in touch with ever since and she's now a foreign correspondent for The Independent in Moscow."

"Has she heard of Boris?"

"Sure, everyone's heard of Boris, and some say he's on Vladimir Putin's payroll."

Dale reckoned that just about summed it up. "Well, I've 'ad an 'ard day and I fancy a pint of Old Wallop, 'oo's coming?"

"Sure, what are we talking about?" said Anita.

"It's the beer in the pub across the road."

"Oh yeah, the Villain's Noose, I saw it when I crossed the road, maybe they want a stripper too."

"I fink Cedric does," said Dale, "are you coming too Loretta?"

"No, I just dropped by for five, I'll catch you later."

Dale and Anita both said cheers as she set off to go. I like her said Anita the moment she was gone. Me too, he added. They lit up another fag before walking down the stairs to the Villain's Noose.

Gaspard was nowhere to be seen.

28

Okay, so the line up for Boris's top table at Tzarbinski's that Saturday night was as follows. Christopher Carrington and Muriel Carrington because Boris had invited them at Effie's prompting. Dimitri was there with Svetlana and Anita because Boris said it was time to get them socialising and establish contacts. Melissa was there because Muriel had had a quiet whisper with Effie. So too was Ian because he had managed to find a baby sitter after all. Melissa was somewhat miffed about this although she certainly wasn't going to say so. Gaspard was there too because Boris had personally invited him which Effie thought was extremely generous. Gaspard had not confided in Effie that Boris wanted to stage Aida whereas he had set his heart on The Trojans. He had dropped a red hot snapper to the section about Gloria Fitzbagley and with any luck, if that somehow led him to Gloria and Rodney's daily schedule, then Boris might feel more disposed to consider the heroic vision of Hector Berlioz and how he, Gaspard de la Grant, would demonstrate brilliantly how to show the Trojan Horse on stage without loss of stature.

For once, Loretta was not there. She had cried off. She told Boris that she wanted to rest her voice and body and sink into a hot relaxing bath and yeah, thanks, she had all the right stuff to put in it. Freddie wasn't there because he wanted to work at his missile research centre which, for some strange reason he had started to refer to as 'the Rio office". For obvious reasons this terminology was restricted. Effie thought he was just immersed in the same old stuff as always and where else would he be except at DERA? Inwardly, she was only too pleased that he wasn't with her tonight because he would be like a wet grey blanket constantly dragging her down. Without him she could flirt with Boris, enjoy the food and wine, and chatter to all and sundry until the evening collapsed. She ended up sitting more or less opposite Ian, which she wasn't too happy about, because he was so monosyllabic. Neither Dale nor Roz were there because everyone knew that they wanted to spend some time with each other and with Roz being in the show every night, well, you couldn't be in two places at once. Sitting next to Ian, on the opposite side to Melissa was Anita. Effie met Anita for the first time in the Tzarbinsky antechamber when she entered with Dimitri and Svetlana. They hit it off instantly.

"I'm dying for a cigarette," said Effie, "anyone got a light?" Anita whipped hers out of her pocket while Igor was asking Melissa if she would like him to hang up her chiffon scarf.

"Sure, go for it," said Anita, "I always set the flame on full blast."

And the two of them lit up together.

"I believe this is your first time here?" said Effie

"Yeah, and what about those huge black ashtrays downstairs on the floor level, you could get high by just being a waitress."

And the two of them laughed together. Effie with her roaring, screaming, phlegmatose wretching, and Anita with her quick, high, staccato burst which became more harmonically diverse the funnier she found things. Ian smiled gloomily and tried not to scratch himself too much. He had never seen Melissa's chiffon scarf before and for a fleeting second he thought it might be an ideal method to strangle

161

oneself if ever the need became pressing. Melissa was immediately struck by the brilliance of Igor's blue eyes and his dishy romantic looks. And of course he was so much taller than Ian which helped.

"You have a beautiful neck," he whispered quietly, "you should not keep it covered."

She wanted to say something incredibly erotic to him but she was constrained by the circumstances and her upbringing.

"It's nice to be noticed," she replied, and flicked the subtlest of glances in Ian's direction. Ian was staring after Effie and Anita who had gone on ahead. Boris was already seated at the table waiting for them. Some kind of Godfather-like habits he couldn't seem to get rid of. He had ordered the curtains and drapes to be parted as wide as possible; this was a night for showing off.

Dale sat alone with the Yum Bum. At that very moment, Roz was on stage and would not be joining him until the curtain came down as near as possible to ten o'clock. After the matinee there was only one evening performance but she would be knackered nonetheless. She was playing Joan of Arc which meant she couldn't wear her glasses. Somehow the heat from the lights always aggravated her contact lenses and made her eyes sore. They had agreed that sitting in the middle of the Yum Bum with two four-packs was better than the smoky atmosphere of the Villain's Noose. Dale had his hand between the leaves and was stroking them gently. He had developed a technique whereby he could gently sweep his knuckles over the tips of the nodules and pick up the Yum Bum's secretions. It was not a sexual thing although it was very enchanting. After a while, the sticky patches appeared to react to his body heat and would swell out into little puddles of soft, translucent jelly. When they first ran down his knuckles his natural reaction was to rub it in. He could feel that there was nothing in the strange liquid, (it reminded him of cheap bath gel) that was burning his skin or causing a nasty reaction, in fact, just the opposite. The muscles in his hands had been punished a lot these last few days but the staircase was almost done. When he rubbed in the Yum Bum, it was if his muscles had

162

been masseured in rum and honey then cooled with ice in cucumber and gin. All tension left him and when he rubbed the remainder into his skin it would make his hands feel supple and sinewy and something to feel good about. He had used a variation of this technique to scoop up enough secretive jelly to put in a little glass jar. Well, two actually. One for Boris and one for him and Roz. They kept it by their bedside table which was in Dale's flat. Dale was building Roz a large walk-in cupboard for all her clothes. In fact he was building her an entire dressing room almost six metres square on top of the flat roof of the flat. Effie said there was nothing in the documentation that prevented that and since there was loads of space and he would be building onto a strong criss-cross base made of oak beams six inches thick and nine inches deep, why not? So there was that little project on-going like. He would give the other jar to Boris and he could do what he liked with it. He wasn't bothered but he would chat to Roz about it later tonight.

"Okay rocket daddy," purred Loretta, pour that stuff that looks like liquid gold over my toes and rub it in."
Freddie grinned and did as he was told. The whole set up at the Rio office was just fabulous. Not only did he have his operations centre and research and test facilities under one roof but Boris was now building a missile launch site which would be electronically integrated into his mission control suite. And if that wasn't enough, he could always knock himself up a quick cup of tea and a toasted cheese sandwich in the kitchenette. Tonight he was in the main bathroom with Loretta.

Boris had asked Lotte Polanski to design something glamorous and sexy and she had come up with yet more Mucha lads and lasses in gentle mellow marble like stilton cheese. But they did the trick. Water of any temperature or solution, (and you could alter your aromatherapy oil mix at the press of a brass button) issued forth from the usual orifices. A penis there a breast there. And the usual gentle flood. It was more than a bathroom, it was a palace of watery delights. Bright halogen up-lighters would cut through the heavy steam and sparkle on the gold edged floor-to-ceiling oval mirrors. It was the best impression of a Sultan's palace north-east of Portsmouth that you could get and Freddie and Loretta were enjoying it.

"I've been thinking about a lot of things lately," said Freddie, rubbing her toes with oatmeal and cinnamon oil.

"Tell me about it."

"I must have integrity of my project."

"I thought you'd got it, Boris is just the supplier, only you know how it all works, and I don't understand it, so where's the moral dilemma?"

Freddie as usual, was initially pole-axed by her remarks but then gained clarity of his senses enough to say, "I think it might be a good idea if you were aware of its basic concept."

"Freddie, this isn't rocket science time, its massage my tootsies time, okay? We'll get back to Cassandra all in good time because I'm genuinely interested in what you do but you gotta understand that on some levels our brains are on a different planet."

Freddie gave due consideration to her comment and continued to enjoy the feel of her toes in his fingers.

Christopher Carrington loved to show off but unfortunately couldn't hold his liquor. His capacity for alcohol was nonetheless staggering and his ability to remain standing and coherent, albeit blurred at the edges, was legendary in London City banking circles. He was known in the usual cellars as the blustering balloon. His silk waistcoats were always bright and shiny and gaudy and he didn't care a shit whether his belly fought the buttons or not because he made a lot money and he knew how it could be worked. He knew that Boris understood that fundamental principle too and they were getting along like two fat toads on a griddle. The dinner party was in full swing by now.

"I say Boris," said Christopher, "I must show you my Billy Bunter impersonation sometime."

"Who's Billy Bunter?" said Boris.

"He's a big fat jerk who jerks off with chocolate and ice cream," said Melissa, with untypical abandon.

164

"Yeah, maybe we better keep him under wraps for tonight, huh Christopher?" chipped in Anita.

Ian was sat between them and was desperately itchy. He needed something to take his mind off the irritation or he knew he would go mad. Every time he tried to marshal his senses his thoughts were overwhelmed by Project Cassandra and what Freddie might be planning to do with it. Melissa was ignoring him, of that much he was aware, but this young woman called Anita, this Russian with extraordinary green eyes and panther-like musculature, was not. In fact he was beginning to find her rather engaging. She never listened to an answer properly, or at least, she appeared to interpret them in a very idiosyncratic way. She was very direct too.

"So why don't you go to the John and have a good scratch? If you want some cream I've got some in my handbag, it's not enough to cover your whole body but you can maybe hit the worst spots and let me know how you get on."

How could he not refuse? When he returned to the table ten minutes later, Melissa was passing a note to Igor as he went around re-charging their glasses

"How d'you get on?" said Anita.

"Fine," he said, "it helped a lot."

"Okay, so listen I'm a stripper, what do you do?"

Although Ian had been drinking heavily he would still able to appreciate the irony if he remarked that he was a private dick. But he did not. Life was complicated enough without attempting to justify an alternative existence that had been thrust upon him from a great height.

"I'm a scientist."

"No kidding, clones or bombs?"

"Neither, I specialise in strato-ionic mathematics."

"That sounds a bit painful, what do you get out of it?"

He could hardly say fun, so he quoted his salary instead. She didn't pick up on it but merely went on about how she hoped to earn five hundred a night in this new cabaret that Boris was funding. Ian knew nothing about this. He was too stressed out chasing after Freddie and trying not to let Melissa or anyone else know about it.

"Perhaps I could see you perform sometime," he blurted involuntarily.

"Sure, why not, see how this Haystack gig shapes up, yeah?" Ian nodded and supped his wine. His mother was chatting madly with Effie, Christopher and Boris while Melissa was being elegant and tantalising with that Tzarbinski maitre de. Anita seemed a nice girl.

Dale passed Roz a third can of Tetleys and they supped ale together in the comforting fronds of the Yum Bum.

"I reckon Boris will have access to some of the best Russian laboratories," said Roz, "he'll find out what kind of DNA structure the Yum Bum has and just take it from there."

"Should we be worried then?"

"About what?"

Dale pondered long and deep and supped his beer and breathed in the pure fresh air of the Yum Bum and felt his mind flow in amongst its green and purple hues and glittering secretions.

"Dunno really."

"See how it goes then. I'm pretty knackered, shall we go to bed after this one?"

"Yeah, why not?"

Loretta was now rubbing Freddie's shoulders with jasmine, juniper and eucalyptus oil. He was naked except for a soft hot towel around his midriff. Her bath had been good and she was totally relaxed. She did not want sex right now and was content to just massage Freddie's shoulders gently and enjoy the moment. The future looked good. The signs that a show could actually be put on were promising. The production team was real, it had people in it doing real things and it was coming together. She liked Effie too, and that helped. And Boris clearly liked Effie and that helped even more. Perhaps it would stop him listening to Dimitri so much? She could handle Svetlana if it came to a problem and Anita was a bit of a blast. She didn't mind if she was in the show. From what she could see of the natives of Fropsham they already had their fair share of wankers so a few more wouldn't go amiss.

166

Dale was a regular guy and she knew a good staircase when she saw one. He was a craftsman and no denying it. And that Yum Bum tree was just something else.

"What do you make of the Yum Bum tree, Freddie?"

"I don't know, I have only seen its seeds."

"You mean you haven't seen it since it was potted?"

"No."

"I really think you should, it's amazing."

"So is Project Cassandra, I have to focus on that to the exclusion of all else."

She was surprised at how little interest he really showed in what was gradually becoming quite a talking point about town. She had chatted with the Haystack actors who attended her audition and they said that they felt their encounter with the Yum Bum had been almost spiritual. She knew Achmed the taxi-driver in Tunisia and he was a conniving bum. The seeds had to be a joke and yet the results showed that they most definitely were not. Freddie had actually handled them but he clearly showed no interest in their outcome. Maybe he really was too screwed up about Effie and could only deal with it by blotting certain bits out?

"Well, Cassandra or not, you did a great job on my toes."

'Thank you," said Freddie, "this is good too, I never realised how tense my shoulders had become."

Loretta circled her palms between his blades and over and around the tops. He had a slight frame and every time he got undressed he reminded her of Woody Allen, especially when he left his horn-rimmed spectacles on.

Gaspard was trying to attract Igor's attention but he always seemed to be floating on the other side of the table whenever there was a chance to signal him. Gaspard was seated between Christopher and Muriel Carrington and felt rather hemmed in by the arrangement. Christopher behaved like a bloated sea-elephant that had sat on a blunderbuss while Muriel waggled her face this way and that as would a demented puffin. Intelligent conversation had now reached zero if, in fact, it had ever started. He craved for Igor and decided that he would attempt to talk to him en route to the gentlemen's lavatory. But Igor was still on the wrong side of the table attending to that Melissa girl whose gestures over the course of the evening had become ever more balletic. He rose anyway and just as he did so, Christopher Carrington said:

"Can you ask Igor for a repeat of the champers, he seems to have deserted us."

Gaspard made his way round to Igor like a crêpe in search of a suzette.

"May I speak with you one moment?" he asked legitimately. Igor unlasered his eyes from Melissa's and smiled kindly at him.

"Of course, shall we move to the sweet trolley?"

The implied intimacy of the sweet trolley made Gaspard nervous in a divine sort of way and he had to snatch a napkin to stop himself dribbling.

"Do you by any chance sing?" he enquired.

Igor smiled indulgently but kindly, "yes, now and again but I'm not a trained singer."

That did not matter to Gaspard who felt he was looking at Aeneas, the heroic tenor who would capture the heart of Queen Dido in the Trojans. Pray God he was a tenor.

"What is your voice?"

"Excuse me?" said Igor politely.

"Bass, baritone or tenor?"

"Tenor," replied Igor.

Gaspard's fingers sunk into the mandarin gateaux, he could see Igor's well-oiled warrior body glistening on stage already.

"Bloody hell Gaspard, we're bloody well gasping over here," shouted Christopher Carrington, "Igor dear boy, where's the rest of that bloody champers?"

Igor nodded and moved towards the doorway.

"Here, take my card," said Gaspard, furtively, "we must talk about singing lessons."

Igor stuffed it in his breast pocket and went for the champagne. Gaspard was torn between the gentlemen's lavatory or another drink. As he dithered, he caught sight of Melissa pretending not to have noticed that Igor was gone. He returned to the table with a smug, satisfied grin.

The dinner party had reached the stage where there was little else to do except drink and talk and it was getting pretty noisy. Svetlana shouted across the table to Anita in Russian. "My mum says you look like a nice boy," said Anita to Ian, "but I told her you were married."

"How did you know that?" said Ian, "I'm not wearing a wedding ring."

"You're not talking to you wife either," she replied. He grimaced sheepishly. "Have you got any kids?" she went on.

"Sebastian, he's only six months."

"You're wife's certainly got her figure back."

"Her mother paid for a personal trainer."

"Some mother. I can't have a kid just yet, it would ruin my career."

"I can imagine."

"Lots of strippers do, don't get me wrong, but it takes a while to get that really sexy look back, you know what I mean?"

"Yes, I think you look very sexy tonight," Ian blurted. The wine had clearly taken over and it was too late to withdraw the remark, not that he was really bothered one way or the other. For the first time in months he was feeling relaxed and his itching had stopped. Melissa was flirting with Igor again who had returned to serve them with fresh champagne.

"Do you like your wife's body?" asked Anita, lighting a cigarette.

"I don't get to see it much."

"It's probably just a phase, don't worry about it," she blew her cigarette smoke across the table, "does she keep her nightie on when you make love?"

Ian heard himself saying, "we don't make love." Anita took another long drag on her cigarette then bent a little closer. Her perfume smelt exotic and he desperately wanted to touch her breasts.

"Listen, I live in Cedar Park Mansions or some place, here's my telephone number" she scribbled on a table napkin "I gotta start making contacts, you understand?"

"Yes of course," he stuffed the napkin in his trouser pocket and realised he'd got an erection.

169

At about half past eleven, two cars swung through the gates of Frank Files' warehouse and drove off in opposite directions. In the red Mazda sports car was Loretta and she was feeling good. Freddie had wanted to dump about Project Cassandra and she knew that she could bring him back on line whenever she wanted to. All in good time though. Tonight had been the first occasion when they had used the Rio office and also the first time that she had cried off from Boris's agenda since her return from Tunisia. He probably wouldn't ring her tonight but she couldn't be sure and would prefer it if he didn't get the answerphone. The thought struck her that maybe the Rio office was bugged, perhaps even with hidden micro-cameras. She wouldn't be at all surprised. Well, she said she was taking a bath and that's exactly what she had done. Given the choice between Lotte's marble palace with all the fun things and her own, who could blame her? Besides, Boris had installed it at her request anyway.

In the metallic blue Rover 75 was Freddie and he was feeling good too. The computers Boris had supplied were much faster than the DERA ones and Project Cassandra was coming along a treat. Soon he would be testing the launch simulation programme and that would be a defining moment in realising his dream. Tonight he had wanted to tell Loretta what it was really capable of but she had declined to show any interest. With hindsight perhaps it was better that way. Her real passion was singing the blues and it was sufficient that she remained engrossed with the production of her cabaret and the occasional rendezvous with him. There had been no sex tonight but it didn't matter. If the truth be known, he was beginning to find it a little exhausting.

Thank God he no longer did it with Effie.

29

"We've got to do something about this prick," said Gloria to Rodney as she swung her legs out of bed and lit up a Silk Cut, "and please don't say 'we?' again because I'm seriously pissed off."

She was of course referring to Gaspard. Rodney looked at her back and admired the curvature of her spine. It was scooped beautifully into her buttocks and although it might give her a few slipped discs if she tried to toss the caber beyond official retirement age, right now it was a most stirring sight to behold.

"Okay, what's he done now?"

She took a plastic Have-a-Nice-Day folder from her handbag and slid it across the duvet to him.

"He's only gone and submitted an expense claim for a surveillance weekend of which we know nothing about."

"So tell him to piss off."

"I would except that – and please look in that folder I gave you – he's provided us with his air ticket stubs, a boarding pass list issued at Gatwick on the way out and Tunis on the return, Barclaycard receipts, sundry till receipts including one from Waterstones marked Piero della Francesca, The Arezzo Frescoes, *and* he's only bloody well sent a note of the bellhop tips on hotel headed paper."

Rodney slipped the papers out their folder. The first thing he noticed was that the date on the Hotel Yamhalia receipt was the same weekend that one of their agents had reported seeing Blodvrinsky with Bannister, the DERA scientist. He hadn't mentioned that to Gloria yet. Things could be tricky because there had been an unconfirmed report that the CIA were there too. Blodvrinsky was becoming increasingly active and the fact that he had now bought several million pounds worth of property in Surrey and Hampshire, to say nothing of a prime pad in South Kensington and, for all he knew, an island in the Hebrides, made him a pain in the arse. He looked at the photograph of Loretta in bed with Freddie. He could tell it was extracted from videotape. Her features were clear but he did not recognise her. Who's side was she on? Vladimir Putin's ? Blodvrinsky's ? CIA? Or was she one of Gaddafi's girls? They had been recruiting across Europe quite heavily for the last few years and it was feasible that they had now got someone in post. He tried to change the subject but found that as soon as he started talking about his meeting with the Defence Minister it came back to Blodvrinsky.

"All we know so far," said Rodney, easing his balls, "is that one of the guys the Serbian police arrested who they suspect is involved in Arcan's murder used a false identity and they've just found out that his real name is Pyshnyi and he's got family connections with the Chechen rebels and we are investigating the possibility that he may be linked to Blodvrinsky's orang-utan."

"Jesus, you could be in the shit," said Gloria, rubbing her legs with an anti-foliate cream.

"There's more to come," said Rodney, getting out of bed to dab his fingers in a pot of her Clarins day cream which he then applied to his dick.

"Go easy," she scolded, "that stuff's expensive."

"And this is precious too," he replied, waggling himself, "anyway, as I was saying, we've also had conflicting reports that a Syrian palace spokesman was sighted with General Lebed in Siberia."

"So what?"

"Well the second report claimed that it was Blodvrinsky not Lebed that was seen, you know how familiar the two men are."

"Well, it should be fairly easy to verify Lebed's movements."

"Yes, we already have, and on the days in question Lebed was in Tunisia."

"And where was Blodvrinsky ?"

"In Tunisia too, same hotel, same dates."

"So who was the Syrian with?"

"We don't know, but now that I know this fucking, over-educated, stern-tube artist Gaspard Grant is involved it won't be long before we get a mega-spray of the old brown smelly stuff when Mr fucking high IQ puts his foot in it!"

Gloria inhaled deeply and streaked the dressing table mirror with an agitated tracer of smoke.

"Perhaps we should ask the Minister to authorise Grant's expenses?"

"At four thousand pounds there are boys on the bill, forget it."

"Perhaps we should take him out altogether."

"Well, it's an option, isn't it?"

Gloria blew another tracer of smoke at the dressing table mirror and looked at Rodney to see how serious he was about it. He had an erection.

"So now what?" said Effie to Boris, as she swung her legs onto a curved Swedish bench chair, in her main theatre office. Boris had in front of him the DNA report from his Siberian scientists and it didn't add up to much. All that they could establish was that it had a DNA profile that loosely resembled the Mediterranean grape but was also capable of sustaining bacteriological growth at minus seventy degrees centigrade. The gel itself was extraordinarily rich in proteins and there was some kind of aerobic association which accounted for its ability to filter toxins out of the air and thus create a friendly environment. Lower down the bio-chain they had discovered a strong tendency towards the rubber species and they were anxious to see photographs of the Yum Bum to aid their research. In short, they hadn't a clue what it was but reckoned it was safe, which was another way of saying that they had found nothing poisonous or life threatening in it. The conclusion simply stated, 'Believed benign pending further investigation'

"So what we do next," said Boris triumphantly, "is to pay Dale to collect the gel on a regular basis and pot it and label it. We think up a fancy name and sell it."

"We'll need government authorisation for various licences before you can do something like that in this country."

"So what, I'll deal with them."

"Who's going to pay Dale?"

"He's on my payroll from now on."

Effie felt threatened for the first time, Boris was becoming rather aggressive. She didn't doubt for one minute that he could pull the operation off but she was aware that she was becoming increasingly dependent on many of his actions. The trouble was, she liked him and yet she knew he was trouble.

"Okay," she said, "I manage the Yum Bum administratively and you take care of operations and capital projects."

"Agreed," said Boris.

"I'll speak to Dale a.s.a.p. and get him signed on. He won't object if we include in his responsibilities the care and maintenance of the Yum Bum, the surrounding staircase and adjoining floors because that way he can continue to supervise any refurbishment projects and it will help to keep him on board. By the way, how much are you paying him?"

"Two hundred pounds a day and no expenses unless agreed beforehand."

"He'll enjoy that. Right, I will also contact the Department of Fisheries and Agriculture for licensing advice and let you know their response."

Boris came to the end of his Gauloise, he had not as yet offered Effie one, and stubbed it out so resolutely in the already overflowing ashtray that its contents started to jump out. His smile was fierce and his frame loomed like a battleship in the chair. He took a slug of neat vodka from a hip flask and stopped smiling.

"Effie," he said, "we do it this way. I get the Yum Bum gel, and sell it. You apply for the bits of paper when I've cleared a million pounds stirling. Get it?"

She got it. It was not altogether pleasant but she had to consider various compensatory measures in the context of her strategic life plan. She had a chart somewhere, left over from her business administration studies, which had a bullet point against the statement: first identify your resources. She had done that. It was Boris, Freddie was a write-off. Dale was featured somewhere on the page devoted to scatological charts. He was an empirical cognisance resource. As for Gaspard, well, he hadn't the sense to realise that Boris was going to use him for his own ends. The poor man was going to be so dreadfully let down. But she would be alright. Boris was surrounded by Dimitri and now, to a lesser extent Svetlana and Anita, but she knew that she was gradually finding her way into his heart and that would eventually lead her to his bed. And why bloody not? Muriel slept in a separate bedroom from that overweight farting walrus Christopher and look at the lifestyle she enjoyed in return. Effie knew she couldn't go on working all her life and when retirement beckoned, the combined value of her and Freddie's pensions heralded an existence as fulfilling as the local hedge-hog's. As far as she was concerned, Boris was glamour and fun and success all rolled into one and she would tolerate his occasional threatening bursts. Besides, it looked like the Yum Bum could become a nice little earner in its own right. Boris was leaving her to deal with all the administration anyway.

Dale thought the idea was great and went full steam ahead and finished the staircase. From the concrete base of the Seventh Cavalry area, right up to the top where the little thatched roof allowed the spring air to waft under its generous eaves, was Dale's conception entirely. When he had showed his prototype design to Gaspard, as much out of respect for his professional judgement as anything else, Gaspard had dismissed it out of hand.

"I would have thought that merely bracing the existing structure was sufficient, besides, your proposal will cost a fortune and I would have thought that the available funds could be better spent elsewhere, for example on my forthcoming opera production."

"Oh, I didn't know nuffink abart that, p'raps I should speak to Effie or Boris and see what they fink?"

"If I were you, I'd get an estimate from Travis and Perkins for the requisite length of sturdy angle-iron and leave it at that."

Dale saw Effie who said go see Boris, and when he showed his draft drawing to Boris, he was puzzled by his first comment but not his second.

"You gotta think big," said Boris, "money's not a problem, I sometimes fund the IMF".

"So 'ow big like, gimme an idea."

Boris took Dale to the very base of the Yum Bum where its giant tentacles held the concrete floor like an octopus contemplating its supper.

"That's where the VIP's are gonna come from," he said, pointing beyond the Yum Bum and across the huge floor to the warehouse doors on the opposite wall, "so we need something there," he pointed to where the Yum Bum rose in a sturdy curving arc and up into the sky and who know's how far beyond in the end, "something to welcome them in, say hello and split a vodka or two, then proceed with their entourage and maybe a few press photographers all the way round and as high as you can get them, that sort of thing."

"Oh right, gotcher, leave it wiv' me, mate, I'm on the case already, I'll come back wiv' another drawing soonest."

"Dale," said Boris, putting his arm round his shoulders like a big uncle, "do the drawing, fine, maybe you gotta work out where everything goes, but don't show it to me, okay, just do it, I trust you."

"Oh righto," said Dale, "I've got a few ideas up me sleeve like, I'll jus' get on wiv' it."

The final result had everyone gasping, including Gaspard who was appalled at the cost and consumed with jealousy over Dale's achievement. The trouble was he had very few people in which to confide, although one of them was Cedric."

"The point is," said Gaspard, very precisely and with a bacardi and lime juice to hand, "I am not suggesting for one moment that the boy has no talent its just that he's poorly educated and has no formal qualifications beyond some vague kind of matriculation certificate for woodwork and carpentry."

"I know just how you feel, squire," replied Cedric, with a babycham and whisky that Gaspard had just bought him, "I've been up against the hoi polloi all my life, that's why I'm here."

"As you know, Cedric, I have been appointed head of production and design for a grand opera which will open when the theatre is extended by courtesy of the Blodvrinsky Arts Foundation, and I have an immense amount of forward planning to achieve."

"Oh quite understand old boy, don't tell me about it, I was the operations director for East Anglian Breweries until they appointed some high flyer with an MBA and a pair of silicon tits."

"That grand staircase and absurdly jingoistic reception pavilion must have cost at least one hundred thousand pounds, which is almost half of the entire donation sum, and yet they won't even let me see the invoices."

"Walk away it from it, Gaspard old chum, take my advice, walk away from it and do something else before it buggers you up completely. Would you like a shot of rum in that?"

The term The Yum Bum, as it was now publicly and quite simply known, incorporated Dale's design and construction of what amounted to a major project in wood. It cost two hundred and fifty thousand pounds and the only people who knew that were Boris, Effie, and Dale, and also Roz because she took care of all Dale's paperwork and tax returns and had naturally added up all the timber bills and prepared a proforma invoice.

At the side of the Yum Bum's huge circular base, Dale had conceived a grand pavilion with a long veranda which extended sideways across the Yum Bum's tentacled roots like a low-lying walkway to open out into a full size staircase wide enough for six abreast including elbow room to answer their mobiles. The staircase had risers all the way up through the

177

first floor so that people who suffered from vertigo wouldn't feel exposed to the vast expanse of the Seventh Cavalry area. Above that level, where the Yum Bum's branches became accessible, the staircase narrowed to four abreast. Every so often, as it wound its way gracefully round like an elegant helter skelter, an octagonal platform had been built at a spot where the scoping valleys of lush green foliage seemed to afford the most memorable gaze. It was a superb construction with lots of long and short-nosed mortise and tenon joints and interlocking butts. The support railings were chamfered octagonally too. These viewing platforms occurred at various intervals, usually where the Yum Bum leaves had spread their farthest, and all of them afforded a pleasurable view of its inner fronds and glistening whorls.

The pavilion itself was a grand and almost pompous affair that seemed heavily influenced by the colonial style, almost British Raj. Dale had taken advantage of the available height and made a feature of the roof. It had a separate balcony just above gutter level with a full balustrade and platformed walkway for the super-VIPs which linked directly to the main staircase. The entire building was constructed in Finnish Pine and yet the overall impression, when viewed from the massive warehouse doors, (which was the only place to appreciate the scale of things) was not so much Scandinavian, or even British Raj, as Bridge over the River Kwai.

There were few dissenting voices, in fact, it had become a significant local attraction that the Haystack Theatre Company was justly proud of. The Fropsham & Farnham Gazette had described it as magnificent and Dale and his team of chippies had their photograph on the front page. When the local hack asked Dale whether the staircase itself would be open to the general public, Roz managed to jump in before he could say dunno and issued a statement to the effect that a final Health and Safety Certificate had to be granted before such a decision could be taken. From that moment on, Dale and Roz always worked closely together when preparing his statements to the press. Roz had a natural gift for that sort of thing, in fact, she became something of a roving ambassador for the Yum Bum and was often able to de-fuse various situations when they looked like getting out of hand. Take the actors for example.

They wanted to be in on things and were angry and felt insulted that they should not be allowed to freely promenade up and down the Yum Bum steps any longer on the flimsy excuse that certain biological tests had to be completed and certificated in the interests of public health and safety first. In the end, Roz explained to Boris and Effie that actors were by and large utterly fed up to the back teeth with being called luvvies and treated as if they were stupid, and that the Haystack Management Committee would do well to understand that their existing contracts should be viewed as a considerable, but as yet, under utilised asset, that could become a polished and articulate, if not inspired and daring conduit of humanistic awareness, for the benefit of Fropsham and the wider community. And to imply that they were considered to be sufficiently childish and unrestrained as to completely ignore a very reasonable request to comply with the Health and Safety Regulations, to say nothing of the Performance Building Special Revision Amendment (1976), was frankly well nigh injurious to their self-esteem. Accordingly, the ban was lifted and the Haystack company in toto, all its actors and technicians and production and administrative staff were permitted to wander up and down and round and about the Yum Bum from seven in the morning until eleven at night. This made everyone happy and the local Equity rep said he reckoned they could push it to midnight provided everyone observed the no smoking ban which management were obliged to insist on, due to restrictive clauses in their buildings insurance which, if not complied with would incur Draconian financial penalties that could not be forseeably sustained without some adverse effect on overtime. Well, what with all that wood, it made sense didn't it?

And so it came to be that the magical valleys of the Yum Bum always had one or two people drifting happily through its succulent vegetation whilst practising the delicate art of nodule knuckle grazing. Most folks followed their instincts and rubbed the Yum Bum gel into their skin and with amazing results. It was particularly beneficial on the face. It cleaned all the heavy stage grease paint out of the pores and fed the skin with a lovely, fresh, light, clean and utterly invigorating after-glow. Roz let on to her best mates that it was great as a sexual lubricant too and in fact actually made them feel more randy, not that they needed any encouragement these days. Actual fornication in the Yum Bum was forbidden by the silent majority, however, no one would dream of such a misdemeanour because, after a while, when everyone had overcome their initial wonderment, the Yum Bum became the place to stimulate your mind. Its effects were extraordinary and long lasting. Everyone realised it too. People would have endless discussions to try and pin-point the exact nature of its benefits and yet it somehow remained elusive. Gradually, everyone settled for the general feeling of being grateful for a happy life and how much they felt inclined to give the rest of it an upbeat swing.

Everyone that is, except Gaspard. His jealousy of Dale ate into him deeper and deeper and fed his increasing paranoia and general insecurity. Eventually, he could stand it no longer and arranged a private meeting with Boris in his apartment in South Kensington.

30

Boris gave Gaspard a bear hug that nearly crushed him then let him slip into the comfort of his high cushioned sofa. He hadn't seen him for a while and was surprised at how pale and tense he was. Clearly, the man needed company.

"Sit down Gaspard," said Boris enthusiastically, "it's been so long."

Gaspard sank into the sofa and felt grateful that he had finally plucked up enough courage to confront, yes confront if that was the word, his biggest remunerative employer outside of the Haystack Theatre, for which, in the latter case, he was paid eighteen and a half thousand pounds a year.

"I'm so glad you could see me, things have been rather difficult of late and in the most peculiar of circumstances."

"I know how it is Gaspard, I face it every day, now whaddya want to drink?"

"I'd quite fancy a Stone's original green ginger wine, I've become rather partial to them of late."

"Okay, that's no problem I'll fix it for you, just gimme a moment."

Boris prepared the drink and then sniffed it.

"D'you take this with meths?"

"No thank you," said Gaspard, "I prefer it as it is."
He took the glass, sipped apprehensively and then faced his mentor.

"I've become terribly jealous of Dale of late," he said, clasping the glass, "I know he's incredibly talented with wood and I can forgive him for not having read a word of Dostoyevsky but does he really have to absorb the resources of the establishment to the extent that I have not even been able to create my own production company for an opera that has yet to be decided upon?"

Boris took a hard look at Gaspard and tried to sum him up. The man was a snob. The man was a poofter. But the man had a soul. He would have to deal with him. He wanted more than anything else to have a grand opera production but this twat didn't seem able to get it off the ground. What was he waiting for? The go signal? Why did he have to do everything himself? Why couldn't somebody else just take the strain now and again? Why did his mother die in a lunatic asylum? Since meeting the Yum Bum, he knew that all such answers would eventually come to rest and everything would be alright as long as he just kept going with the next project. He wasn't where he was today without having fired from the hip.

"Gaspard," said Boris, with a glass of neat vodka in his hand, "it's like this. You think I don't know about The Trojans? Tell me, where were you on August the fifth, nineteen sixty two?"

"I'm afraid I can't remember," said Gaspard, completely taken aback by the question, "in fact I cannot even remember where I was when John F. Kennedy died, my parents disapproved of world events and shielded me from the news.

"Well this will surprise you Gaspard. I was in the Royal Albert Hall to see Colin Davis conduct the London Symphony Orchestra in a performance of the Symphonie Fantastique that blew the cream out of the fannies and the spunk out of the pricks. In the second half he did Stravinsky's Oedipus Rex and it was like some mad Greek tossed an electric toaster into the bath. I was sixteen at the time, I was a good student, I played bass trombone in the Chechen Schools Philharmonia and attended all the rehearsals. The state recognised me and I was invited to attend an education symposium and give my views on society. What could I do but accept? I knocked them out with my eloquence so they gave me a place on the Soviet Cultural Exchange Programme for students with established contacts in writing. I think that was pretty adventurous for my age but you tell me you can't even remember what you were doing?"

"Well, I may have formed a view by now," said Gaspard, realising that Boris must have had quite a good education, "but please don't let me impose."

Boris had no intention of letting him impose or whatever else was jangling around in his mind, he simply wanted to say that Svetlana had put her foot down about sharing the dog arena with a dozen elephants, so mentally speaking he had put Aida on the back burner. He would love Gaspard to do the Trojans, if only the guy would stop sulking and bitching and just get on with it instead of expecting him to sort it all out. But the man was scared. He wanted somebody else to paint the flag green. Boris continued.

"So there I was, a star Russian school kid at the Royal Albert Hall, a promenader at the BBC Proms with a KGB minder sitting on a chair by the fountain. The colours changed and the water looked good but I couldn't run as fast as Nureyev. I went off the rails in later years but look where I am today. So where were you on the night in question?"

Gaspard looked flustered and took a big swig of his drink, he was ready for another.

"I cannot remember precisely but I do recall that my governess said that the Proms were rude and excitable and should be avoided at all costs."

Boris felt like hitting him but he knew it wasn't his fault. He was damaged material. The man needed motivation and support. He'd give him a kick up the arse he wouldn't forget.

"Gaspard, you think I don't know about Sir Colin Davis and Berlioz?"

"No, no," gasped Gaspard, "I wasn't for one minute suggesting-"

Boris cut him dead. "He was a hooligan along with the entire London Symphony Orchestra but when he sliced the air with his baton they all took off like snot in a rocket. Now everybody loves him and even the French have pinned a medal on him and not before time, if I may say so. But you gotta think big, Gaspard, you gotta see the angles. Colin's doing his monumental Berlioz Odyssey at the Barbican all this year and you want to embarrass him by staging the Trojans at the Haystack? Think about that Gaspard, bit of a cultural maelstrom don't you think? Now why don't I top up your glass?"

Gaspard accepted a recharge and felt a certain throbbing of the temples. Everything was in tatters anyway. He had been promised a production but all anyone could talk about was that infernal cabaret. He didn't want to cause offence and had never realised until now how cultured Boris really was. His apartment was magnificent and the fixtures and furnishing were utterly ravishing. Fancy him being at the proms in nineteen sixty two, no wonder his table at Tzarbinski's resonated with the Royal Albert Hall, how incredible to carry a vision like that for so long.

"The point is," said Gaspard, diplomatically, "even if we do Aida, we shall still need an orchestra and you appear to have more contacts than I do."

"What I'm saying," said Boris, easing himself beside him in the luxurious cosseting of the silk cushions, "if we're gonna do Les Troyens justice, then I'd better give Colin a ring and invite his mob over, the trouble is, I don't have his number, and how much longer do I have to wait before I get your first draft stage design?"

Gaspard reeled and tried to gather his senses. You mean The Trojans were on? There would be an orchestra? There would be singers? Oh My God! What about Igor? Would Sir Colin allow amateurs into the company? Boris had asked him for the set design and he hadn't got one! He tried not to panic.

"I need a production team to support me."

"You already got one, you want me to put the bums on the seats for you?"

"No no, not at all, I was merely pointing out that I was unaware of the administrative arrangements."

"Administration is Effie, you know her better than I do, what are you waiting for, a starter's pistol?"

Boris had called his shot and he would have to leave and get on with it. He tried to give the impression that he knew what to do next.

"Right then Boris, if I can have your assurances that I will receive your support in every way I'll ring for a taxi."

"I'll get Dimitri to give you a lift but before that, come and look at this."

Boris took him to the lounge window with its splendid view of the Albert Memorial glistening in the spring sunshine.

"There's no denying it's immensely impressive," remarked Gaspard, sensing that it would be prudent to express appreciation. Boris put his arm round his shoulders, clasping him like an uncle.

"It's impressive alright, and why? Because when it was built your nation were getting a lot of things right in a very big way. Sure, you were bullies and had got a thing about cucumber sandwiches and rubber stamps, but you weren't afraid to slap people around a bit to get them on board with the big idea. So I'm wondering how much longer do I have to wait until you give me Gloria and Rodney's weekly schedules?"

Gaspard clutched his second glass of Stone's original green ginger wine. He had got nowhere with the section because, as usual, they were being completely uncooperative. Perhaps he should tell Boris the truth.

"I'm afraid the section is blocking my moves, I cannot understand their motives, the trouble is, nobody likes me, they deliberately keep me out in the cold, it's so terribly vexing but what can one do?"

Boris released Gaspard from his hug, he could tell the man was uncomfortable with intimacy. What he needed was a backbone.

"Okay Gaspard, so I'm gonna apply a bit of leverage to our little tango dancers, leave it with me and I'll get back to you."

Gaspard was visibly relieved and gulped his ginger wine gratefully.

"There's something else you need to know," said Boris.

"Well it makes a change to be included," replied Gaspard, beginning to feel a bit better now.

"Of course, and as head of production for the Haystack's Trojans you need to know that Lotte Polanski is designing the costumes."

Gaspard froze. The truth of the matter was her décor and designs at Tzarbinski's had impressed him, in fact, he felt threatened. She was good and quite feisty too. What if she wouldn't accept his authority? Would she by-pass him and go straight to Boris? He saw yet another disappointment looming.

"I shall look forward to a mutually rewarding association."
Boris gave him a big hug and summoned Dimitri on his mobile. It was chucking out time.

"I'm right behind you Gaspard, and just remember, as my great grandfather used to say, what you shout at the forest the forest shouts back."

"How frightfully pithy."

"Sure, he was from eastern Karelia before the border disputes broke out but don't worry about that, you've got enough on your plate."

As Boris kissed him on both cheeks and steered him towards the door, he knew that to be true.

31

Effie was having tea with Loretta and Anita in Dunkerbell's. Ever since they had met, the three of them had really hit it off and Effie enjoyed getting away from the theatre. She had seen quite a bit of Loretta at the Haystack and they seemed to have formed a natural alliance that was developing into friendship. Loretta liked Effie's joi de vivre and Effie loved the way Loretta kept the boys at bay. She admired her talent too and was under no illusion that she was going to be the hit of the cabaret. Anita had taken to hanging around the theatre and generally doing anything anybody asked her to, provided there was the odd quid in it for her, here and there. She said she didn't want people to think that her adopted uncle Boris was giving her a free meal ticket because he wasn't and she had always taken care of herself and mum. She was crazy and hyper and great fun. Loretta liked her too because she had this amazing guile and could suss out where somebody was coming from in about ten seconds. She liked her act too. Both she and Effie, and all the stage crew, and every actor that was not rehearsing, and any admin. or production staff that weren't actually on the phone, watched spellbound at her rehearsal. Her naked body was extraordinary. Short and square with muscles like a wood block engraving. She was strong and sinewy and her sexual attraction was of the lioness. Her green eyes when spotlit in a full frontal glinted in a remarkable way. Off stage she carried this aura quite unselfconsciously. Both Effie and Loretta adored her self-confidence and hedonistic charm.

"Well it still looks like cum to me," said Anita, putting away her freshly labelled jar of Kool, which was the Yum Bum gel's new name, "but as I said before, when I took a day trip to Helsinki last April, all the supermarkets were selling packets of rye biscuits, y'know those dark heavy Ryvita things that look like the sole of some beatnik's sandal, and it was called Kunto, so I guess Kool is pretty okay for when we expand into the European market."

Effie was laughing and wheezing already and Loretta was feeling good about just doing something ordinary and nice, assuming of course that selling a wonder cream whose strap line was *it's kool on any part of your body"* without a licence, could be considered nice. What the hell, she knew that whenever some civil servant came along waving the book, Boris would take them to one side and show them their future in no uncertain terms. The arrogant and stupid ones usually ended up experiencing the more imaginative of Boris's life revelatory scenarios. She was using the cream itself and it was definitely cool.

"Well I think Kool is cool and it's gonna sell like hot cakes."

"Don't you mean cool cakes?"

By now Effie was in serious need of a spittoon.

"Y'know," said Anita, who always carried on relentlessly whenever somebody was doubled up in fits, "when we had that fantastic binge at Tzarbinski's I was chatting to this guy called Ian who suffered from some kind of eczema, so I lent him a tube of dermatological cream that I usually carry around with me and he fixed himself up with it in the john. He probably gave himself a quick hand job too 'cos he couldn't stop looking at my tits all evening and he told me he doesn't do it with his wife any more. I reckon he could do with a tub of Kool but I don't have his telephone number."

By now Effie had partially recovered although Anita's latest revelation almost sent her off again.

"Oh dear," she said, wiping her eyes, "we'll all be thrown out if we carry on like this."

"You mean *you* will, me and Loretta will just carry on knocking back the cappuccino's."

Effie managed to contain herself, "I think you were referring to Ian Trubshaw whose wife Melissa was flirting with that gorgeous hunk Igor."

"I didn't find him that gorgeous," said Anita, "in fact I thought he was a bit wet."

"Sounds like you've had a lot of wet men around you," said Loretta, "maybe they need drying down not creaming up."

They all fell about laughing again and a couple of ladies in twin-set and pearls decided that Dunkerbell's wasn't quite like it used to be.

"I can tell you all about Ian Trubshaw," said Effie, "because his mother and I are life-long friends, we were even at school together, and his late father Ted was Freddie's closest colleague."

"Wow, like some family mafia," said Anita, "what about his wife? I only got to speak to her when we were putting our coats on in that weird room that reminded me of some kind of antechamber that they have on death row in the movies and she didn't have much to say for herself."

"Melissa is a snob, take it from me," said Effie, "and Ian is as dull as ditch water. He works with Freddie and Freddie is always complaining that he's got no initiative and follows him around like a shadow all day."

Loretta did not miss the remark but remained silent.
Anita carried on.

"I got the feeling he was incredibly shy, he had to drink a lot of wine before he could hold a conversation with me and then he told me I was sexy and blushed so much that I wrote my telephone number on a table napkin and told him to give me a ring sometime but I guess that glacial bitch of a wife of his has probably got him on a tight lead."

"Well apart from the fact that he's married, I think you'd be better off dating one of the Haystack's actors, at least they're not half-dead."

"Most actors are too vain, I'm kinda into brains at the moment although I wouldn't want to wreck a marriage."

"Doesn't sound like they've got one," said Loretta, "maybe you'd be doing both of them a favour."

"Yeah, the scarlet woman, maybe I could build it into my act somehow, y'know like have him on stage begging to be whipped and then she rushes on and wants it too."

Effie convulsed again and had to light up another cigarette to calm herself down.

"Well," she said, "only in the interests of promoting Kool, I shall give you his office telephone number but tread warily."

"Sure, I'm a big girl now."

Effie scribbled a number on a piece of paper, "just remember that Freddie might answer it too."

"Yeah okay, I'll have a question ready on strato-ionic mathematics, just in case."

They all laughed again but inwardly Loretta was concerned. She recognised the term from when Freddie had been telling her about Project Cassandra.

Gaspard was feeling very happy these days too. His meeting with Boris had been eminently successful. Boris would now deal with Gloria Fitzbagley and Sir Rodney Snodder himself and, ipso facto, keep the section off his back. No doubt he would still be required to undertake those ridiculous telephone calls but now at least he would have the upper hand. The production of Les Troyens, which he now insisted it should be billed as, was on green light for go and the possibility that Boris would be able to secure Sir Colin Davis and the LSO, if only he could find his number, was beyond the more than exciting.

Additional good news was that Effie had given him a production office twice the size of the Cabaret team's, (which he sniffily noted had not yet come up with a name for the show) and he was in the process of taking down the room numbers 502A and 502B, and pushing back the large, heavy, wood panelled partition. There weren't actually five hundred rooms or more in the Haystack but there were five floors with narrow corridors and no lift. However, the admin section for house maintenance, who were all part of the general staff and on a bona fide payroll, had very thoughtfully pinned a small plastic encapsulated notice to the entrance of each floor with a footnote explaining that the first numeral of the room number indicated the floor it was on, the second numeral signified the agreed level of service, (details of which could be verified by ringing ext.246), and the third numeral was the actual room number itself. There was also a sub-note printed in bold capitals: DUE TO FIRE REGULATIONS, NO SMOKING IS PERMITTED. Needless to say, nobody took a blind bit of notice and there were loads of aluminium take-away cartons sitting in every nook and cranny. Gaspard abhorred the habit but, like most people in the theatre, had learnt to cope with it. This time however, as Head of Production (Les Troyens) he would enforce the ban. The first move was to ask Dale to get rid of all the cartons. Now that his creative genius had been unleashed, Gaspard was no longer jealous of Dale's success and they had been getting on quite well. He still wanted his body, yes, but not as much as he wanted Igor's. If Dale had been Adonis then Igor had become Aeneas. He would be seeing him later in the morning after he had issued his administrative orders. He could hardly wait. It was pleasure and pain combined.

"Dale, I am going to produce Les Troyens."

"Oh that's nice, I'll give yer an 'and."

"Thank you, that would be most welcome. The first thing I would like you to do is to clear away all those ashtrays."

"What all of 'em?"

"No, just throughout floor five."

"Oh righto, I'll just bung 'em in a black plastic bin liner and see 'oo else wants 'em like."

"That is up to you, however, I should be obliged if you would apply your mind to the creation of a Trojan Horse and let me know what you think."

"That's not a rocking 'orse, is it?"

"No, it is something vastly bigger and capable of carrying an army of well-oiled, pectorally distinguished men with spears and shields and magenta skirts."

"Yeah, I remember now, you showed me that picture but I don't remember the 'orse but the bloke looked great."

"What horse are you talking about? What bloke?"

"I can't remember it Gasp, but you writ it down for me like 'cos there was a load of foreign language, I'll letcha know when I find it."

Gaspard was relieved to have sorted that one out and began to sketch a large freehand drawing of a Trojan Horse. The only thing that concerned him was that he didn't know the dimensions of the new stage area that Boris had promised him. Work on that had not even started. But that was down to Boris and he trusted him because he was a fellow aesthete. He would finish the drawing, let Dale have a look at it, and then proceed in his car to Tzarbinski's where he would meet with Igor and audition him for the part of Aeneas. He hoped and prayed that Igor would have sufficient strength in his lungs to be a true heldentenor rampaging through Carthage.

"Can I leave you with this?" he said an hour later, handing his drawing to Dale."

"Yeah okay, I done them cartons by the way, cor this is bloody good, is this the Trojan 'orse?"

"It is my first impression of it."

"Yeah, like it, definitely, 'ow big's it gonna be?"

"Possibly as big as the Yum Bum."

"Oh you've got over yer catatonic trance then?"

"I beg your pardon?"

Dale could see that Gaspard could not understand a word he was saying so he decided to carry on as if nothing had happened.

"That's quite a size then, same as the Yum Bum, if you include the Seventh Cavalry assembly area I reckon it won't be far off two 'undred feet."

Gaspard managed to fathom his senses and felt relieved that he was able to quote Boris's axiom.

"One must think big, Dale, this entire production is a monumental epic portraying the highest human drama."

192

"Yeah, life with Cheryl, tell me about it."

They laughed convivially and went about their ways, Dale to apply a final coat of wax on the handrails of the Yum Bum's staircase, and Gaspard to his car.

As he crossed the shingle towards his shining black 1968 Citroen DS21 Pallas Automatique, he decided to make a phone call from the public kiosk.

He tabbed the number in and waited.

"You recognise my voice of course."

"Yes number six."

"I am still awaiting reimbursement of my expenses, what is the reason for the delay?"

"It is being dealt with."

"I should earnestly hope so, please note that I am unavailable for field operations until I receive it."

And then he slammed the phone down almost giggling with glee. Not for nothing was the upholstery in his gleaming black car, Jocasta Red. He turned the ignition key and the car hissed into life like a slumbering snake. Tzarbinky's was only a twenty-minute drive at this time of day.

Melissa dropped Sebastian off at the child minder's and rang Ian on her mobile.

"Sebastian's with Sandra and I'm aiming to catch the ten forty-seven to Waterloo, what time will you be home tonight?"

"I'm not sure, it depends on Freddie."

"Why does it depend on him? I thought you said that a major project had been cancelled and he didn't know what to do with himself?"

"That was three weeks ago, things have changed now."

"You never tell me anything."

"Sorry....I don't know when I'll be home."

'Well Sandra can't keep Sebastian later than seven o'clock, I'll ring you if I get in difficulties, bye."

And with that she was gone. Ian turned round to check where Freddie was and saw that he was in his inner office, cleaning his glasses. As soon as he replaced the telephone, it rang again.

"Propulsion department."

"Hi can I speak to Ian please?" (it was Anita).

"Speaking."

"Oh hi, I thought it was you but I didn't want to say too much because of security and stuff like that, listen I've got a jar of Kool for you, y'know the stuff produced by the Yum Bum, and I thought it would be great for your rashes, so maybe we could meet up this lunch time, whaddya think?"

Ian was flummoxed. He knew it was Anita but he didn't know how to handle himself. He was supposed to be watching Freddie.

"Er, uhm, I'm not sure, I would need to ask my manager."

"What for, a lunch break?"

"Well not exactly but just to agree the time."

"Okay, so look I make it nearly eleven o'clock, how's about we aim for twelve o'clock at Dunkerbell's and take it from there."

Ian noticed that Freddie was on the phone, he would have to make a decision first and hope for the best afterwards.

"Yes, okay."

"Great, have you still got my mobile number, y'know the one I wrote on the Tzarbinski napkin?"

Ian began to panic, where was the napkin, he couldn't remember?

"Um, er, p'raps you could give it to me again just in case?"

"Sure."

Anita repeated the number and he wrote it down on a sheet of graph paper.

"Okay, I've got that, I'll see you at twelve o'clock."

When he rang off, Freddie was still on the telephone.

At Tzarbinski's, Mitzi from Bistro soups on level three flicked through the pages of music on the piano. It was a doddle, she could handle it. Igor was looking quite excited and so was Gaspard if it came to it. They had met and chatted in the Bistro for a while and when Mitzi had said ready when you are, the three of them had walked through the other levels and across the floor to a green room behind the bar and down one flight of stairs to the basement.

"I thought it would be a good idea to sing some Berlioz," said Igor.

"Marvellous," replied Gaspard, 'what is it?"

"Villanelle from Summer Nights, and naturally I shall sing it in French."

Gaspard nearly swooned at the thought of it. It did not matter that it was not heroic it was sufficient that it was all about love. He sat back in the low armchair and waited. Mitzi smiled at Igor.

"I scolded my fingers on a hot plate this morning so I hope I've not lost my touch."

Igor smiled beatifically because he was psyching himself up for the part. Mitzi felt for the pedals in her high heels and began playing. The piano was actually in tune and her hands sent out fluttering heartbeats of chords that hung expectantly in the air. Igor began right on cue and issued forth a vocal radiance full of ardent longing. It was all that Mitzi could do not to lose her place, never before had she heard such beautiful singing. Gaspard was transfixed to the chair. Tears began to streak his cheeks. This was a voice to die for. A little on the light side admittedly but then the song was not dark or brooding. By the end of it, he was totally besotted and almost incapable of speech. It was Mitzi who broke the silence.

"That was gorgeous, I never knew you could sing like that, shall I make us a cup of tea?"

Mitzi left them to put the kettle on and conclude their business.

By the time Melissa's pea green Punto roared into the main car park, Gaspard had said his goodbyes to Igor and was accelerating towards Fropsham. The morning had been blissful, easily the best in years. Igor understood the situation entirely. He may or may not have to audition for Sir Colin Davis, but until then, steady as you go. Gaspard would arrange a singing teacher to expand his vocal cavities and encourage him to project a bit more. The scene dock was acoustically ideal for that sort thing. Costume fittings would come later.

Melissa checked her eye make-up in the mirror and sent a fine spray of perfume across her neck. Igor could start right there as far as she was concerned, he had said it was beautiful. They had agreed to meet on the second floor which seemed to be the level where people took least notice of each other. Igor was a common site on all the floors and his comings and goings were just part and parcel of what went on. He would often chat with casual visitors or company reps whilst taking coffee on a four-up table. That was where he joined Melissa.

"Would you like a sticky bun with your coffee?" he enquired, tilting the pot and engaging her with his brilliant blue eyes. He thought she looked the perfect English Rose, such a pale delicate neck. Being mindful of later she chose to decline.

"No thank you, I don't want to lose my figure again, it's taken rather a lot of work to bring it up to standard."

"You certainly set yourself high standards," he replied, not being ashamed to let his eyes undress her admiringly. Melissa basked in his gaze. She thought he was looking particularly radiant that morning and said so.

"You seem excited about something, tell me."
Igor smiled and regaled her with his story. She could see that he was consumed with enthusiasm. He was becoming very sexy.

"So, there you have it, I am a Russian about to become a Trojan warrior."

"That's wonderful Igor, but you must keep in shape, no eating chips."

He gave her a long suggestive gaze, "my appetite is for other things, that is how I keep my shape."

By mutual consent they finished their coffee and Igor led the way downstairs and across the floor towards the basement. His bedroom was not very large but that only increased the feeling of intimacy as they lay side by side on the double bed.

He kissed her neck and slid his hands down her back, seeking to find a means of opening. They undressed until they were almost naked and then slid coyly under the duvet. Igor dimmed the lights with a remote control and then turned to meet her embrace. Soon their passion rose and as he tore her remaining garments off, her mouth fell upon his chest and she marvelled at the unblemished smoothness of his skin. He had a chest like a warrior's shield and she wanted to pour oil all over him and mount him as if she were astride the Trojan Horse. Her hands slid downward across his taut abdomen and she felt him rise to greet her. Wet with anticipation she kicked the duvet off the bed and flipped herself on top of him. He was enormous. A truly Olympian dick. She was about to position him for entry and then froze. It wasn't a dick she had got herself on top of, it was a bloody great dildo! In a frenzied mixture of incredulity, frustration and anger, she tore it aside and there beneath it was a vagina. She gasped, and groaned and screamed all at the same time.

"Oh my God!"

She tried to leap out of the bed but he grabbed her.

"Stay with me Melissa, stay with me!"

"I can't, I can't, you're a woman!"

"I know, but I want to be a man, I'm still waiting for the operation."

"God, this in unbelievable."

"Stay with me," he grabbed the dildo and began to re-fasten it, "this is merely a temporary measure."

Freed from his grasp, Melissa seized her opportunity and jumped off the bed and grabbed her clothes and ran for the door. But it was locked.

"Open this door immediately" she screamed.

"Try to understand Melissa, I want you as a man."

"You sick bastard, where's the remote control?"

It was on the bedside and they both made a lunge for it simultaneously. Melissa got there first. She stabbed at the buttons madly, her panic rising. The door lock clicked and she raced towards freedom. Igor was now in tears and demonstrably upset.

"Please Melissa, please, this is a transitional period, I still have needs, I still have feelings."

"Fuck off you pervert!"

And with that, Melissa flung the remote control on the floor where it landed on a button that activated the bed.

Igor attempted to leap aside but the spring mechanism was too powerful and quick. It snapped shut against the wall and he disappeared inside, splayed flat like a cartoon sandwich.

A hand, a dick and a receding figure.

32

Ian drove along Fropsham High Street trying to find a place to park near Dunkerbell's. It was a lost cause. There were restrictions everywhere and those who sought to flout them were whipped into place by a small but highly organised team of traffic wardens. They were polite and efficient and ruthless. Ian had no wish to tangle with them. He was about to ease himself back into the flow of traffic again, having realised that his front bumper was at least two hundred centimetres into the Blind Dog Owner's Trolley Cart Parking Only bay, when he spotted Anita crossing the road ahead. She was incredibly agile and could sprint and turn like a big cat. As a courier parcels delivery truck tried to upstage her, she leapt six feet in the air and spread-eagled her legs in a ballerina's split. When she was level with the cab, she yelled out wanker and tossed off her hand in mid air. Ian drew close but did not sound his horn for fear of drawing too much attention. There was enough of it as it was.

"Anita," he said, projecting his voice through the car window, "would you like to get in?"

She recognised him immediately, "oh wow · great timing – don't stop – keep moving – I'm gonna leap in – NOW!"

She slid into the passenger seat beside him and slammed the door, he was still only doing twenty miles and hour. Her face was a picture of fun and joy.

"Hey how yer doin?"

"Rather busy at the moment and things have been tending to oscillate between demanding and impossible."

"I know how you feel, what if the guy driving that truck had slipped on the steering wheel, I could be dead, Jesus there are so many prick drivers in this country where do they all come from?"

Ian wondered whether it would be appropriate to suggest the sink housing estates that were attached to Fropsham like an umbilical chord when he recalled that his stepfather had demolished a bollard near Sainsbury's in his Rolls and somehow managed to successfully sue them for insufficient safety notices. He remained one of their best customers and yet Ian couldn't help thinking that in every other sense he was a prick driver too.

"Driving standards are becoming more European every day."

"Talk to me about it. In Paris if you're lying bleeding on the roadway they blast their horns because they just want you to get the fuck out of it and in North Africa, y'know places like Nabeul and Hadjeb El Aïoun, I've actually had a police car spit at me."

"Were you breaking the law?"

"Well I certainly wasn't calling them wankers, but I mean really, when you're inside Russia, yeah maybe I give them a bit of cheek because we both know we're pulling the punters for what we can get, but in a foreign country and especially if there's some lunatic dictator running the show, no way José. Anyway, where are we going? Obviously Dunkerbell's is a miss, we passed it fifty metres back and there wasn't enough space for a brick and with all the road signs you got in this country it looks like you've gotta quote your table number before they'll even consider putting you on the list."

Ian hadn't a clue where he was going or what he was doing meeting Anita in the first place. Melissa had now insisted that they sleep in separate bedrooms until his eczema cleared up and since his Doctor had told him that it was stress related the prognosis for a nuptial reawakening looked bleak.

He reckoned that Anita was too much of an odd-ball to be really interested in him and she was probably just trying to be helpful by giving him a jar of Kool, or whatever it was. He needed to find somewhere that would allow maximum anonymity without costing an arm and a leg. For no particular reason, the ground floor bar of Tzarbinski's popped into his imagination, so he suggested it and she agreed.

"Great, hit the gas and let's go for it."

They eventually cleared the local melee and drew speed along a dual carriageway. As they approached a roundabout a pea-green Punto tore across in front of them and struck the central reservation's concrete kerb. The front tyre blew out and the vehicle spun wildly through three complete circles, eventually coming to a halt facing backwards on the wrong side of a feeder entry.

"My God, that was Melissa!" exclaimed Ian.

"You any good with first aid?" said Anita, "or do we call up the paramedics?"

He pulled along side her and they both leapt out. The seat belt had saved her from fatal injury but unable to speak, she was clearly in a state of extreme shock. What he could not understand was why her bra and knickers were on the dashboard and she was naked except for a petticoat.

"Maybe her car heater's jammed?" said Anita helpfully, "the electrics on some Italian cars can still be a bit dodgy, nevertheless, from what I know of her, which isn't much, I reckon she was in some kind of emotional trauma before she got in the car and judging by the look in her eyes she's probably been raped."

The thought of an enforced sexual act on his wife, who only recently had banned him from her bedroom, was not a concept that Ian could mentally grasp at that precise moment.

He could see that Melissa was in need of urgent hospitalisation and borrowed Anita's mobile to make the call.

The ambulance arrived in twenty minutes during which time they did their best to keep Melissa warm and comfort her. But she was a blank. She had become as pale as a statue and without a flicker of emotion. In the hospital Ian telephoned Freddie to apologise for his extended lunch hour.

"I got your note explaining your reasons for leaving," said Freddie politely, "and I'm very sorry to hear of this afternoon's development, please take however long you need to sort matters out and we can reconvene this conversation at an appropriate moment."

"He was very understanding," said Ian, "I can have as much time off as I want."

"That's great, see, everything works out fine in the end provided you just keeping pushing for that little bit more," said Anita, "okay, I don't mean to be insensitive to Melissa's condition but if you only look back as far as you were when we said hello in the car, you can see how far you've come already. No work stress! Pretty good. Okay so now we spend some time together, if you want. I'm not saying forget Melissa I'm just saying hello from me, with no strings attached. That's the deal. "

Ian looked around him and considered her offer of friendship to be an acceptable one. Yes, he knew he would need help. He needed help on just about every level of his daily life with the possible exception of strato-ionic mathematics. She was the only one around and thank goodness for that. Already he could see that the events of the past hour or so had caused a radical change to his normal routine and there was no knowing what might happen as the days unfolded before them. Already he had mentally included her in his life but typically, had forgotten to tell her.

"Hello Anita, what shall we do next?"

"Let's grab a cup of coffee from that vending machine and see how long it takes a Doctor to get back to us. My guess is she's in a coma and they'll keep her in overnight while they do some more tests or something."

Not being able to think of anything better he walked with her to the vending machine and they started to amalgamate their cash.

Igor was barely able to fight his way out from behind the bed. He had to summon the strength to pull himself into a ball and then push with his back to the wall and both legs forcing the bed out in front of him. At one point he thought he was going to suffocate and nearly passed out, but he was physically fit, (although, in his mind's eye, the wrong physical shape) and eventually collapsed half on the bed and half on the floor.

He lay there wondering why his life was in such a mess. It wasn't his fault that in the eyes of the world he had yet to become a man. As far as he was concerned he had been one for as long as his wakening conscience was there to remind him. But nobody could possibly imagine the degree of torment he suffered. He had been putting on a brave face for almost twenty-six years now, trying not to let his inner turmoil take over. When Boris offered him the job he had jumped aboard without hesitation. It meant subjugating his acting talents in the performing sense, but in return, the chance to forge a new identity and find a sympathetic surgeon. Now the genie was out of the lamp. He had been called a pervert and a sick bastard by the very one he had so desperately sought to love. His public humiliation would inevitably follow and would probably cost him his job. Boris was a compassionate man on some occasions but he did not like to attract the wrong kind of attention unless he could control it. What had happened in this bedroom was between Igor and his God. But he did not have one.

He was spiralling downwards towards a place where naiads and fauns had boyfriends called trolls and the nebelungs danced with the frogs. He was a woman who wanted to be a man.

He was halfway there but until his genitalia had been altered he remained in no-man's land and he did not know how much more he could take of it.

203

33

The Yum Bum was now becoming a successful business and Cedric was hoovering up the spin-off trade in buckets. Due to a generous amount of PR footwork, willingly given by the Haystack actors who had become fantastic sales reps because they used Kool themselves every day and knew what it could do to one's general feeling of well-being and togetherness, actual over the counter sales of Kool at Effie's Cascade flower shop were surprisingly buoyant. Even Dale did a stint behind the counter but it was generally agreed that his talents lay elsewhere in the care and maintenance of the Yum Bum and its surroundings.

Roz was so closely connected to the Yum Bum and now so hopelessly in love with Dale that she would spend every spare minute she could either in the shop or helping him harvest the Yum Bum's gel. A few of the cast passed bitchy remarks but they were politely advised by most others to talk it through directly with Roz and preferably underneath the Yum Bum tree. Whether or not a situation like this was the origin of the Yum Bum pavilion's success as a tea house, we may never know, but Dale's magnificent construction in Finnish pine was beginning to worry Dunkerbell's who feared that if it opened during the weekdays it would probably eclipse their own business. It was actually Anita who suggested the commercial opportunity to Effie and even volunteered herself to be its first manager provided somebody else did the paperwork. Effie said give it a go and on the first Saturday it opened, she knew she had a success.

Very prudently, Effie kept her plans to extend the opening hours beyond Saturday mornings, to herself. Equally astute was her decision not to allow members of the public to use the Yum Bum's staircase. She wanted them to admire the Yum Bum in the vast perspective of the Seventh Cavalry area but not pinch its gel. The supply lines of Kool had to be protected. Being the general public they simply ignored the traffic cone Dale had placed in the middle of the stairs and he often had to escort them down again. He began to get a bit fed up with that so he built a wooden arch in the Kwai style and hung a door with widely spaced vertical bars so that you could easily see beyond them to the fronds above. It also had a sturdy lock and a wooden notice made from Japanese Maple that said: NO ENTRY. KOOL FARM. (Trained Foresters Only)

There had been considerable discussion with Norman, the local Equity rep, about what he termed 'a flagrantly restrictive practise that flies in the face of the splendid PR that my fellow members have given the venture free of all professional charges'. When Dale realised he had completely overlooked their access rights he had a chat with Norman and they came to an immediate agreement. Although Dale would not say so himself, he was rather proud of his super-VIP walkway running behind the balcony on top of the pavilion roof. It had a neat staircase leading up to it and when Norman followed Dale up and out across the roof, with its superb view of the general public en mass below, he knew the actors would love it.

"No skin off my nose if they wanna come this way," said Dale cheerily, "I built it to be used so I'd be 'appy to see 'em use it like. In fact I'd welcome an extra 'and filling up them jars of Kool, the ol' Yum Bum's producing sap like syrup running down a gutter."

Norman skidaddled back to the actor's green room to tell them the news and receive their further instructions. Before very long, a Yum Bum harvesting rota that embraced the entire Haystack Theatre Company had been drawn up.

In exchange for an hours's work under the attentive supervision of Dale, 'Koolers', as they were now referred to, would receive one free pot of Kool a week. Norman did not think he would be able to get that written into their contracts just yet.

Dale had noticed that the Yum Bum seemed to be at its best at sunrise. It was as if it awoke fresh every morning after a deep relaxing sleep and had to release the sap it had accumulated overnight. Like taking a slow motion piss, as Dale so eloquently put it. Koolers who took the sunrise slot received two free jars a week. When Roz let it slip that a full jar, when agitated vigorously under a hot tap, produced a truly transcendental soaky bath trip, it became a hotly contested hour.

As time went by, the Haystack Theatre Company developed into a Yum Bum culture. This was typified by a generally courteous way of going about one's daily activities and when challenged to lose one's rag, to be able to see the other person's point of view, clearly and profoundly. Needless to say this made for a fair old bit of dynamic but there was an exhilaration about the place that set everyone buzzing. Great ideas, great zeal in the face of adversity, people who would hold your hand if you openly wept and those who would openly applaud you if you won. So many people, so many endeavours. That was the culture of the Yum Bum. As sales of Kool continued rising, it started to spread. An ambience of loving kindness was everywhere. Well almost.

The only person out of step was Gaspard. Fired by love of Igor and the forthcoming production of Les Troyens, he had somehow managed to completely by pass the Yum Bum culture and conducted himself in a remote and critical manner. Effie had become pissed off with his endless carping and as soon as she heard from Boris that he actually was going ahead with Les Troyens provided he could get Sir Colin and the LSO on board, she manoeurvred her weakest staff into position and handed them over to him. Gaspard was delighted. Twenty servants at his disposal. He could ask for no more.

"Sally, would you be so kind as to rinse my paint brushes in warm soapy water and let me have them back with their bristles wrapped in kitchen towel."

"Why, shouldn't someone else be doing that?"

And so it continued until he simply ignored her and pretended she did not exist. He was no longer on the plane that dealt with human interaction. He was creating one of his own and he was going to fly in it. A new theatre would be built. There would be grandeur and spectacle. An immense operatic drama that would catapault him to international stardom. He would design the agenda for the world to live in and he and Igor would become lovers fêted on the world celebrity circuit. But there were other forces about him that were not part of that agenda.

Gloria parked her car two bays down from Rodney's in a shabby side road not far from Victoria station. Each time they slept together they both used different cars. But it was not enough to fool Reginald Ponsonby-Spratt. His intelligence, as in the context of spying was incredible, and there weren't many people in the Establishment, from politicians to the judiciary, whose size, colour and shape of their excreta remained unknown to him. His use of Ian Trubshaw was merely an operational necessity. Nobody else could understand strato-ionic mathematics and without it, Operation Cassandra was a mystery.

The Sprout knew he was facially repulsive but it did not stop Gloria Fitzbagley from giving him the odd jump now and again which he very much enjoyed. But she was leaking secrets all over the place with her louche behaviour and it had to stop. He decided that a direct confrontation was the only course of action. He would not bother with photographs or blackmail, he would simply make his presence known to all parties present and that would be sufficient to sort matters out. The last thing he wanted was for some over-zealous agent to go barnstorming into Freddie's Rio office while Blodvrinsky was funding the entire project.

Of course Project Cassandra was the work of a madman, but that's why they wanted it. No other nation's scientist could have flipped their lid to the extent that Freddie Bannister had, and as such, his work was the ultimate deterrent. But far too hot for Her Majesty's government to handle directly (not that that was any of Gloria's business). Underground it would have to go, and there they were, all nicely set up, and then these two fornicators had started to wreck it with their incompetence.

He watched Gloria enter an inconspicuous side entrance and waited for about twenty minutes before entering the same building. It was a knocking shop as well he knew and it didn't take him long to find out which bedroom she was in.

He gave the door a massive straight leg kick which sheared the handle shaft and sent the entire door and its hinges flat on the floor. Rodney was on top of her and he had a spotty back. He lept off her and dived frantically for his pistol under the pillow but could only find a packet of condoms.

She swung her legs together and sat up in bed, defiant and glowering.

"Reggie, you bastard," she said.

"I think I have made sufficient statement," he said, and then turned and walked out.

"How the hell did he know we were here?" snapped Rodney, still shielding his penis.

"I don't know. Who besides our PA's know where we are?"

"Nobody."

"Wrong, somebody does, and I intend to find out, now pass the tissues and stop waving your dick about."

If that was Rodney's idea of constructive assistance she would seriously have to reconsider her position. Coitus interruptus was one thing but sperm in her perm was unacceptable behaviour.

She knew that The Sprout was going to freeze MI5 out and also that he was capable of doing it. Rodney had no idea what they were up against and with Blodvrinsky involved it was fast becoming the intelligence gathering operation from hell.

There would be no support from above and the newshounds would feast on an orgy of discarded entrails.

She wondered whether there was anybody in the House of Lords who could help her?

34

Melissa was now in a private mental hospital. The NHS had done their best and the pressure on beds was simply too much for the Registrar to argue that a physically fit young woman with a supportive husband in secure employment and with no mortgage arrears should remain there. Since her arrival, the only word she had uttered was dick, which was somewhat disconcerting. She was too far gone for a place on the Care in the Community programme and would probably have to be force fed if there was no change in her current condition. Ian had been looking after Sebastian, with the help of Anita who, it was noted, spent a lot of time with him. Muriel, his mother, was somewhat ambivalent about the liaison, however, when Ian told her that The Sprout was offering to pay for Melissa's treatment and award him two incremental salary steps if he returned to work forthwith, she urged him to accept. And he did. It was a significant change of routine, but with Anita now looking after Sebastian and taking care of the house, the rhythm of his life began to change. Naturally, he visited Melissa as often as he could although he had to admit that he was finding her monosyllabic utterance rather tedious. Anita suggested that he drop his trousers and pants in front of her to see if it elicited any reaction but the psychiatrist said it was making too many assumptions about the root cause of her restricted vocabulary, and in any case it would be advisable if such actions were left to professionals like himself.

So, Ian and Anita became something of an item and both were to be seen with little baby Sebastian, every Saturday morning in the Yum Bum pavilion, or Kool Farm House as it had become generally known. Svetlana was employed in the kitchen and also waited on the tables when things got pushed. Surprisingly, quite a few of the Haystack actors offered to help out with odd tasks when they were not fortunate enough to be playing big roles. There was a feeling of what goes round comes round sort of thing and everyone seemed very happy to lend a helping hand no matter what. Svetlana's English noticeably improved and she became as popular as Anita for the very same reasons; she was confident, natural and up front. In fact the Kool Farm became something of a Pryshnyi family affair because Dimitri also put in regular appearances and enjoyed nothing more than sitting in the corner, puffing on his Gaulloise and sucking the froth off his cappuccino elite through a bendy straw. He was a hands-on man too and once cleared the toilet when somebody tried to shoot the contents or their prawn vindaloo and Old Wallop down the pan and missed. Effie and Boris paid occasional visits too and sometimes Loretta was there and nearly always attracted attention.

The cabaret was now coming along a treat and the production team were buzzing up to here with their progress. Kool Kat, as the cabaret was now to be called, featured Anita in the title role with Loretta taking the star place as a vocal commentator on the unfolding tale. The story itself, and indeed it was a story and not a series of quick unrelated vaudeville sketches, as Patrick O'Quinn the Haystack's resident writer was quick to point out, explored the depths of blues anguish to reveal the raw pain of human existence and the transient pleasures that some attain.

This gave every opportunity for Loretta to plumb the depths of the blues repertoire and go beyond the golden oldies. For sure there were a few of the undisputed classics like The Man I Love, and Until the Real Thing Comes Along which Loretta was particularly fond of, but apart from that, it was gloves off and into the arena. Loretta also did this other number called The Rags on Scott Joplin, which was basically a hickory beat jangle to which Anita would strip in bow tie and spats.

They discussed the end of the Joplin number one Saturday morning while taking a break in the Kool Farm House.

"What about my G-string, should I keep it on or off?" asked Anita.

"Take it off, but see if you can do a quick swap with one of your spats," said Loretta.

"You mean cover my fanny with a spat?"

"Yeah, why not, pussy spat?"

And they fell about laughing.

At the same time, Ian was giving Sebastian his bottle in the kitchen and trying to explain to Dale the meaning of strato-ionic mathematics.

"I understand 'ow you got to twenty-five like but you lost me on the bit abart three thousand in a single moment of time," said Dale.

"Yes, it's a difficult one that because it effectively means that you have bought yourself to a total and absolute standstill before deciding whether you want to select a series of projected results that could take you from one extreme to the other."

"Yeah, well life round 'ere can be pretty extreme at times but I s'pose it's all down to 'ow you go about treating one another like, or is that what you're talking about?"

"Ultimately, yes."

"That's good innit? We was on the same wavelength there. 'Ere watch out, Sebastian's dribbling, d'you wanna kitchen towel?"

Gaspard, on the other hand, did not frequent the Kool Farm cafeteria as he preferred to call it, because he found it vulgar and populist. That was until Dale asked Lotte Polanski to design a bar top that would seat fifty people in a curving line and she had delivered and he had built it and it was a hit in its own right. Until then, Gaspard was seldom seen outside the Les Troyens production office and when his interest in the Haystack repertoire diminished entirely, Lotte was engaged by Effie to take over his position as in-house stage designer and she occupied Gaspard's now deserted office in the scene dock.

Lotte leapt at the opportunity like a pike on a tight line and her sets were dazzling. Dale led a three man team of carpenters and Dimitri supervised the supply of timber through Frank Files' new warehouse in Aldershot. When Gaspard summoned Lotte to his office (an action that members of his production team referred to as, going up the wall of Troy) she failed to appear. Phone messages were left in the Kool Kat production office where she was also busy with her responsibilities as stage designer and lighting consultant but to no avail. Eventually, Gaspard forced himself to take a morning coffee one Saturday sitting in the Kool Farm.

Lotte came to see him at the table with a huge artist's folder under her arm. It was tied with pink linen ribbons and looked like a giant solicitor's brief. Just as she pushed it across the table, somebody yelled to her that Loretta's costumiers were on the phone and could she take it?

"Yes of course, give me ten seconds, listen Gaspard, I got to go now, please look at these, they are my costume designs for Les Troyens let's talk about it later."

She was gone before he could even think of a reply and since no one appeared to be taking any notice of him, he unslipped the bow ties and looked at them. They were magnificent. He could not fault them. They practically smelt of Greek Tragedy. The costume for Aeneas sent his mind spinning. He must show it to Igor at once, it might cheer him up. He did not know why, but ever since his audition, Igor had become strangely withdrawn and quiet. When Gaspard rang him to inform him that he had found a suitable singing teacher he commented no further than to say that was nice. He seemed to be avoiding him and that made him feel rather apprehensive. After all, if the producer and principal tenor couldn't hit it off, what hope was there for the rest of them?

As he began to mull over the stages of their relationship, if only to gain some insight into where it was now, he became aware of a handsome woman with a beguiling perfume slipping into the chair opposite him. It was Gloria Fitzbagley.

"Good morning Gaspard, I have your cheque."

Gaspard didn't flinch an inch. Well, four centimetres, maybe.

"How much for?"

"Four thousand, one hundred and sixty four pounds and two pence."

"Thank you."

She took it out of her handbag and slid it across the table.

"There's one or two things I'd like to talk to you about."

His eyes sped round the room. Nearly all the tables were full and the air was vibrant with chattering. Perhaps they would be less conspicuous if they stayed put.

"Well, that is your privilege to do so," he said.

"Thank you, it's nice of you to say so."

They eyed each other up. She knew that Rodney hated his guts because he feared his intellect. The fact that Gaspard was a homosexual probably disoriented him a bit too. There were some straight men, and Rodney was one of them, who felt uncomfortable in the presence of gays. She had no such problem. The fact was, she could no longer rely on Rodney to feed her with information concerning Project Cassandra. Reggie had messed that one up for her and he was using his relationship with the Defence Minister to freeze her out. She had to take the initiative if she was to win and for better or for worse, that initiative was now sitting right opposite her with an expression on his face that seemed to imply that someone had just farted.

She noticed the huge folder on the table with its loosened tassels and a plain white sticker that said: Les Troyens. She stirred her coffee, gathered her senses, and smiled as normally as she could. She knew many men were attracted to her handsomeness and consequently she adopted a vaguely butch-gent kind of attire. She didn't know why, it was just part of her nature to indulge in subtle flirting.

"These look interesting," she said, "are they yours?"

"Yes," replied Gaspard, "I am designing for Les Troyens."

214

"Gosh, how wonderful, I love Berlioz."

"Oh really, I find that most commendable, would you like to see them?"

"Ooh yes please, I'd love too."

Gaspard proceeded to position the folder as Gloria yelled gotcha inwardly to herself. It was only because Classic FM had played the Roman Carnival overture that morning and she had picked up some LSO publicity material from the Barbican, that she even knew who Berlioz was. Her preference was J.J.Cale and Sade, and occasionally Johnny Cash when she was alone with a bottle of vin rouge. Also, Tchaikovsky at a pinch; the finale of the Fourth symphony was her favourite. That really got her going.

Now that she had gained an in with Gaspard she would have to accommodate his every nuance until somehow or other he would be in a position to cooperate fully with her. Her aim was to get as close to Freddie Bannister as possible. He was the key to everything. She knew that Bannister's wife Effie was a regular consort to Blodvrinsky and that Bannister himself was occasionally getting his leg over with Blodvrinsky's moll. There was no such thing as a safe route and it looked as if Gaspard would have to be the first step.

She had heard from the Haystack grapevine, via Reggie who was also fond of actors, that Gaspard's nose was currently out of joint. Kool Kat was the hot gossip and he was simply fading into the twilight of his own production office up on the fifth floor. Loretta Regina was too streetwise to fall for any subterfuge although it might be possible for her to somehow latch onto the coterie of admirers that were gradually growing around her. It was a tricky scenario. When she had first lured Reggie into bed, their session had been such fun that he had lain exhausted, supported only by the wrist straps, and told her that some ministerial staff had actually been pushing to have Freddie committed to an asylum and from whence to carry out a covert operation on Project Cassandra. Only he had managed to convince the Minister of the only viable alternative. Project Cassandra was cancelled without the Prime Minister even knowing about its existence in the first place.

She looked at the costume designs in front of her.

"These are remarkable," she said, "they are so bold and heroic," then she noticed Lotte's signature in the corner, and caught Gaspard's eye as she did so. A difficult moment hung in the air as she tried to work a diplomatic way out in case he disagreed with her.

"They are just what I envisaged myself," he said, in a fairly neutral tone, "naturally I gave Lotte Polanski the designer a detailed briefing."

"She certainly seems to have listened carefully."

"That is more than I can say for some other people."

She knew immediately to whom he was referring and decided to bite the bullet.

"Yes, I am now aware of the difficulties you have been facing with the section over the past few months and I wondered if you would care to consider reporting directly and exclusively to me on twice the salary you get here?"

There was a discernible flicker in his eyes before he replied.

"I cannot possibly leave the Haystack Theatre at this present moment."

"Of course not, I'm not even suggesting that you should. I fully understand that the opportunities you need to create often take a great deal of forethought and planning, in that sense we need only liaise when necessary."

"Well, I'm relieved to hear that at long last *somebody* appreciates the complexity of the job."

Gloria was also relieved that she had not stumbled at the first post.

"Perhaps if you could take note of this special number and we could further our conversation in private?"

Gaspard realised that he was being somewhat impolite and took measures to correct that.

"Yes, of course, may I suggest that we adjourn to my personal office, perhaps I might even show you my set designs for Les Troyens?"

"That would be lovely," smiled Gloria and they rose to go.

Just at that moment Dale and Roz squeezed through the throng and approached their table.

216

"Ello Gaspard, I can't 'elp finking I ain't seen you for a bit, wotchoo up to?"

Gaspard was on the threshold with Gloria, he could not avoid introducing her.

"May I introduce Gloria Fitzbagley an associate of mine, this is Dale our chief carpenter and this is Roz a member of the acting company."

"Nice to meet ya, Gloria, I can see you're just leaving, 'ave you got yer jar of Kool yet?"

"Dale, don't be so pushy," said Roz, not everyone has to have one just because they're here."

"That's okay Roz," said Gloria, I know they're popular so I fully intended to slip into the shop before leaving anyway."
Then Gaspard said, "we were just about to commence a business meeting in my production office, Dale."

"Sure no probs, well nice meeting ya Gloria, don't forget yer Kool then, I reckon it would clear that neck rash up a treat."

Roz quickly elbowed Dale into a chair to give Gloria the escape she needed. The four of them said goodbye.

Roz watched Gaspard and Gloria thread their way through the tables.

Somehow, she couldn't help thinking that she'd seen Gloria somewhere before, maybe even on television.

35

Loretta was sitting alongside Freddie at his control console and looking at an image of the world on three enormous screens above their heads. She did not really want to know what it could do beyond what he had already told her. However, she felt that having expressed an on-going interest in Project Cassandra, admittedly as a casual remark when he was massaging her toes in the bath, it would be a bit insensitive not to let him have his day. They had already agreed to skip strato-ionic mathematics and just run with the main thrust of the project. As far as she could ascertain, this meant firing ballistic missiles in defence and attack. To do this properly you had to know what was going on in all sorts of ways. Some agent with a secret satellite dish high in the mountains of Albania would send a signal about Serbian troop movements and Project Cassandra would be updated with a special troop icon. All this sort of stuff was integrated with a mass of launch and tracking data. Estimated hit time and capillary blast reaction countdowns sent a line of figures spinning in several monitor windows and this all linked up with something else that was also going on simultaneously elsewhere and it was like there was nothing possible left to leave out. An all singing all dancing, super hi-tech ballistic missile programme, designed by Freddie to operate in theatre war scenarios encapsulating the full political monty.

"Which was the bit The Sprout objected to?" said Loretta, watching the screen fast zoom from outer space to the Bayswater Road not far from her flat.

"That was to do with using the enemy data to our advantage."

"No kidding, I would've thought that was a bit fundamental to the desired outcome."

"It is, but Cassandra is capable of locating and reading the enemy's launch data and can manipulate it to the extent that it can fool the enemy into believing that it has achieved a direct strike when it hasn't."

"Sounds brilliant to me, so what's his beef?"

"Some peculiar streak to do with being English, I think. The belief that you can beat the hell out of somebody provided that it's all part of playing jolly fine cricket. You know there are quite a few members of the establishment that still feel guilty about the bombing of Dresden."

"Well, my history's a bit shaky but I thought it was a case of one lot kicking the shit out of the other for kicking the shit out of them first."

"But kicking the shit out of somebody is not playing cricket. The idea is to win, and then efficiently log and record the victory, but not to destroy."

Loretta shrugged her shoulders. It didn't matter anyway because Freddie was steaming full ahead regardless. The potential for human destruction was chilling but Freddie said the sophistication would serve the nature of defence as equally as attack. What Freddie had not explained to her was the Ergonomic Psychology factor. He sensed that her wish for information was driven more out of courtesy than real need. He was determined that nobody should understand Cassandra's real sting until it was fully operational and being built and sold to every regime, corrupt or otherwise, in the world. It would be too late then to hang anything on him.

"So when d'you get to fire this thing?" she asked.

219

"It's up to Boris to find a launch test site, which, for obvious reasons cannot be within mainland UK"

"Shame, I've never seen a rocket close-up before"
Freddie looked at her in a quizzical, almost school masterish sort of way.

"Perhaps you'd better come this way."

She followed him and they made their way out of the main operations and research centre and along the corridor towards the back of the main warehouse. There was a steel gantry, open and exposed that ran like a catwalk from the back of the main warehouse to the smaller one behind it.

"What the hell's that?" said Loretta, pointing at Svetlana's dog arena, with its wooden palettes stacked in levels like a Roman amphitheatre.

"I am told that it is a temporary rehearsal room for the Haystack Trojans until the new auditorium gets built," said Freddie, not showing any signs of interest and continuing to walk on ahead.

"Well it's nice to know that somebody on that production team has actually got their arse in gear and done something constructive," she replied.

They continued walking in the gloom until Freddie reached the far end and opened a steel door using a switch card to clear security. A raised hit-button on the left of the wall lit a corridor that was almost, in its totality, one long descending flight of steps. There were a couple of breathing places, so to speak, no more than six foot squares of landing really, and the entire staircase was a fair old hike. Freddie turned right at the first landing and stood in front of yet another heavy steel door that was painted deep green as opposed to the battleship grey everywhere else. Another switch card action and they walked through the doorway and stood on a steel gantry platform about twenty metres above floor level. Loretta grabbed for the handrail as Freddie slammed on the flood lights.

There in front of her, mounted on a twenty-four-wheel articulated low-loader, was a long, slim, stainless steel rocket. It was the most awe-inspiring sight she had ever seen. She couldn't work out its dimensions but common sense told her it was huge. The transporter on which it rested in a sort of giant cradle was easily as wide as two buses and as long as six of them. All the stuff she had ever seen on Star Trek and in the sci-fi magazines always seemed to favour a proliferation of things grafted onto the outside but Freddie's rocket was completely clean. It was as unencumbered as a silver bullet. She had no point of reference other than her own experience and on that count she thought it was beautiful, chilling and unique.

"Jesus Christ, Freddie, I didn't know you'd got this far!"

"Well, Boris has been simply superb with the resources as indeed you assured me would be the case," he said.

"Is this ready for take off?" she said, still holding the handrail and watching fascinated as the arc lights bounced off its mirror surface.

"Yes," said Freddie matter-of-factly, "but I still have to conduct actual flight tests and I'm waiting on Boris to let me know when he has made the necessary arrangements."

Loretta gazed at the rocket for a few more minutes and then looked at Freddie for the first time since they had stepped into the hangar. No wonder he was so quiet and thoughtful with all this sort of thing bouncing around in his head. In bed she had found a human button that released him and in so doing, and to her utter amazement, had released something in her too. In the face of what must have been incredible disappointment he had struck lucky and found a way to realise his dream. Years of research followed by public humiliation and ridicule had not stopped him from carrying on regardless. She was striking out too, but in a different way. Drive and guts came into the equation somewhere and maybe Freddie was X and she was Y? Likely as not, they would both be going places this year.

"Freddie, I think your rocket is the most beautiful thing I have ever seen, apart from the Yum Bum tree which is totally different."

Freddie tried to understand her use of the word beautiful in the context of his rocket and concluded that the aesthetic aspect of Project Cassandra must have been something to emerge from his sub-conscious. It was true that he had created a computed-aided design of the body shell with all the relevant stresses and strains calculated and the dimensions extrapolated therefrom but that was as far as it went. As for any comparison with the Yum Bum, well, he had heard about it incessantly, almost ad nauseam from Effie and yet he just hadn't got round to seeing it. It was a question of priorities. If it really had grown into a rooted tree the full height of the Haystack building (and there were so many exaggerations flying around) then it would probably have a life span of at least thirty to fifty years and possible more, whereas Cassandra would become dead and buried in a vastly shorter period of time. He would visit the Yum Bum after Cassandra's first successful live launch.

"Shall we return?" he said.

"Yeah, let's go to bed."

Freddie shut down the lights and they turned through the doorway and made their way back up the long flight of stairs. Freddie opened the door at the top. It was dark in the adjoining warehouse save for the eerie glow of the emergency exits lights down below. Freddie produced a small pocket torch and shone it behind him like a cinema usherette. Loretta followed in its dim ring of yellowy light. The catwalk seemed longer going back and because it was so dark and high up she couldn't fathom how far they had to go to reach the other side. The only sound was the subdued thudding of their feet on the metal grid-irons. And then came the scream.

It was a long, agonised, hideous shriek. A human reaction to some terrible pain. Freddie and Loretta stopped immediately,

"What was that?" gasped Loretta.

"I'm not entirely sure," said Freddie, "but it came from down there, quick, follow me, I know the way."

They raced down another flight of factory style stairs and emerged breathless and agitated at the entrance to the arena.

Freddie swung the light switch down and the arena was flooded with light. There in the centre was a naked body slumped half upright in a pool of blood. They ran towards it and stopped short when they realised who it was. Seated on the floor, legs wide apart, was Igor Tzarbinski with a Trojan sword thrust deep into his genitalia. The wound was so

222

horrific and the blood loss so great that it was impossible to see that he had attempted to slice open his vagina. Freddie and Anita exchanged frantic glances. They knew that to call an ambulance meant involving the police and that was not an option.

In desperation, Loretta grabbed her mobile and rang Boris.

36

Boris took care of everything. Igor's body was whisked away and nobody in authority, or anyone else for that matter save Loretta and Freddie, knew anything about it. The word was put about that Igor's mother had died unexpectedly and he would return from Moscow in the fullness of time. Breaking the true news to Gaspard was not going to be easy because everyone knew how infatuated with Igor he was. It naturally fell to Boris to undertake the task. He invited Gaspard to join him for lemon pepper biscuits, vodka and iced tea in South Kensington one Sunday morning.

Gaspard welcomed the invitation for many reasons, not the least being that he would demand to know when work on building the enlarged stage and auditorium would commence and could he please have a set of architect's drawings in order that he may design Les Troyens as an actuality rather than an illusion. Boris welcomed the meeting too. He needed to put Gaspard right on a number of operational matters particularly the one concerning Gloria Fitzbagley. He would remind Gaspard of his special status within Blodvrinsky International Artists, and that a formal contract would be offered following an appropriate staff appraisal at the end of the probationary period due to expire in six months time. The Agency was nothing if not generous. The point he had to get across was that laying a false trail for the British Government took priority over Les Troyens. He wasn't calling it off, but he was talking reciprocal action here. Gloria was the best feed-in he had and he didn't want any cock-ups. Gaspard would have to understand that although the truth of Igor's death genuinely shocked him too, it did not mean that he could tolerate sodden tissues for ever and a day. Igor had left a suicide note which simply said, 'tell Gaspard the truth'. So that's just what Boris did.

"I had no idea he was a woman," he said to Gaspard, who was still white as a sheet after Boris had given it to him cold turkey about five minutes ago, "to me he was always a man.
I met him as one and he behaved as one. It's tragic I know, but what can I do about it? Nothing."

"You might have let me see the body before sending it to Russia," said Gaspard, "all you have left me with is a tormented memory."

"You gotta understand Gaspard, there are a number of very important issues at stake here, I'm talking global and I'm talking politics. Project Cassandra is about to leave the country and I've gotta make that happen in secret. Having to explain a dead body to the police while asking them to look the other way while I move a rocket, is pushing it a bit."

But Gaspard was in floods of tears again and it was a full half hour before he had properly gained his composure. Boris summoned Dimitri who had driven him up from Fropsham. Now it was time to return before the entire apartment ended up looking like a Kleenex paper chase.

As they climbed into the Bentley, Dimitri couldn't help noticing a fundamental change in the man. On the way there he had behaved almost imperiously and yet now, slumped in the back seat, all he said was 'put this on' and passed him a CD pack. Dimitri did as he was asked without comment because he could see how upset Gaspard was. The music lasted all the way from Kensington Gore to Fropsham High Street and there was enough of it to keep on going afterwards.

Dimitri found it rather scary and concluded that the guy who pressed the disc must've been a nutter. When Gaspard got out of the car he handed him back the discs.

"Which group's that?" he asked.

"Berlioz," said Gaspard flatly, and disappeared into the theatre.

At three o'clock on a Sunday afternoon, it was deserted. He did not retreat to his production office but went instead to the scene dock where he slumped dejectedly on a bench and took stock of all around him. Lotte's influence was everywhere and so was the scenery for Kool Kat. It dominated the area with its loud, vulgar, garish, brash, flash, exhibitionist display of ill considered gut reaction to the tools of the trade. The whole conception seemed to mock and deride him with a kind of up yours and in your face attitude. Les Troyens was no more than a promise from Boris. And an empty one at that. Igor was dead, Aeneas was dead, and so too was his dream of fame and success.

With a feeling of total isolation he wandered through the scene dock with all its apparitions glinting and sparkling until he arrived at the Yum Bum. He knew that things could go no farther. There in front of him was a plant that he had observed with his own eyes that had sprung into raucous life in a manner that was almost human. It had completely dominated everyone and everything around it and was practically becoming a place of pilgrimage. It had stolen Dale from him too. Ever since the day it self-rooted Dale had spent all his energies renovating the floors, building a staircase and erecting a highly idiosyncratic entrance house, or villa, or pavilion or whatever it was that everyone called it. He had not even come back to him with his thoughts on the construction of the Trojan Horse. Clearly, he was not interested. His energy, and he certainly had some, was being dissipated by his relationship with Roslyn combined with that disgustingly unbridled commercial enterprise with the stupidly simplistic name of Kool. Back in the days of their quick little chats, Dale had told him that when Effie had set up a group of creatives to choose a name, he had suggested Yum Bum Cream but everyone said that was too obvious or misleading. Either way

226

he still thought his name was quite good but wasn't going to create havoc by sulking and would prefer just to get on with it.

Gaspard noted that Dale never seemed to have any problems in getting started on anything. It was as if he were permanently plugged into the national grid and when the right switch was flicked he was off and away. Well, two could play at that game. He Gaspard de la Grant was about lay a veritable cape of in-put. A right royal hunt and storm.

He strode quickly to a corner of the scene dock which was set aside as an armoury and selected a huge, heavy mediaeval axe, the type that could cut a man in half or fell an oak tree. Then he strode back to the centre of the building and looked down to the Seventh Cavalry area and then upwards towards the lighthouse which he had still not experienced due to his fear of heights. Standing there in front of the Yum Bum he savoured his moment of revenge.

Taking full advantage of his height and with an immense swing, he plunged the full force of the axe blade into the Yum Bum's trunk. There was an immediate and spectacular reaction. An intense jet of amber coloured sap burst forth like a broken sluice gate on an ocean dam. It tore the axe out of Gaspard's hands and then, engulfing him too, sent him hurtling backwards on a gigantic wave towards the side of the building. Such was the volume and speed of the sap that it reached the wooden slatted sides of the building before him and burst through into the open air carrying him with it. It was at that point that the Yum Bum went public. Not only were the sides blown away like so much firewood, but everything gave way with an incredible bang. It was enough to lance the Sunday afternoon stupor and crowds gathered instantly.

The Villain's Noose emptied immediately including Cedric who hoped that this was not going to be Fropsham's first IRA bomb. The Yum Bum's sap had blown away the entire windmill section of the building but the thick brick walls of the Seventh Cavalry area remained untouched as did the remainder of the theatre itself, including Effie's shop and Dale's flat above it. Now the sap was rising fast and pushing upwards like a big long party balloon to cover its farthest extremities. Not only was it balloon-like in shape but also pneumatic in sound. The pressure required to raise a lake of sap and push it higher than Nelson's column was staggering, as one of Cedric's customers observed somewhat big headedly.

"How do you know how heavy the sticky stuff is?" said somebody.

"How do you know the stuff is sticky?" said another.

"Well, even if it's no heavier than a balloon and not sticky, it started out with enough force to demolish the building, and I'm just wondering whether it's safe to be standing here, I mean what if it bursts?"

Fortunately, Fropsham had its own Fire Station although it had to share its two engines with Farnham. Both were on the scene by the time the sap had reached the top of the lighthouse which, rather amusingly, remained intact. The podgy-fringed thatched roof sat there like a benign blob of soft marzipan beaming at the gathering crowds below. The Yum Bum was now encased within a beautiful, translucent, rubbery sheath that dominated the skyline like a giant golden condom.

As there was no fire, the fire brigade concentrated on rescuing Gaspard who had ended up being deposited at the far side of the shingled car park on top of a silver birch. It was a straightforward ladder job although he was badly shocked by the event and was transferred to an ambulance that had just arrived. The police were on the scene too, only one patrol car and two officers at the moment but they radioed for help immediately.

"Explosive incident at the Haystack theatre and possibility of fatal injuries. Paramedics and one fire appliance in attendance and request immediate back-up for crowd control."
As it became perfectly clear to the Chief Fire Officer that Gaspard was the only serious casualty and there wasn't the merest suspicion of a flame anywhere, he realised that his moment of glory was fast fading. The police had called in more paramedics to treat a dozen or so passers-by who had received slight bruises and the occasional splinter in their head or forearm. His main focus became the building, or at least the bottom half of it.

He drove his fire engine to the opening of the big warehouse doors and walked into the Seventh Cavalry area. The main brick walls looked untouched in every way. He could see no potential hazard unless you included the Yum Bum itself. The Kool Farm House, which he had taken his kids to only yesterday, looked the same as ever, except that it was completely encased in a thick rubber skin about a foot deep, (he made a mental note to call it thirty centimetres when he wrote his report). The entrance and stairway were similarly encapsulated. The rubbery skin around the base was a deep amber whereas the remainder, that soared into the sky, had now changed from its initial gold to a deep lustrous bronze. This magnificent phallus thrust heavenwards, through where the ceiling used to be, to culminate several hundred feet up, with a beautiful deep brown areola and fulsome chocolate nipple. The Yum Bum itself was completely unharmed and perfectly contained within this fantastic translucent condom.

Fearing no immediate danger he called in a team to inspect the remainder of the building which, to their amazement, remained completely intact as far as the ground floor was concerned. Everything above that level had been blown away but in effect that was only the slatted sides of the windmill section. It looked as if the first floor ceiling had somehow been pushed down from above and its remains deposited at the foot of the walls in a kind of haphazard perimeter dump. No fire anywhere, nothing to hose down except a fine spray to settle the dust. He moved closer and noted that there was no feeling of heat anywhere near the Yum Bum's rubbery surface and, since it was possible to see inside the balloon, albeit as if you were wearing a pair of sun glasses, there was nothing to get excited about, apart from the sheer spectacle which was like nothing he had ever experienced before in his entire fire-fighting career.

He pushed his hand into the wall of the Yum Bum. It was rubbery and springy and he could make no impression. There didn't appear to be anyone inside but he had to make sure, so he unclipped his hand axe and tried to make an incision but it simply bounced off. The rest of the team had now joined him and one of them offered him a Stanley knife. It was equally ineffective. The Yum Bum's skin wouldn't yield, or split, or cut, or open in any way, no matter what implement they utilised.

The Chief Fire Officer was about to radio for help when Dale and Roz appeared with one of the policeman. They had been downing the ale in the Villain's Noose and naturally took a personal interest in what was going on.

"I live 'ere, d'you wanna 'and like?" said Dale obligingly.

"I need to isolate the gas and electricity," said the Chief Fire Officer, "but I can't get through this protective skin."

"Well, I'll give it a whirl, if you like."
As recent events were completely outside everyone's experience, nobody saw fit to object. Several of the lads wanted to take a run at it but reckoned it would be just like jumping on a trampoline. They would rather let Dale make a fool of himself and with any luck they might be included in a hot press shot with Roz.

Things were looking pretty horny as Dale approached the Yum Bum and put his hand flat against its skin. It felt like jelly so he turned his hand sideways and gently pushed it in. This time there was no resistance and the skin opened out like two soft deep lips. Dale stepped through the gap and the lips met and resealed after him.

"Ow 'bout that?" he exclaimed, unaware that he had just done something intensely erotic.

"Can you get out again?" said Roz, who found herself blushing.

Dale repeated the action and stepped through a fresh set of lips jubilant and grinning.

"Eezy peezy when you know 'ow, wodjafink?"
They all had a go but to no avail.

Only Dale had the magic touch to enter the Yum Bum.

37

So the situation was like this. Within twenty-four hours of Dale's mind-boggling through-the-rubber-lips-slit-Narnia type act, the national TV and press were there in force and CNN were flying in their correspondent from Ireland. Every hotel and guest house within a ten mile radius of the Yum Bum was taken up by journalists. Cedric tripled his prices immediately and steadied himself for the inevitable local flak. Sod 'em, the Villain's Noose was slap-bang opposite the biggest potential tourist attraction in western Europe and he intended to enjoy his privileged position. Besides, the press drank a lot and needed a publican who treated this basic requirement with as much respect as final edited copy. Cedric secured his supply lines and prepared to be mine host, available for news interviews and well-informed opinion.

The police weren't quite sure what to do about Dale because he had not committed any offence, in fact he even let the gas and electricity guys in to check the supplies for safety and all was intact. Since Dale was the only person who could effect access to and from the Yum Bum, they could see little point in asking him to move elsewhere. They couldn't get in without him so they let him carry on with his daily routine and maintained the most cordial of relationships. They had responded positively to a request from Roz to secure the perimeter around the building in order to give them some degree of privacy. Dale was very good with the press although he hadn't a clue why. They asked the questions and he did his best to answer them as honestly as he could. His photograph was all over the place and was given almost as much exposure as the landscape shots of the Yum Bum that were now buzzing around on the internet.

Gaspard had stayed in hospital overnight but discharged himself the following morning. It was a mistake. He was hounded by the press and had to request police protection until further notice. It was granted by the local Chief Constable when he learnt that Gaspard was a close friend of Dale's. When the initial frenzy had died down a bit they both hoped that he would be able to visit the Yum Bum and have a general chat, until then, he stayed at home with a patrol car prowling around out front.

Boris and Effie had retreated to South Kensington in the hope that the press wouldn't find out about their unlicensed Kool cream operation. Boris was furious at what had happened and instinctively knew that Gaspard was at the bottom of it. However, he too would have to keep a low profile for the moment and conduct his business by telephone and satellite. Dimitri was able to give him the local scene first hand and was pleased to report that Svetlana had set up a dog fighting syndicate with some journalists who seemed a pretty good lot. One of them believed strongly that every local nick should have a twelve-pack of Pit Bulls to maintain public order. He knew of another syndicate just outside Cardiff that they could organise bouts with. So things were on the up and up.

Melissa remained in her catatonic state and people gradually dropped off seeing her. She did not recognise Sebastian, or even Ian for that matter, so he continued to co-habit with Anita for the baby's sake if not for his own as well. Freddie and Effie hardly spoke to each other and when they did, he was careful to avoid mentioning Boris in any context other than as her business associate and temporary landlord. For obvious reasons, Loretta kept her counsel down the Bayswater Road and met up with Boris at Tzarbinski's where it was business as usual. Elsewhere the pace was hotting up.

Civil disorder contingency plans were being discussed as it became apparent that the south-west exits from London were fast becoming log-jammed as the ghouls and crackpots, historians and archaeologists, scientists and sci-fi anoraks were drawn inexorably towards this unique bio-chemical ejaculation. Millbank was working overtime to quell the speculation that a secret government biological laboratory had suffered a nasty accident that was beyond their control. The Prime Minister was handed a note from a press aide informing him that a certain Mr Freddie Bannister, who was one of their most senior and experienced missile scientists, was married to the woman who controlled the Fropsham Haystack Theatre but he was not under surveillance.

"Well he bloody well ought to be," snapped the Prime Minister, "for Christ's sake get on to it and let me have Gloria's report tomorrow morning."

The Defence Minister shot off to make the necessary arrangements but was forestalled by Gloria who told him that she had already taken care of it. The Minister was visibly relieved. He was even more pleased when she told him that she had planted a highly skilled and very special agent close to Bannister in order to monitor the attentions of a Russian mafia boss who it was widely believed had become active in the international arms arena. The Defence Minister liked Gloria and felt safe in her hands.

Gloria was no longer sleeping with Rodney for professional reasons and their daily interactions were now mostly confined to intelligence jousting. The Sprout was still moving in as a malevolent force and neither Gloria nor Rodney would admit that they were a tad apprehensive about the nature of his endgame. They did not know what he knew nor what he intended to do with his information. Gloria had dredged through every agent's section report and found out that Bannister was closer to Blodvrinsky than she had first imagined. She needed to know whether the Yum Bum phenomena had other applications and whether they were anything to do with the Tunisian situation that Rodney had tipped her off about before putting his penis on ice, so to speak. She decided the time had come for another tête a tête with Gaspard. She was alarmed at the changes she saw in him but sought to take maximum advantage, after all, her own survival was at stake.

He spilled the beans in a torrent of loathing. Clearly, he felt as let down by Effie as he did of Boris. He was convinced they had conspired against him.

"I can't imagine what they see in each other, they are completely incompatible."

"Are you sure Effie knows nothing about Loretta?"

"Absolutely nothing."

"And Freddie doesn't care about Boris?"

"No, he still trusts him, which is more than I can say for myself."

Gloria realised that her earlier decision to concentrate on Freddie was the right one, but the problem, as she saw it, was with his wife. She was amazed, and not a little bit relieved that the press hadn't yet made the connection between Effie and Freddie and the Yum Bum, to say nothing of Effie's past affair with Dale and her current relationship with Blodvrinsky. It wouldn't be long before they did and she was acutely aware that she was in a race against time. From which ever angle you looked at it, Effie seemed to be the common denominator. Gloria could hardly risk dropping by on a casual visit to the Albert Hall Mansions, any more than she could risk ringing Reggie to enquire whether he fancied a spot of anal sex enhanced with a liberal dose of Kool cream, just for old time's sake.

As is so often the case, other events occurred which nullified her dilemma, the first one being that the press got hold of the link between Freddie and the Yum Bum. Needless to say, Dale did not believe he was dropping any kind of clanger when he revealed the Yum Bum's origins to a dozen or so reporters and it was only because Roz was there at the time and was able to let them take a photograph of her and Dale at the small

234

table in the lighthouse where the Yum Bum had been potted, and where they had exchanged their first kiss, that they did not dig deeper there and then.

As a consequence, Freddie disappeared permanently to the Rio office and a growing number of residents who were domicile within the Royal Borough of Kensington and Chelsea, complained to their recently appointed high flying MP that they were sick and tired of the small army of journalists who had taken to eating their sandwiches and swigging their hip flasks on the steps of the Albert Memorial. So Freddie relied on Boris totally to protect him from the outside world and this he did brilliantly. The Rio office was Dimitri's masterpiece in bugs, surveillance cameras and electronic security fencing. Even The Sprout couldn't get in.

The second nullifying event was that the Yum Bum ceased to produce its wonderful sap beyond a mere trickle of ten cubic centimetres. Whether this was due to its recent massive ejaculation of life protecting forces or not, we shall never know. The fact of the matter was that having the blade of a medieval axe slammed into your guts was something deeply wounding in a very profound way. It was as if you had no right to be there even though you didn't know why you were in the first place. After-effects were surely understandable?

Dale collected the Yum Bum's sap from the highest nodules. It was the only place where it was producing it. He caught it in an upturned toothpaste cap and later transferred it to a glass jar; there were stacks of empties all over the place. Bodily functions propel us all forward and Dale took it as it come like. He was no good on strategy but the here and now he could deal with. Up to a point of course, but then you just had to keep on going and not lose yer rag like. He rang Effie at Boris's.

"Ello, 'ow yer doin?"

"Ghastly, how about you?"

"Brilliant, got 'em all dancing."

"Jolly good, keep up the show, what next?"

"The Yum Bum's drying up, I ain't got enough sap to clean me teeth wiv'"

"Can't you water it?"

"I fink it needs summik more basic than that, anyway, I'll keep me eye on it. Now, what abart these government geezers all over the place? They can't get in 'cos they don't know 'ow to."

"Neither do I Dale."

"Yeah, well I dunno what to make of it meself, it's difficult to explain."

"Well try, you must know something you can tell us."

"It's jus' summik that 'appened Eff, I jus' fort to m'self, everyfing's good around 'ere, so I'll apply a bit of the ol' tender loving kindness an' all that stuff and don't close up on no one like, and before you could say Oil Slick, it jus' opened up, but I can't understand why no one else can't do the same like, honest, I can't, I mean that's it."

Effie realised that she would have to put in a lot of work with Dale to get to the bottom of it and certain things were going to have to shift in order for that to happen.

"Well look, I'll run with whatever you think is best at the moment, it's rather difficult at this end because I think Boris is suffering from some kind of identity problem and I ought to see him through it as a true comrade and business partner so to speak."

"Oh righto. By the way, I'm gonna see Gaspard tomorrow, anyfink you want me to tell 'im?"

"Not really, but try to get him to relax and enjoy himself and perhaps remind him that he's still on the Haystack Theatre payroll so no need to worry about earning a living."

"Okay, well ta-ra then."

Dale rang off and tried not to think too much about things. There were a lot of people in the Haystack Theatre Company who had got themselves arse about face by trying to work out all the angles before anything happened.

"You can only plan when you know what you're planning for," he had said to a lone reporter, "otherwise you might just as well leave it alone."

The following day in the Daily Mirror it was a front page quote under the banner headline GURU DALE SAYS LEAVE IT ALONE. Roz said that she thought things might be getting a bit out of control but Dale said don't worry about it, just keep

236

both feet on the ground and everything will be alright. When she sat back and thought about it she came to the conclusion that he was probably right. It wasn't that she was stupid or anything, far from it, but she had only really twigged in the last couple of days that Dale was in a unique position to call all the shots, to all the people, all of the time. Perhaps, instead of trying to head off some imaginary scenario in the future, her energies would be better spent by managing the situation now with a spot of adroit PR.

No sooner was it twigged and tended when Norman the Equity rep rang the front door bell. He had made an appointment and notified the police constable on door duty because, as he said at the beginning of their meeting, 'you are dealing with a professional negotiator here'. She was pleased to see how Norman and Dale had struck up a friendly relationship and particularly because Norman, representing as he did, a substantial number of creative minds, was never short of a good idea. He was there to discuss one now.

"So the bottom line of everything that I've been saying," said Norman, "is that all company members unanimously agree that they would be delighted if you would open up the Yum Bum so that the Kool Kat cabaret could be performed around the Yum Bum itself, with Lotte's scenery adapted to fit your magnificent staircase, and with Anita in the title role and with Loretta as the star, plus all the Haystack actors, and with the resources of the Blodvrinsky Arts Foundation to underwrite negotiations for world television and film rights with the highest bidder"

Roz practically leapt over the table whereas Dale just remarked:

"Sounds brilliant, let's get cracking, I can't answer for Boris though but I'm sure 'e'll be willing to listen, so I'll 'ave a word wiv' 'im if yer like?"

"That's great, I'll tell the members that the big show is on."

"And I would like to issue a press statement on behalf of Dale," said Roz quickly, "and also to give the media something new instead of all this Millbank stuff about how many scientists are on the case and why they can't force Dale to take a medical because we live in a democracy etcetera."

"I've got no problems with that," said Norman, "let's fan the marketing publicity."

"Yeah, let's 'ave some fun, go for it!"

Dale and Roz were buzzing so much with the thought of what a fantastic show they were all going to be in that Dale got on the phone to Effie right away. Effie was won over instantly and so too was Boris. Effie told Dale that since their last call she and Boris had been having a really good chat and had come to the conclusion that as they were no longer selling Kool Cream, they could only be guilty of past misdemeanours if the Crown Prosecution Service could prove it. What's more, Boris had made it abundantly clear that he'd seen off bigger fish than the CPS before now, so as far as both of them were concerned, the CPS could stuff the rough end of a pineapple up their wotsits.

"Sounds great," said Dale, "so will he underwrite the world TV rights an' all that stuff?"

"Yes, and what's more, he thinks we should go ahead with The Trojans so tell that to Gaspard when you see him."

"Okay, I will, so when are you two coming down?"

"Tomorrow."

38

The Prime Minister had called a special cabinet meeting because things were getting completely out of hand. Not only was the Tunisian government claiming that the Yum Bum belonged to Tunisia and wanted it back, but the White House had telephoned this morning to say that the President would prefer to give the Dome a miss and visit the Yum Bum instead; and all this after a high wire safety net had given way during the third Dome manager's recent suicide attempt. To make matters worse, the President had expressed a personal wish to attend the opening night of the Kool Kat cabaret and say hello to the cast at the party afterwards. The date of his visit had already been planned months in advance so there was little chance of altering that. The UK mainland was virtually under siege as millions of tourists poured in through every possible air and sea port. The entire transport infrastructure was nearing collapse and the mayor of Fropsham had called for a state of emergency to be declared plus a bullet proof car for the school run. And still nobody could tell the Prime Minister what the Yum Bum was made of or how to get inside it without ingratiating themselves to an inarticulate carpenter who had left school at fifteen without a single O level or recognisable career plan. If things carried on like this, the British government would become the laughing stock of the world, never mind the rest of Europe. The only cold comfort on offer was that Tunisia was also being besieged by tourists looking for Achmed the taxi driver and a handful of Yum Bum seeds. The trouble was that every taxi driver in Tunisia was now called Achmed and there had been near riots at the airports as passengers were forced to hand over their packets of goat's dung to the police.

And behind all this lay the spectre of Blodvrinsky.

The Defence Minister had anticipated being exposed to some heat and had asked Gloria to submit written daily reports. Sometimes she would pop in and see him which made for quite an agreeable break even though what she told him wasn't always as optimistic as he would like it to be. As far as he could tell, the shit was on the knife-edge. The CIA had confirmed to Rodney that they had been tracking Blodvrinsky ever since he had slipped through their hands during a big Colombian drugs baron bust some while ago. The fact that Blodvrinsky had now duplicated the banned Cassandra project with the help of one of his own ministry's scientists who the world's press were looking for, did not seem to bother them. And the fact that he was holed up with a rocket just round the corner from this bloody Yum Bum thing was an absolute nightmare. Gloria told him that Rodney had said that the CIA didn't like being upstaged with the action and had therefore told the President that there was no foreseeable security threat although their presence during his trip would be advisable as per normal routine. He made a mental note to check this out with Rodney and listened intently as Gloria told him that she was in direct contact with one of their best agents in the field who would be able to supply them with a genuine sample of the Yum Bum sap now that the black market was flooded with fakes made from shampoo gel.

"What about Reggie?" he asked her.

"He's under surveillance too but there's no evidence to suggest that he's in bed with Blodvrinsky, if you'll pardon the phrase."

"Perhaps it's his sleeping partners that I should start getting interested in?"

"I can explore that avenue of enquiry if you so wish," replied Gloria, with the utmost seriousness.

The Defence Minister felt he had been burdened enough as it was and his immediate problem was how to translate his intelligence into a plausible statement that would not herald the kiss of death, primarily his own. The cabinet meeting could become a bit sticky.

"Right, what's the defence angle?" said the Prime Minister bluntly.

"We have everything under control," said the Defence Minister, "the CIA are co-operating closely with us which means we shall be able to head off any awkward press enquiries with confidence. We have Freddie Bannister at a safe house and I am expecting to receive a full scientific analysis of the nature and structure of the Yum Bum shortly."

"Okay fine, now what about the President's visit?"

"Here again, we're working closely with the CIA and the usual security agencies. We don't anticipate any incidents, in fact I believe the Home Secretary may wish to comment on the general crowd control situation?"

The PM raised his eyebrows expectantly and the Home Secretary took his cue.

"The extraordinary thing about this whole situation is just how good-natured everybody appears to be, if there's a problem at all it's really a question of volume and transport, I don't know if anybody wishes to comment on that?"

"No, I don't want any comments on that," said the Prime Minister, curtly, "I'm sick to death of hearing everyone's comments on transport. So, are we saying go with the show and yes to the President being there?"

There was an embarrassing silence after which the Foreign Secretary, knowing that the PM's personal ratings were plummeting daily, said: "the President feels it would be a good PR opportunity for you both."

"What's the show about?" asked the Prime Minister, without blinking, "all I want to know is whether it's free of banana skins."

"I believe the Haystack Theatre is issuing a press statement about it today," said the Home Secretary.

"My department has not received anything on that," interjected the Press Secretary.

"Well get on to it right away," snapped the Prime Minister, "and have a press statement ready for my approval before midday,"

The Press Secretary scribbled on his Have a Nice Day jotter pad, "assuming it to be wholesome family entertainment, what else would you like me to say?"

"Jesus Christ, do I have to do *everything* myself!"

The Defence Minister smirked at the Press Secretary's discomfort. Considering that his opposite number in Belgrade had just been bumped off he was relieved that he did not have to watch his own back to quite the same extent. Blodvrinky's suspected involvement in the Arcan murder had yet to be verified and on that count he just wished the CIA would stop dragging their feet. Rodney's de-briefings were become more and more erratic and to make matters worse, it looked as if that ghastly, pock-marked gargoyle Reginald Ponsonby-Spratt was deviating seriously from his original remit. For a second or two, the Defence Minister toyed with the idea of backdating a report to the PM about Project Cassandra but ruled it out by the third second as being too risky. Ponsonby-Spratt was an ambitious bastard who could no longer be trusted. For the time being, all his chips were on Gloria, and she was certainly no bacon butty.

Later that afternoon Roz read out a press statement to the world'smedia. She was speaking on behalf of her principal client, The Haystack Theatre Company but was pleased to confirm that it had also been cleared by her colleagues in Millbank.

"The Haystack Theatre Company is proud to announce that the Prime Minister, accompanied by the President of the

United States, will attend the first night of an exciting new cabaret called Kool Kat on Thursday the eighteenth of May. The performance will take place in the Haystack's recently extended auditorium otherwise known as the Yum Bum. As a result of its wonderful translucency, plus recently installed stage lighting, the Yum Bum's cabaret can be viewed by the general public outside and the rest of the world simultaneously via satellite TV. The Haystack Theatre company has never shrunk from its responsibilities as a bold interpreter of today's often controversial issues, nevertheless, it can assure its audience that Kool Kat will present a dazzling and innovative approach to the fundamental forces that drive us all as human beings in a new emerging world, often as mystical as it is earthly. The Prime Minister and the President of the United States have both accepted our invitation to party with the full cast after the show in the Yum Bum."

The statement went round the entire globe, through the nearest hole in the ozone layer and back down again in matter of minutes. It was the high spot of Roz's new career in PR and a personal best in her capacity as the leading partner in De Winter PR, an agency she had recently created with Effie and Anita, (Dale was an advising consultant although he did not get involved with the actual writing of press releases and similar documents).

Understandably, it also put the Haystack Theatre on the world map, due cognisance of which, Norman politely reminded Effie, would have to be taken into account when certain members' contracts came up for renewal. Effie could not envisage any complications arising from that and everyone agreed how fantastic it was to have her coughing and shrieking all over the place once again and what a splendid couple she and Boris made with no disrespect to Freddie who must be having a very challenging time of it right now.

Everything was electric. Everything was alive with anticipation. Everything was going so well. Dale was installing his modified set of Lotte's scenery on the Yum Bum staircase and rehearsals were reaching a peak. To be a

243

Haystack actor in Kool Kat at the Yum Bum was the best job in the business.

Whether it was the best time to be a secret service agent was debatable although not as far as Gaspard was concerned since he was having the time of his life. For once he was in control. Not only did Gloria Fitzbagley, the Head of MI5 visit him regularly to consult on security matters, but she kept his former boss, Sir Rodney Snodder, the Head of MI6 (and a monumental charlatan if ever there was), completely off his back. As a consequence, his relationship with Gloria was extremely cordial and was enhanced by the fact that she unaware that he had his own gameplan up his sleeve which bore no resemblance to hers. They had agreed to meet in Oded's Bowl, a popular Israeli restaurant in Earl's Court where the noise levels were so high as to render electronic eavesdropping completely impotent. Gaspard rose to greet her.

"Gloria, how lovely to see you again and on such a gorgeous spring day."

When she had first met him, Gloria had found Gaspard rather stiff and starchy and with very little self-motivation, but now he was relaxed and seemed more open to her direction.

"Hello Gaspard," she replied, "what are we having?"

They settled for a whole range of little bits and pieces that included one of Gaspard's favourites, to wit, Shallot Confiture.

"This is one of Oded's personal adaptations from an ancient Middle Eastern recipe," he said, knowingly.

"Tastes lovely."

"Yes, it's cooked in a spice syrup."

They dunked their falafels in it together . Gaspard had never felt more at ease with a woman than he did now.

"So, Gloria, did you want to ask me something?"

"Yes, the PM feels boxed in and the Defence Minister is about to shit himself, so I need your help."

"Well, by virtue of my payroll advice slip, I believe I am here to do precisely that."

"Oh great. Gaspard, you've no idea what a bloody uphill battle it can be when dealing with bureaucracy and back-stabbing at Ministerial level."

Gaspard could but sympathise. He had an inkling of what was about to come next. As long as Reggie kept his end of the deal, he would be alright.

"Anyway, not wishing to dump like an out-of-time appraisee," said Gloria, "but I need a sample of the Yum Bum sap urgently and since you have a close relationship with Dale, who my superiors think may be linked to Freddie in some way although personally I doubt it, I'm relying on you to get it."

Gaspard was delighted at her response. He needed to get back inside the Haystack with some measure of dignity and here was the perfect excuse.

"Dale has the ability to involve himself in everything and everyone, he cannot help it, it's an unconscious habit that tends to attract all sorts of people, however, we do have a special relationship, in fact we met recently and he said how nice it would be if I were to reappear."

At that point Gloria inwardly crossed herself as only a good Christian should. A lucky break at last! If she could get a swap-over of the Yum Bum sap before Reggie got his hands on it, she would still be in the race.

"Well, I need a sample of the Yum Bum sap and its got to come direct from Dale. The PM is going to kneecap every member of his cabinet if they don't find out what the Yum Bum is made of before the President's visit."

"I shall get on to it right away, now what about Boris Blodvrinsky in all his disguises? Is it to be crucifixion or immolation?"

"Steer well clear of him for the time being, the Defence Minister suspects that he may have done some kind of deal with Reggie."

"I shall tread carefully," said Gaspard, stabbing another shallot.

Anita and Ian were sitting with Sebastian in Dale's living room. Roz was in the kitchen on a secure line to the White House press office.

245

"I can't see what the problem is," said Anita to Ian, "if Dale has given a genuine sample of Kool to Gaspard as well as to you, what the hell does it matter? It doesn't prevent you from giving your boss what he wants, so where's the hassle?"

But Ian was still uncomfortable. "The Sprout is up to something, I don't trust him but I don't know what to do about it either."

Ian was getting quite intense. Maybe going back to work wasn't such a good idea after all? Before, he would just go along with things, albeit in some agony, but now he felt as if he had been pushed around long enough and yet he didn't know where and how he should make his stand. He was sure it was to come.

"Don't worry abart it," said Dale, "I can always get Roz to knock up a press statement, no trouble, and then if anyone wants to bang around wiv' the facts, well that's up to them, innit?"

Sebastian burbed and Anita winded him. She couldn't understand why some Brits got instantly stroppy with any form of authority whereas others, like Ian, were so afraid of it. The easiest way in both cases was to go underground where there were no other rules except those of survival. Having said that, things were so buoyant. She knew Ian had a backbone somewhere or other, it just needed finding then propping up. She was on the case.

A few days later, a very worried looking Gloria entered the Defence Minister's private office.

"Tell me the worst," he said, reading her face in an instant.

"There's a compound in the Yum Bum sap that when mixed with tea makes it as volatile as a litre of nitro-glycerine within a cube of sugar."

"By that, I take it you mean rocket fuel?"

"Exactly, and we must assume that Reggie knows about it too."

"What about Bannister?"

"We don't know for sure. He's shown no interest in the Yum Bum to date but it's not inconceivable that Blodvrinsky may have passed some of the sap on to him previously. There is also the unanswered question of whether all the seeds Freddie smuggled in from Tunisia have been used in one planting or not."

Now the Minister looked as worried as Gloria. If he passed this information to the CIA they would probably insist on storming the Rio office, (as he now learnt from Gloria, Freddie's missile centre was called) with hand grenades and stun bombs.

He wondered whether there was anybody in the House of Lords who could help him?

39

Gaspard's sleek, black, shark-shaped Citroen with its upholstery in Jocasta Red, slid smoothly into a small copse overlooking the town at Fropsham Heights. Effie was with him and she was not amused. The fever back at the Haystack was just fantastic and the last thing she wanted was to be dragged away by a disconsolate Gaspard on his insistence that what he had to say concerned national security. Nevertheless, that is exactly what had happened and now she hoped that his explanation would do it justice.

"I shall come straight to the point, Effie," said Gaspard with an air of authority.

"Well it will be a personal first, I can assure you, d'you mind if I smoke?

"Well if you must."

"Yes, I must, now has this thing got a dashboard lighter?"

"You'll find a packet of Swan Vestas in the glove box."

Effie fished them out and lit up. Gaspard pressed the window button for Effie's side but it didn't work, so he hand wound his own side down by a couple of centimetres.

"You may not like what I am about to say but it is too late now for me to bother about that. There are some unpalatable truths which I wish you to be aware of. The first is that I am an undercover agent for MI5, having been transferred from MI6 because I did not wish to travel this year. The second is that Boris Blodvrinsky is the most powerful of the Russian mafia to operate criminal activities on a global scale and both the British and American governments are extremely concerned about his presence in this country. The third is that Freddie is a traitor and he is sleeping with Loretta."

Effie spluttered in derision, "I don't believe a bloody word of it, you're completely off your rocker."

"I anticipated that reaction," said Gaspard calmly," may I suggest you concentrate on this."

He placed a small portable television on top of the dashboard. He slipped a disc in the side and pressed play.

A slightly grainy but quite distinct colour picture came up. It was the video of Freddie and Loretta in bed together in the Hotel Yamhalia in Tunisia. There was sound too. Effie fell silent and did not take her eyes off the screen. When the picture blinked and faded away another one replaced it shortly afterwards. Freddie and Loretta again, this time in Suite 42 of the Great Cumberland Hotel. The antics were more uninhibited. That too came to an end, and a few seconds later, there they were again, naked and inverted in the Mission Control Centre launch chair. The programme came to an end and a blank screen flickered and then went dead as Gaspard switched it off.

Effie lit up another cigarette and dragged deeply and furiously. Gaspard ejected the disc and replaced it carefully inside his breast pocket. He wound his window right down slowly and deliberately and enunciated clearly.

"Freddie was officially banned from continuing with a missile programme that the British government felt was too unstable to be safe. He ignored that instruction and became ensnared by the Russian mafia. Blodvrinsky has funded the operation and the intelligence services have discovered a covert missile launching site within this vicinity. Expert opinion believes Freddie is deranged. You are the only person capable of talking some sense into him for which immunity from any kind of prosecution will be agreed. Please consider your response carefully."

Effie grabbed her handbag and the box of Swan Vestas and got out of the car.

"Stay there," she said, and walked into the trees. A grey squirrel pounced on her cigarette butt as she flicked it to the ground. She kicked the squirrel and lit up another cigarette. It was a full twenty minutes before she re-emerged and returned to the car. She slid into her seat. Her eyes were red but her features were determined.

"When do I get to see him?" she asked grimly.

"Thursday the fourteenth of May, after the first night party is well under way. It will be a tricky operation that civil police will be unaware of. I must swear you to absolute secrecy. Everything will be off if you break your silence."

"No chance," she said, and lit up another cigarette.

All she wanted to do now was get hold of Boris's stiletto dagger.

40

The sheer scale of the Presidential razzmatazz was staggering. It was like Michael Jackson dancing naked at Prince Charles' coronation. The Prime Minister was furious but there was nothing he could do about it. The Dome had gone into receivership and its sponsors had turned politically nasty. If this event flopped then it would lead to a vote of no confidence in the House which he knew he could not win.

As for the President himself, he had issued instructions that he did not want to upstage his British friends, but on the other hand he was damned if he was going to be overshadowed by some republican limey's metaphorical clever-dick act. However, come Thursday 18th May, the atmosphere at the Yum Bum was enough to consign every nation's millennium celebration memories to a deep freezer.

Inside the Haystack the pre-show nerves were almost at breaking point. They had done a technical run-through and dress rehearsal in the old auditorium so as not to be seen, but now they had to perform in front of the entire world, and around a mystical tree over two hundred feet high that had acquired the status of a peace icon for the twenty-first century.

Every dignitary that had climbed to the top of it had sworn blind afterwards that they had seen a vision of peace and happiness the like of which they had never experienced before. Every time it was Dale who welcomed them through the lips of the jelly bronze Yum Bum and accompanied them up his beautiful staircase. Everyone of them gasped at the sheer diamond twinkling brilliance of the leaf pods and said they had seen angels and gods sitting side by side on magnificent golden thrones.

Dale was now a famous Guru of the tell-it-how-it-is school. Tonight, Roz had spent an hour massaging aromatic oils into his body before draping a simple over-the-shoulder robe about him. He claimed he had seen, with his super vision at the top of the Yum Bum, a fight outside Burnt Oak Broadway underground station which must have been a good sixty miles away. He simply willed the combatants to stop kicking the shit out of each other and so they had! Roz consulted the local police who confirmed that they had been called out to an incident on that particular day and at that particular time but there had been nothing to deal with when they had arrived apart from asking two blokes who were kissing each other in front of the ticket machine to move along.

On another occasion, the Tunisian Ambassador had asked Dale whether he thought it would be possible to re-plant the Yum Bum in Tunis as an Arab statement for peace and prosperity in the region.

"Dunno really," said Dale, "I reckon yer best bet would be to flush out the original Achmed and start potting, it does its own fing when it gets bigger so you don't 'ave to worry abart nuffink."

The Ambassador had smiled for the cameras. Anyway, tonight Dale had opened the Yum Bum for the entire company and in a few moments he would slam on the spotlights and the opening number of Kool Kat would commence.

The Presidential entourage, the Prime Minister's gathering and an army of security guards and selected media and celebrity stars were packed into the Seventh Cavalry assembly area and everything was hot and ready to go. Sale of Kool Kat logos had already made Lotte a millionaire on paper

Several miles away The Sprout was assembling his vehicles and synchronising watches. What he didn't know was that hidden from sight behind him, in a huge circle that ringed the entire industrial complex where Project Cassandra was housed in, were fifty SAS soldiers backed up by several elite regiments of specially trained combat support operatives. Nobody was taking any chances.

British Intelligence had reported to the Defence Minister that The Sprout was planning to storm the Rio office during the height of the Kool Kat party when the eyes of the world would be on the two political leaders. The CIA had promised to stake out the President and Blodvrinsky just in case The Sprout and Blodvrinsky were ready to spring a joint operation of some kind. MI5 had infiltrated a top agent, (who knew both the Bannisters socially), with The Sprout. The agent knew how to amend the launch data and neutralise the fire command.

The Prime Minister was unaware of all this, and the fact that he was, made the Defence Minister wonder whether he hadn't left things a bit too late? Gloria had moved heaven and earth to keep one jump ahead, whereas Rodney had just chased his own tail round and round in circles until it looked like a renal assault.

The Chief Constable of Surrey was personally aware of the registration number of Gaspard's black Citroen DS21 Pallas Automatique, and had issued strict instructions that he was to be allowed unimpeded access to and from the Yum Bum together with his passenger, Mrs Effie Bannister. There were many people who were crossing their fingers tonight.

The opening number of the show went off like dynamite. Anita made her entrance at the end of it and jacked up the audience temperature a few degrees by simulating a strip-tease dressed only in crocodile-skin nipple covers and a mink thong. The Prime Minister buried his head in undisguised anguish. He had been promised solid family values and already the President was shouting and hollering along with his aides.

The cabaret switched from music to drama and the actors pole-axed everyone with a series of sharp snappy portrayals of the temptations in contemporary society. The Prime Minister felt his stomach churning. This was going to be full frontal satire. The world would witness the collapse of his wunderba regime and vanquish him forever to some elephant Valhalla where the white bones of failure would grin and mock him until he went crazy.

Back stage, Effie and Boris were circulating amongst the company which included a sizeable contingent of security men. Boris was in his element, playing the benign and avuncular arts patron whilst all the time goading and enjoying the suppressed hostility of the CIA. Effie was her usual life and soul getting ready to party, although one or two people agreed that she did seem unnaturally tense at times. Notwithstanding these observations, the show was on the road and the audience were loving it.

Ian was back stage helping Anita to change in and out of one costume after another. Sebastian blew bubbles at himself in the dressing room mirror. In the audience was Melissa, accompanied by Svetlana. The psychiatrist had agreed to her visit and even came along himself. When Melissa saw the Yum Bum, she no longer said dick, but Igor. Her psychiatrist punched the air in elation.

"That's an incredible breakthrough!" he shouted.

"Yah," said Svetlana, "he turned out to be a crazy woman."

The applause drowned out any further conversation.

Loretta made her entrance. Even before she began to sing, the applause was sensational, and then she socked it to them. I'm Reeling in the Line by Sid Hawkeswood made it clear that Loretta was about to take everyone's psyches away and jab at them with a moral ice-pick. She was slinky, she was sultry, she was sodden with suggestion. The President whispered to his aide that he wanted to see her alone if possible.

Meanwhile, in a basement room in Tzarbinski's, sat Dimitri, loyal as ever, scanning several television monitors as they relayed pictures of the Rio office in live time. Freddie was working the same as ever, sat in front of the huge screens and checking and cross-checking logistics data.

"Nothing happening boss," said Dimitri to Boris on the mobile.

"Have a vodka, relax, it's after the show when the fun starts."

And the fun was certainly piling up in the Kool Kat cabaret. The full company were now assembled around the height and width of the Yum Bum and Anita was writhing and twisting with a fake python and a large eating apple. Loretta, dressed in a dazzling white sequinned dress, took full spotlight and gave them a showbiz stopper. In the end she was gyrating as sexily as Anita and not even the Prime Minister could take his eyes off her legs as they interlocked with Anita's. There was joyous frenzy everywhere. Yo, let's all be brothers and sisters, screamed Loretta, and the world screamed its approval. When the finale finally ended the audience went berserk.

"Hey, get that eruption," shouted Anita to Loretta above the commotion.

"I'm getting it, I'm getting it," yelled Loretta as she stepped forward to tumultuous applause.

It was a good half hour later before the President and Prime Minister finally made it to the entrance of the Yum Bum. Flash lights went off incessantly as security tried to prevent a media scrum. Dale stood inside the Yum Bum and fashioned two parted lips as the Prime Minister gestured to the President to go first.

"Hi Dale, how goes it?" said the President.

"Yeah, doin' alright I reckon, 'ow abart yerself?"

"I'm right there."

"Well that's good innit, come on then, let's get stuck into the party, there's a load of booze like."

And the celebrations began. And it was just fantastic.

The Prime Minister felt that the world's obvious jubilation with the sincere and open message of the cabaret to unite in friendship and love was proof enough that this time, somebody had got something right. And now, all he had to do was get the Tunisian ambassador rat-arsed on Elderberry wine and he would be over the next hurdle. The President was pumping the flesh and working the scene and obviously enjoying every minute of it. This was the life. Now, where was the Defence Minister?

Effie slipped into the front seat of Gaspard's car and they whisked themselves away. Nobody noted their absence because they were having such a wild time. The car veered along a loop road and dropped down onto the main road that led to Tzarbinski's roundabout. A few minutes later, it pulled up outside the restaurant.

"It's all clear," said Gaspard.

There was a shuffling behind the front seats on the floor and Ian emerged from underneath a grey blanket.

"Good night Effie," he said, and walked inside the building.

Gaspard pulled away and they neither of them said a word until they arrived at The Sprout's rendezvous.

"We're ready when you are," said Reggie.

"Okay, let's proceed," replied Gaspard.

Down in the basement of Tzarbinski's, Ian took a fire axe off the wall and severed the main electricity supply cable in one hit. As soon as he was plunged into darkness, Dimitri leapt up and kicked down the door of the surveillance room. Ian wasn't sure whether he had taken the right corridor to go back upstairs.

The Sprout de-polarised all the Rio's security locks and they moved in. The SAS watched carefully, awaiting the order to capture him. Gaspard led Effie to the central control room.

"I have important technical work to do, I will return at an appropriate moment. Please do your best with Freddie. Good luck."

And then he left her there.

Effie pushed open the door and strode angrily towards Freddie who was sitting hunched in his chair. Good luck didn't come into it.

"You bastard!" she yelled, slapping him across the face. Freddie leapt back in hurt and amazement. He pressed some switches on his console but nothing happened. Effie was not going to strike again, he could see that. Well, who was the guilty party?

"You have lied to me," she spat out her accusation.

"And so have you."

"Well that doesn't quite make us even."

Freddie had regained his composure but not so Effie who he knew from year upon year upon year of co-existence, was about to blow again.

"This is my lifetime achievement," he said carefully.

"And I suppose this is your extra-curriculum study?" she snarled, and flung down some video print-outs. That somehow lit the fuse and Freddie felt a streak of indignation rising.

"I have devoted all my energy and concentration to this one project and even now they want to destroy me."

"I'm supposed to talk to you reasonably but quite frankly I'd be perfectly happy to join in with the other side."

"Please don't antagonise me," said Freddie, becoming white with anger, "I have created the ultimate weapon and if you don't believe me, just read the fourteen hundred pages of this project manual." He grabbed a large, heavy, ring-binder and flicked its sheets in a gesture of completion. An expensive pair of silk knickers fluttered forth from the pages and fell, in coquettish convolutions, to the floor.

"You fucking bastard!" she yelled and whipped out Boris's dagger from her handbag. Freddie saw the lunge coming and leapt aside. Effie crashed past him and landed heavily on the control console as the dagger clattered to the floor. Unfortunately, she had landed on a big green knob marked GO and before the dagger had even reached the floor, there was a massive thunderclap of ignition blast which shook the entire building.

Downstairs, feverishly re-programming the launch data with a lap top in the cab of Cassandra's low-loader, was Gaspard. The blast blew him out of the cab to the sides of the wall. Then the main propulsion engines fired and the Cassandra rocket lifted into the sky. Gaspard was incinerated in a moment, or perhaps, in view of the extreme temperatures, we could say, instantly vaporised in.

Upstairs in front of the control console, Effie stepped back in alarm.

"What was that?"

There was real fear in her eyes but Freddie had become unnaturally calm.

"You have just fired my rocket."

"Jesus Christ you lunatic, where will it land?"

"It will return right here, it is irrevocably programmed to do so."

"What the hell are you talking about?" shouted Effie.

"I'm talking about the ergonomic psychology factor," Freddie retorted, raising his voice, "it will always return to kill its own base but its operators can never know that."

"You're stark staring bonkers."

"No, it's the rest of the world that is mad. Don't you see? Don't you get it? Placed in the hands of the right type of salesman, we can sell Cassandra to our enemies and they will blow themselves to kingdom come when trying to destroy us. World domination will simply be a matter of a viable sales plan. No one will be strong enough to resist it, I have calculated the strato-ionic helix within the ergonomic psychology factor and have concluded that, as a human race, we are mathematically incapable of resisting temptation."

"My God Freddie, you really have gone mad!"

"No, this is rocket science Effie, and we have exactly two and a half minutes to live."

Effie screamed and ran for the door.

Within seconds of Cassandra erupting into the sky, computer screens and alarm signals were bursting into action as the Royal Air Force put its fighters in the sky. Roger and Tally ho did not come into it. This was the age of the hard computer. The Cassandra rocket was plunging towards the Yum Bum at a speed of about thirty miles an hour. Considering that it was capable of mach one, something was clearly wrong. Freddie's computer told him that he was about to be obliterated in two minutes and ten seconds but the reality was that Gaspard, having tinkered with the trajectory settings before his personal vaporisation programme kicked in, the Yum Bum was about to receive a direct hit.

The world's media could see it too and they dived for cover. Some of them stuck their cameras on automatic and hoped for the best. There was also panic inside the Yum Bum. Everyone could see the huge shaft of flame that was dawdling towards them with inexorable insouciance. But Dale was the only person who knew how to get out and he really wasn't too bothered

"It's nuffink to get worried abart, we're better protected inside than out."

As if to verify his statement, the Cassandra rocket plunged into the side of the Yum Bum. It did not explode. The Yum Bum absorbed Cassandra deep in its rubbery folds then bent over a bit before catapulting it with a great whopping BOINNGGG sound. The reaction inside the Yum Bum was not like being on the Titanic. They were safe. They were alive (apart from a few fatalities arising from heart attacks). So the band struck up again, the champagne flowed and soon everyone was getting stuck into the canapés again.

The Cassandra rocket was now spinning towards the Rio office like a slow motion flymo blade or a Fuzbee's Buzbee. Effie dived towards a concrete bus shelter as Cassandra crashed through the roof. It did not explode.

"I knew you would come back to me," said Freddie, smiling with delight before it crushed him to death. Cassandra's engines blasted an intense stream of heat and the building was on fire in a matter of seconds. The Sprout had been standing on the first gantry trying to check on Gaspard's trajectory settings when it had taken off! Now he was no more than a boiled husk. His peculiar sprout-like face more nearly resembling a braised turnip.

Effie managed to stumble towards where she thought Gaspard had parked his car. She was in luck. She had a spare set of keys. The extent to which Gaspard trusted her was quite touching. Inside the car she felt under the driver's seat and fished out a quarter bottle of gin. Three large swigs and a fag or two and things would be alright.

Anita took a call on her mobile. It was Ian. She got her shot in first.

"Hey what happened to you after the show? I've been struggling to free my dress zip with a pair of nail cutters."

"I had to assist your dad with some data protection files."

"No kidding, I didn't even know my dad could read."

"Anyway, I'm coming back in, sounds pretty lively from this end."

"It's a total rave. There is absolutely no animosity anywhere. It's the most fantastic state of being that anyone can imagine. And there's food and booze coming out of our ears. Anyway, get yourself over here fast because I want to introduce you to the Defence Minister who keeps asking me to dance with him. Y'know he's quite a gas and I reckon he's got the hots for this slightly horsey but really nice girl called Gloria Fitzbagley."

"Hey Roz," said a honky Puerto Rican reporter with CNN, "how's about a real French kiss with Dale, y'know like unmistakably raunchy."

"We don't do raunchy," said Roz, blushing, " we're in love."

"Yeah," said Dale, "besides, you gotta behave yerself in public like."

And so they kissed gently and tenderly and in so doing were transported to some far off Elysian field where little fluffy lambs jumped over a rainbow gate and children played with buttercups in the sun. It was the first time in their lives that either of them had really fallen in love.

The President's aides had gradually siphoned off the crowds by leading him upwards towards the lighthouse. Most serious party goers had wisely chosen to give the stairs a miss and were pasting their brains in the air on the ground floor.

"We have something interesting for you, sir" said the President's aide and withdrew tactfully leaving him alone.

It was a warm spring night that few would ever forget, least of all the President. Standing there in the magical twinkling of the Yum Bum, he felt at one with the world and himself. Far below, the insistent beat of the party music was no more than a background pulse. Up here, all was peace and tranquillity, friendship and trust. If only it could be so for the rest of eternity.

He sensed the unmistakable fragrance of feminine perfume and the gentle swish of an evening dress.

Loretta approached him.

"Good evening Mr President," she said.

He shook her hand warmly, "okay, agent Regina, let's hear it."

"I need to get closer to Dale," she said.

"Uh huh, Mr Magic Hand, can you do it?"

"Yes sir, the signs are promising."

"Good, well you get as close to him as you can because this Yum Bum thing has withstood a direct missile attack and nobody seems to know how, or why, so right now I'm feeling kinda vulnerable, you understand?"

"I understand perfectly sir, just leave it to me, you're in good hands now . . . but I must advise you that the way ahead is gonna be pretty zippy."

They exchanged smiles and the President felt happy once more.

ooo00ooo

EPILOGUE

Readers will be pleased to know that the paper used in the production of this book has not been taken from the Yum Bum tree whose organic structure remains an enigma.

In spite of human misdemeanours, the tree itself continues to flourish and is now under the protection of the Heritage Trust who have appointed Dale as their Patron Emeritus.

To this day, anyone can enjoy the spiritual aura of the Yum Bum at Fropsham in Surrey, but strangely, it has become invisible to those who do not approach it with loving kindness.

Other novels by Martin Pilcher

Visit the author's storefront for direct on-line purchase.
www.lulu.com/aadvarkzap

The Banana Skin Tango

Melvin is a stressed out executive with a broken marriage, a fading career and a nicely developing drink habit. When he beds the local bar maid, he ignores the fact that her boyfriend is a psychotic bi-sexual gangster with half London's bent coppers in his pocket. When finally ensnared, both sexually and criminally, he is at last forced to confront his own dubious morality. Redemption occurs when he realises that if you want to stay alive, you must treat women with respect.

Beyond the S-Bend

Ambrose is a politician who believes he has achieved spiritual enlightenment. The truth is, he's a smug, right-wing, muddle-headed control freak. Nevertheless, he convinces the nation that he will fulfil his manifesto promise 'to put the dignity of human beings above all else'. He becomes Tory Prime Minister in a landslide victory. But, within months of taking office he announces plans to build six new mega-sized prisons and introduce national identity cards. It is all part of his personal vision known as The Great Thrust Forward which includes doubling the police force, immigration service, customs & excise and the national coast guard. When he begins an affair with Helga, a mysterious civil service secretary, with fascist tendencies, everything starts to go pear-shaped. His enemies mount a leadership challenge, but not everything runs smoothly in politics. A tale of political incompetence and human delusion.

AADVARK-ZAP PUBLISHING (UK)